Oth

White Trash Trilogy

Reviving Kendall

Refusing Kendall

Reclaiming Kendall

VanPelts: A White Trash Trilogy Prequel

Logan: A White Trash Trilogy Novella

Lady of Darkness Series

Of Death And Darkness

In Dreams Of Despair

AntiLove Bookclub Series

Love Bitters

Love Starves

New Year Surprises: An ALBS Novella

Omegaverse

Building My Pack

Rocking My Pack

Divinely Damned Series

The Arbiter

Saga of Evanescent Realms

Sunken Empire

Standalones

Identity: A Villainously Romantic Retelling

Zombie Queen

Burying Blayke

Sidra

reviving kendall

brandy slaven

Reviving Kendall

2nd Edition

Edited by Michelle Hoffman

Cover by JODIELOCKS Designs

Table of Contents

Black Trash Bags

My breath puffs out in tiny plumes in front of my face. It's colder than a witch's tit outside, but it's better to take my time on the walk home. I know what awaits me there, the same thing that waits every other night.

Shifting the leftover bag of Mexican food in my hand, I adjust my scarf around my face. The last thing I need is to get sick right now. Got to have money for bills and got to have a job for money. Waitressing requires a clean bill of health. I can't be sneezing in someone's plate of tamales, can I?

HONK!

My palm slaps my chest as I jump back, falling into a damp pile of leaves.

"Stay down in the dirt where you belong, trailer trash!" Derrik, the school jock and womanizer, screams while hanging halfway out his window. He then finishes it off with a howl at the sky like a freaking looney tune.

"Idiots," I mumble, standing up and dusting myself off. Damn it, now I've got to sit up tonight and wash my clothes. This is the only uniform I have for work and I won't have time for it to dry between school and my shift tomorrow.

"Ugh, fucking dicks." I flip them off for good measure, even though they are long gone. I smooshed the leftovers in the bag and they spilt out into the ground. I dump the rest knowing some animal will thank me for that, but I carry the container and bag with me to throw away. The wetness from the leaves soaked into my pants and makes the last bit of this walk absolute torture. So much for being warm.

I stomp into the Sleepy Pines Mobile Home Community, in a foul mood. Fingers crossed that no one will stop me between here and my Gramps's trailer. It's close to midnight, but you never can tell with these folks.

Trying my best to be quiet, it doesn't stop the creak of rusty hinges when I open the door and catch it just in time for it not to slam against the side of the trailer. The smell that rolls out the door makes me gag. I can't stand the smell of cigarette smoke, especially if I'm trapped in a room with it. I take my last breath of fresh air before walking inside.

I don't bother locking the door behind me. There's nothing here for anyone to take and if it happens to be a serial killer, please come put me out of my misery. Choking down the bile trying to rise up, I go into the kitchen and clean up the mess Gramps left on the counter and sink. I swear to God. Sometimes, the man forgets to eat and other times, it's like an aftermath of letting a three-year-old cook. Tonight was one of those nights. I sigh and take off my jacket. I hate bringing it inside. It always smells like smoke when I leave, but if I leave it outside someone is bound to take it. A real leather jacket sitting out in the open around here, yeah, I might as well say, 'Here, what's mine is yours.'

I wouldn't give half a shit if it was mine. No, it used to be Brian's. He let me wear it one night and his mom let me keep it after...nope. Not going there tonight.

Washing the dishes in and around the sink, I wipe the flour and milk off the counters. There's no telling what he was trying to make today. One of these days, he's going to burn this place to the ground. I wish he would, I think, but then feel immediately guilty because

Gramps wouldn't likely make it out.

After drying my hands on the dish towel and sweeping up the mess on the floor, I make a beeline for my room. Gramps is up here by the kitchen and he's got his own bath. The only good thing about this trailer is my own room and bathroom. I knew kids before who had neither and didn't even have a bed so yeah, I'm one lucky B.

I don't bother with the light switch in my room. Instead, I walk straight to the window. Sleeping with it open isn't ideal for me not to get sick, but the stench is overpowering tonight. It's a risk I'm willing to take. Not like the trailer gets all that warm anyways. I've got plenty of blankets piled on my bed to keep me toasty.

Stripping down, I find my favorite sleep shirt tucked in my top drawer. It's the only one I own and will probably try to ever own. Though, it doesn't look like those odds are going to be in my favor considering the holes all in it. Another piece of clothing that wasn't originally mine. But, I did win it fair and square literally off Will's back in a rowdy game of strip poker.

My brain is driving me insane tonight. I don't want to think of them right now. Especially after Derrik and his stupid buddies. That's probably what started the trip down memory lane anyways. If my guys were still around, Derrik would have been too chicken shit to pull something like that. He knows the VanPelt brothers would have stomped him a new asshole for it. Unfortunately, not just for me, the world will never know just what those guys were capable of if they put their minds to it. And I'll never know what could have actually been.

I shake my head and let out a silent scream for letting my brain go there. Taking my uniform into the bathroom, I give it a good scrub down in the sink. A washer and dryer are a luxury around here. Once I'm satisfied with my work, I wring it out in the sink and hang it on the coat hanger to take outside. Not the most brilliant of ideas, what with it being cold, but there's a slight breeze that I hope will help dry it faster.

I make quick work of running it out to the porch and then back inside to crawl underneath my covers. I'm exhausted and I get to wake up and do it all over again in the morning.

A few hours later when my alarm goes off, I want to throw it through the still open window. I don't have the money to buy another, though, so I settle for hitting the off button and getting up.

My sock-clad feet drag as I make my way into the living room. I'm up way before Gramps, but that's no surprise. I normally am. There's a strange ticking noise coming from the porch. Okay, I'm awake. Grabbing the broom, I'm thinking of that raccoon in our garbage last week. It took me over an hour to clean that wreck up. There's no way that I'm doing that again.

Cracking the door, what I find is much worse. The ticking noise is coming from my hangers that I put out last night and the reason they are making so much noise is because they are empty. A note hangs from one of them. I yank it off to get a closer look, 'Even these Salvation Army rags are too good for you. We left you something suitable.'

Looking down, I see one of our black trash bags at my feet with a hole in the side. Mother trucker, they better not have...walking around the side of the house I see that they did. Trash from the bag surrounds the trailer almost like they walked a full circle around it emptying it out of the bag. I just want to sit in the trash pile and cry right now, but I can't. This has to be cleaned before the park super wakes up. Gramps would catch hell for this. That's okay because my day can only look up from here, right? Turns out I am wrong.

Chapter Two

One Sip at a Time

Standing at the entrance with the other kids of Sleepy Pines, we wait for the bus to roll up and take us all to school. Most teenagers would be ashamed to be riding the bus as a senior, but not me. I'm grateful as shit that I'm not having to walk to school in the cold. This used to be amusing when we were younger. Getting to stand here without parental supervision and joke around. Those days are long gone, though. And to think it all changed because Brian decided to work for a roofing company everyday two summers ago. Will, Casey, and I all tried to talk him out of it. We weren't complaining by the time he bought Old Jenning's Camaro. Know how they say hindsight is 20/20? Yeah, I would have protested a little harder if I had known that in less than a year all three of them would die in that car.

I try to clear my mind. They've been stuck there lately, because I miss them more than breathing most days. Right after was the worst. I spiraled out of control and even have the scars on my wrists to prove it. My every intention was to die the day that I found out. Some would call our relationship unorthodox or even disgusting, but I didn't care. Still don't. Most people whispered about a melodramatic teenager from the trailer park trying to kill herself over some twisted version of puppy love. Those same people didn't know that Brian, Will, and Casey were the only people to ever give two shits about me in my entire life. It actually mattered to them if I had food in my belly or if I came home at night. They were my world and I loved them with everything that's inside of me. I've wished a million times over that it could have been me. My therapist used to say that things happen for a reason, but I don't believe in that bullshit. People make decisions. That's why shit happens, not because the universe decides for them. Brian let Casey drive that day. Even though he was already seventeen, he'd only had his permit for a week. It was late on a Monday night and they were coming to pick me up from work. For whatever reason, they left late and they never could stand to leave me waiting on them. So, Casey was speeding and tried to beat the train. They say that he was only inches away from making it and what's worse is that they probably still would have if it hadn't been for that leak in the Camaro's gas tank. I didn't even get to go to the funerals. They considered me too much of a risk to myself to let me out of the hospital. So, my boyfriends...my best friends were put into the ground without even a goodbye from me.

The pain on days like today is excruciating. Those little, white pills from my therapist help some, even though I think I should have doubled up this morning. This day already has a suck factor off the charts.

By the time the bus makes it to school, I've decided that I need all the coffee to make it through the day. I didn't get my cup this morning and had to skip breakfast, too, since I was too busy picking up trash. Too bad the cafeteria doesn't offer us coffee. Some bullshit about stunting our growth or something. Thankfully, this isn't my first rodeo. I've always got my travel mug and a box of those single serve instant coffee packs in my backpack. Now I've just got to find some hot water.

Walking around the side of the building, I tighten my coat around me. Late fall has always been my favorite. All of the leaves have changed colors and their tiny corpses litter the ground, crunching underneath your feet. The bite in the air is just enough to warrant a jacket and scarf, but you won't freeze to death if you don't.

Looks like one thing is on my side today, the side door has been left propped open. Probably to cool off the cafeteria without having to switch the air conditioning on. One of the best things is the fact that there's no one around here on this side. The less people I have to deal with today, the better.

Walking in, I see they're still serving breakfast. My stomach rumbles as I smell the biscuits and fruit. I shove my hand down the side pocket of my backpack in hopes that there might be some change in it. It's a hopeless venture, but it's worth a shot. Nada.

Shrugging internally, I weave my way through the tables. If my stomach hadn't distracted me, I would have already seen the group of jocks sitting at the table to my left. A foot juts out and catches around my ankle. Tumbling forward, I manage to get myself straight before smacking my face on the table next to them.

Their rambunctious laughter echoes around the now silent room.

"Stop trying to bring attention to yourself, trailer trash," Derrik says while his buddies snicker. I ignore them the best that I can, even when the derogatory comments and laughs follow me behind the counter.

"You can't be back here, dear," Jane, the lunch lady, tells me as she tries to shoo me back around the corner.

I put on the saddest face I can muster. "But I'm not feeling well, and I was hoping to get some hot water in my thermos to make some tea and soothe my throat." I realize that I'm rambling, and I'm not surprised. That's what normally happens when I lie.

Something in my face has her taking pity on me. "Ok. Give me your cup and go stand on the other side of the counter."

I dig it out and quickly move to do as she says. This woman is my savior of the day. Of course, I'm going to obey with no questions asked. The sneers start up again behind me, but I ignore them. Until I feel someone behind me that is.

Derrik's voice makes chill bumps break out over my skin and not the good kind, "Need money, trailer trash? I know you do. I've got five bucks for you if you'll meet me after school."

I assume my best approach is to act like I don't hear him, however, it only makes it worse.

"What do you say, baby?" he says and then a little louder, "Stop begging, trailer park." At the last he thrusts his hips into my ass and I jerk forward, bumping my hip bone into the metal counter.

"Young man, that will not be tolerated in this school," Jane says fiercely, coming back around the counter. "You just stay right there. Are you okay?" she asks, turning to me.

Know that old saying, *snitches get stitches*? Yeah, I may not end up with stitches but the pod squad will make my life even more hell.

"I'm fine," I tell Jane. "It's okay. He didn't hurt me or anything."

She looks at me like I'm crazy. "Sweetheart, that was harassment and it needs to be reported."

I shake my head. "It's okay really. He was just kidding."

Derrik nods at us and holds up his palms. "Just playing around."

Shaking her finger at him, she warns, "Don't let me see that again or we will be talking to the principal and you'll be lucky if you're not suspended."

He does his best to look contrite until Jane turns back around to me. Then he puts his fingers to his mouth and licks between them. I fight the urge to vomit as I look back to her.

She hands me back my thermos full of water this time and

also a few packs of honey. "It's for soothing your throat. Just mix it in with your tea and it should take out the ache. Oh, and wait just a minute." Hurrying around the corner she busies herself gathering a few things.

When she comes back, I'm handed a paper sack like our elementary field trip lunches used to come in.

"There's an orange, yogurt, and a peanut butter and jelly sandwich in there," she says. The confusion must show on my face because she quickly adds, "You could use some extra meat on your bones."

My jaw drops, and I suck in my pride long enough to tell her thank you. She just waves me off as she walks away. "It's no big deal, but you're welcome. Come back and see me if you need more water for your tea today."

Her kindness makes me feel bad about lying. Especially when I make my coffee and slide the little packets of honey in my bag. I won't do that again.

With coffee refueling my system, I walk the halls to my locker. As I open the lock, my work clothes come tumbling out. They are shredded almost into pieces and someone has written the words trailer park across what's left of them in some chicken scratch handwriting.

"Too bad about your clothes, trailer park," Derrik says, walking by with his goons right on his heels. "Guess you should have taken me up on that offer." Their laughs make me want to punch things. I work hard for everything that I have and that isn't much. Then to have someone do something like this over a stupid grudge that should have been destroyed with that train, it only makes me that much angrier.

I slam the locker door, take a deep breath, and sip on my coffee. That's how I'm going to make it today. One sip at a time.

Chapter Three

Weirdos

Compared to the morning, the rest of my day is boring and uneventful. Even with the snide remarks from Derrik in the one class that we share together.

I even pat myself on the back for managing to make it to work on time. Sans uniform of course. Luck is on my side for once today. Charles isn't pissed at me for not having my uniform. I think he's just glad that I showed up. Friday nights at the only Mexican restaurant in town can get busy. Add that to the live music that only plays on Friday and our crowd is pretty incredible. So, yeah, any callouts have the potential for disaster.

One of the best things about being busy is I don't have time to stop and think about all of the bad shit in my life. Plus, that means more people and more people equal more tips.

After several hours, I'm sweating enough to miss my lighter uniform. Thankfully, we're only an hour out from closing and I've got a wad of cash from tips in my pocket.

"You've got a table full over on seven," Theresa, our hostess tonight, says as she walks past.

"They'll probably be here awhile, and they always leave good tips." At that last, she winks at me.

If it had come from anyone else, my pride would have been highly offended. Coming from her, though, I don't feel like it's as much of a handout as it is an understanding. I told her what had happened to my uniform earlier. She threatened to go kick their punk asses, but I reasoned that it wouldn't look good on her if a thirty-something-year-old woman beat up on a couple of teenagers. No matter how justified. Instead, she's hooked me up with bomb-ass tables all night. I've made enough in one night to cover the cost of two uniforms.

Pulling myself out of my head, I make my way over to the table with a smile on my face. It drops as I see two heads of hair that look similar to Derrik and his dick friends. Once I realize that it's not them, I snap my smile back into place.

"What can I get you guys to drink?" I ask, making eye contact with the tallest guy in the group. The other three raise their heads. Holy bananas, they are hot. The one I made eye contact with has short, blond hair on the sides while the long, top part waves in front of his green eyes. He's built like some of the men in the NFL. His blue-eyed friend sitting next to him is the one who answers me, "We'll all have water. We're trying to watch our figures." He pats his washboard abs, drawing my attention there and they all laugh.

His eyes crinkle around the edges when he laughs, and I admire the shaggy, dark-brown hair that frames his face. As I take in the other two, I notice that they are all similarly built in variations of tallness. The only one that is smaller in muscle mass is the one with glasses. He's just as hot as the others, though with a strong, angled face, dark-blue eyes, and black hair laid back against his head. Last but not least, is his buddy sitting next to him. With long, blond hair hanging past his shoulders, a smallish nose, and chocolate-colored eyes, he looks like he just stepped out of a surfing magazine.

I crack a genuine smile. "I'd say you guys do enough of that already."

Their expressions are a mixture of shock and amusement. Leaving them like that, I walk back to get their drinks. My smile quickly reverts back to a frown as guilt begins to eat at me. I flirt quite often for good tips, but it's never real. I'm truly attracted to these guys and it's the first time since the accident that it's happened. Tears are fighting a battle behind my eyes as I try not to think of what my boys would say. They would tell me to be happy and get the fuck over it. I just don't know how.

Rearranging my face into something presentable, I make my way back over to give them their waters. "You guys know what you want, or do you need a few minutes?"

I catch the one with glasses glaring at me as if he sees straight through my façade. Shit. There goes that good tip.

The brown-haired one answers for all of them again, "Yeah, we're just going to have the all you can eat tacos."

A smile threatens to break out after his comment earlier. "Ok, anything else?"

Surfer boy grins at me. "Your phone number."

I plaster another fake smile on my face again. "Don't have one."

This makes him smile even wider. "Are you really trying to blow me off?" This guy is, apparently, used to getting his way, especially with the ladies.

"No, actually," I shrug, "I just really don't have a number, because I don't have a phone."

He tries to hide his shock with a smug smile. "Well, how about a name? I know you've got one of those."

I hesitate. Everything seems more personable that way, but I don't want them complaining to Charles, "It's Kendall. I'll go get this in for you guys. Let me know if there's anything else that you need."

Glasses watches the entire exchange without taking his eyes off me. It's unnerving. Putting it all to the back of my mind, I spend the next hour running out taco refills to them.

In between, I sweep up the floors and do all of my closing duties for the night. Once it's time to close up shop, they finally ask for the check.

"Sorry we stayed so long," the green-eyed blond tells me as glasses signs the check. Surfer boy steals the pen as the rest of them slide out of the booth. Glasses looks down at me like he's looking for something. Then without saying a word, he turns and walks away as the other two follow him out. Weirdo. I reach out to take the pen when surfer boy hands it to me. He shoots me a shit-eating grin before he heads to the door. They're all weirdos and that's the official ruling.

Shaking my head, I move to clear off the table. As I go to lift their check ticket, two bills fall out onto the table. My hands close around the two one-hundred dollars bills as my jaw hits my chest. They can't be serious. Glancing down at the scrawl across the tiny white paper, I see why surfer boy stole the pen. *Use this to go buy a phone and then call me.* Followed by his phone number. Accidentally balling the paper up into my fist, I rush to the door in hopes that I can catch them.

"Where's the fire?" Theresa laughs.

The door pops open just in time for me to see their headlights pull out of the parking lot. "Shit!"

"What are you cussing for?" Theresa asks, coming up behind me.

I jerk my face around to her. "Those fucking weirdos that you gave me, dropped two hundred bucks as a tip!"

"That's not surprising," she says even though her face says otherwise. "They used to be regulars in here before you started. That's how I knew they'd tip you good. Maybe they thought you were pretty."

Rolling my eyes, I walk around her. "Yeah, I'm sure they did.

I'll just do them the favor next time and tell them where I live."

"There's no shame in where you live, girl," she says, shaking her head. "It's all about how you present yourself."

I turn her words over in my head as I find a non-existent speck to stare at on her back when she walks away.

Stuffing the cash in my pocket, I take the receipt up to the counter. When I go to put the amount in from it, I realize that glasses put an extra fifty bucks on as a tip. Jesus, what the fuck is wrong with them? Must be nice handing out daddy's money like that. Either way, I won't spend a dime of it. I'm not a goddamn charity case. I earn my way, thank you very much. I'm going to give them a week to come back in. If they don't then I'll use surfer boy's number to get it back to them somehow. Surprisingly, I don't even need the week.

Chapter Four

Surburbiaville

Charles doesn't schedule me for Saturday and I'm okay with that. Says it was to hire a new server or something, but it gives me a chance to go get new work clothes. Plus, drop the rest of my money in the bank where it will go straight to paying the electricity bill. That's one thing that I never want to live without in the winter again. I can sleep in ninety-degree weather with no AC, but I must have heat, even if it is what little bit we are able to contain in the trailer. The only thing that sucks is the smell. Those fucking cigarettes.

I try to tell Gramps all the time that it's going to kill him. It's just hard for a man who lost the love of his life to cancer, and is now suffering the same fate to actually give a shit. Gramps isn't a bad man. He never has been. He and Nana took me in when I was only six and my parents got busted for meth. They wouldn't have to still be serving time if it wasn't for some murder they were charged with on top of the drugs. Yeah, my parents are the epitome of white trash. Dear old mom and pop got prison and I got Gramps and Nana. Things were the best they've ever been for me for a full year. Then Nana got sick. We had to move out of their house they've owned for forty years, just to pay the bills. I was used to the trailer park life. There's nothing degrading about it, because it's the people inside that matter. Not the house. Nana took it hard, though. She left us within the same year. I guess it was just too much for her. Then Gramps started smoking again and got sick himself. Life is a bitch and we drew the short end of the stick.

Maybe that's why Derrik's words hurt so much. I know where I come from and God forbid when something happens to Gramps, I'll have nowhere else to go but that trailer. At least it's paid for and luckily, I'm of age, so I don't have to worry about the state stepping in again.

Now that it's Sunday. I'm in the shower starting my quick getting-ready ritual. It seriously consists of nothing but a shower, brushing my teeth, and a little make up. I don't give a shit about my hair. I just always throw it up in a bun anyways. Stepping out of the tub, I wrap a thin towel around my body and shiver. Damn, I really need to splurge a little and get some new towels. These are so worn that they barely do their jobs anymore. It's just not worth the money at the moment.

Sighing, I wipe my hands across the fog on the mirror. A stranger's face stares back at me. Long, wet, dark-brown hair, greenish-mostly-brown eyes hiding under bushy eyebrows with a small nose and lips a little too big for my face is what I see. The dark circles under my eyes do nothing for the image either. Maybe on a healthy person who isn't so stressed all the time, my looks would be considered classic beauty. Theresa was so wrong. There's no way in hell those guys found me attractive the other night. I'm nowhere even close to their type anyways.

Angrily tossing my eyeliner back into my bag, I wonder why the fuck I'm even thinking about them in the first place. They've been on my mind since Friday night and I can't seem to get them out. Which of course leaves me an angry, guilty mess. It's probably a good idea to schedule an appointment with my therapist soon, but I have neither the time nor money right now. I'll just double my meds today and hope that it helps.

I get dressed and walk into the living room. Gramps is passed out in his chair with a cigarette burnt to ash between his fingers. Snatching it from him, I smash it down inside an old Coke can before tossing it in the trash.

"I wasn't finished with that," he says hoarsely between coughs.

With my back to him, I roll my eyes. "You were out, and it was burned to ash anyways."

He coughs again. "I wasn't asleep, I just closed my eyes for a second."

Right. "Well, I've got to work today. I won't be home till later. Is there anything you need?" I ask with my hand on the doorknob

"I need another carton," he says seriously.

My eyebrows shoot up on my forehead. "That's not happening. Anything else?"

"You're as stubborn and bullheaded as your Nana...was," he says.

I smile. "And that's something she was always proud of, especially when it came to you." Turning back around, I walk over to him. A smile crosses his face as I lean down and press my lips against the top of his bald head.

"I've got to go or I'm going to be late," I tell him.

His voice reaches me about the time the door swings open, "You can always take the car you know."

My steps falter and I find myself staring at the old, blue Chevrolet Malibu sitting in the driveway. His voice turns softer, "It's been two years, Kendall. You already have your license. Keys are hanging in the same place they always are. I can't stand the thought of you walking home at night alone."

"Thanks, Gramps," I say, trying not to get choked up. Then I shut the door on his sigh.

I get lost in my head thinking on his words. It really has been that long and if Will were here, he would laugh at me while he says that my fear is ridiculous. Ever since the accident, I've been terrified to be in a car. Buses don't freak me out as bad and I think it's because they are bigger. Who knows. Maybe I'm just a white trash freak. Or maybe Gramps is right. Maybe it's time to get back on the horse.

I stay on autopilot the entire forty-five-minute walk to work and all the way through dinner.

About thirty minutes before we close, Theresa shines a light through the fog in my head and pulls me out, "You've got table twelve."

I shake my head, "No, that's Becca's section."

Her left eyebrow quirks up and a smile crosses her face, "They asked for you specifically."

There's only two "they" that I can think of that would ask for me, Derrik's dick squad and the strangers from the other night. With the way that she's acting, I'm guessing it's the latter. My head truly hopes that it is. My heart isn't so sure.

Straightening my shirt, I walk around the corner. Said heart does a funny skipping-beat thing and feels like it's going to jump out of my chest.

"Well, well, well. We were hoping that you were here tonight," blond surfer boy says as I make it to the table. Before I can say anything, he continues, "You know, I waited all weekend for a phone call, but never got one."

His dark-haired friend says, "It's true. He hasn't shut up about it since Friday night."

This reminds me of the money burning a hole in my back pocket. I take out the two hundred-dollar bills plus the fifty from the ticket and drop them on the table. "That's because I don't have a phone.

Like I told you before."

"Damn, Teagan. Guess you heard that," the other blond across the table says.

Teagan growls, "Shut the fuck up, Goose. We're not finished here. Are we, Kendall?"

Damn myself for giving him my name the other night and damn Teagan for making it sound so fucking sexy rolling off his tongue.

Guilty anger spikes through my chest. "What the fuck is wrong with you? You can't just charity case someone two hundred bucks to get into their pants. I'm not a fucking hooker!"

I regret the words as soon as they leave my lips, especially since there's a couple sitting close enough to overhear and are now staring. Teagan sits open-mouthed staring at me as Goose and the other blond look anywhere but at us. It's the other set of eyes that throw me off. Dark-blue ones framed by a pair of glasses. His look says he's halfway impressed with the bug under the microscope.

It's awkward for about thirty seconds before keeping my voice down, I say, "I'm sorry. But I'm not taking your money and you're not sitting in my section tonight. Becca will be with you shortly." At that, I walk away leaving Teagan's jaw still on the floor.

I find my way outside to the smoker's spot behind the restaurant. The cold helps clear my head. It's at least ten minutes before Charles finds me. "You okay, Kendall?"

I broke about every serving rule in less than five minutes. There's no way he's not out here to fire me. Fuck, I really need this job. Best to start groveling now, "I'm really sorry, Charles. I shouldn't have said those things."

He holds his hand up to stop me. "I asked if you were okay."

I nod, and he says, "Good. Now listen, I've known you for a

very long time and I know you've been through some real shit in your life. There's no way in hell you would react like that if it wasn't warranted."

I go to say something, and he holds up his hand again. "I don't even want to know. No matter how regular the customer, I trust you."

Tears threaten to spill over, but I yank them back in. "So, you're not going to fire me?"

He laughs, "Not tonight, but I do want you to head on home. Theresa and Becca can finish up closing."

I nod and follow him back inside. When I pass Theresa, she pulls me into a sympathetic hug. Returning it, I then pull on my coat. Now I just have to make it through the dining room. If I'm lucky, they'll already be gone.

They aren't, per my luck and I feel their stares burning holes into me. Once I'm outside, I take a deep breath of cold air. For once, I'm thankful for the long walk home, even as I have to avoid the Dicks pumping gas at the Shell. Not the smartest plan, but I stick to the shadows a little more just in case they drive by.

Headlights flash and a car slows down next to me. Just fucking lovely. I don't want Derrik at my back, so I turn to face the almost stopped car. Low and behold, it's not the dick squad.

"Kendall?" Teagan says from an open window. "Look, I'm really sorry about the way things happened. I was a jerk and I get that."

His apology is sincere, but I'm still frustrated and I'm getting cold from standing still. "What do you want?"

"Well," he says, hesitating like he is weighing his words before saying them, "Do you want a ride home?"

Biting back my automatic sarcastic retort, I say, "No thanks."

He looks at me like I'm crazy, "Are you sure? It's pretty

fucking cold out here." The nice brown-haired one punches him in the arm. "Sorry, I mean, it's cold out."

Shaking my head, I open my mouth and a horn blares as a car zooms by. I have about half a second to realize that someone chucked something out the window. I can't help the yelp that comes out as the cup makes contact with my chest and explodes all over me.

Teagan and Goose, who was riding shotgun, are out of the car and over to me before the cup even hits the ground. I fight tears as I try to wipe the sticky mess off.

"Are you okay?" Teagan asks as Goose at the same time says, "Hell."

"What the actual fuck was that?" a deep voice asks. I glance up to see the other two from the car standing close. The voice belongs to glasses.

"You're still here?" Goose asks him.

His eyes move toward the disappearing tail lights and then back to me. "I thought about going after them, but I'm not leaving you here."

I know that he's talking to them, but it almost feels like he's talking to me. Possibly wishful thinking on my part. Either way, my insides do a flip. "I'll be fine really. It was just the Derrik Dicks."

"You know those assholes?" the nice one asks.

Before I can answer, glasses says, "Get in the car. We're taking you home."

"I'm fi—"

"I swear to God, if you say that you're fine, I will pick you up and throw you in the car myself," he says, pushing through the other two and coming face to face with me.

My nerves have had all that they can take tonight. "I don't even fucking know you! Haven't you ever heard of stranger danger?"

He points to himself. "Maverick, Teagan, Goose, and Lucas." Then facing me he points to my chest, "Kendall. There. Happy? Now get in the car." Turning to walk back toward the car, he gets in and slams the door.

"Fine!" I yell. "You want to take me home? Let's do this." At least this will kill any notions any of them had of being even friends with me. Once they see where I live, that is.

It only takes us ten minutes, but it's pure fucking torture on my anxiety. So much so that I'm borderline panic attack by the time that I say, "Right here."

I hop out of the passenger seat and shut the door of their brand-new Range Rover. The window rolls down and I spread my arms wide. "There it is, boys. Home sweet home. And this is where you run back to Surburbiaville and forget about the poor girl from the trailer park. Thanks for the ride."

I put one foot in front of the other and make it all the way inside before I break down.

Chapter Five

Want to Make a Deal?

After crying myself to sleep last night, I wake up with darker than normal circles under my eyes. Rolling over, I stare at the ceiling and try to figure out why it matters so much. It really shouldn't. Pity parties have no room in my life. Don't have the time and in the end, will get me nowhere, yet here I lay wallowing.

I rub the heels of my hands against my eyes before throwing back the covers and getting up. Tossing my hair up in its usual bun, I dress in a black tank and button-up, red-flannel shirt. The jeans I pull on just so happen to be my favorite. They came from a yard sale about a year ago and are faded with holes in the knees, but I love them. Safe and comfortable is just what I need today.

Running a pot of coffee, I take my time sipping at the first cup. My eyes catch on the glint of silver of the keys hanging by the door. It would be so nice to drive today, but after the almost panic attack last night, it probably isn't such a good idea yet.

I pour the rest of the coffee and a tad touch of creamer in my thermos and grab my leather jacket before heading out the door.

I manage to make it all the way to lunch without thinking about last night. Of course, as lost in my head that I was this morning, I forgot to pack my lunch. On a more positive note, I haven't had to deal with any of the dicks today, so I'm just going to steer clear of the cafeteria and go to the library to work on my research paper that's due Friday.

I should have known that would be too easy. Just as my hand reaches out for the door, it opens and pops me right across the knuckles.

"Oops, sorry," a blonde says coming out.

"Don't waste your breath on trailer trash, new girl," Stacey Marsh says following her out. Just fucking great. The pod squad. You know, I get Derrik's hatred, but I'll never understand Stacey's. It may have something to do with his obsession with torturing me, as if I have something to do with that. Everyone knows they've been dating since freshman year.

"Excuse me," I say to the last of the pods, Sarah, still standing in the doorway, a blonde Barbie just like the rest of them.

She sneers at me, "Hey, Stacey, aren't those the clothes that you donated to the Salvation Army last week?"

I force my way in beside her and leave them cackling at the door. Finding a secluded corner of the room, I hunker down and get absolutely nothing done. Rain spatters against the window and I watch the water run in little rivulets down the glass. Tears roll down my face in the same pattern. I've never cried at school, because these people mean absolutely nothing to me. With all of the other shit going on in my head, though, it's unstoppable. The ache of missing Casey, Will, and Brian is so deep today. It burns me so far down that I feel it in my soul. I'm surprised to look at my hands and still see flesh instead of ash. Depression is its own kind of evil and it's weighing me down. I won't even have the reprieve of work tonight.

When the last bell rings, I'm nothing more than a zombie. A walking bag of skin and bones with nothing firing upstairs. I hear my name being called, but I ignore it. There's no one worth talking to at this place.

A warm hand grasps me at the elbow, "Kendall?"

My first instinct is to punch first and ask questions later, but I recognize the voice. The brown-haired nice guy.

"Did you not hear me calling for you?" Lucas asks.

The bus behind me lets out a whoosh of air and closes its door. It's getting ready to pull away and mine will be right behind it.

Lucas pulls my attention back to him. "Hey, are you okay?"

The rain steadily falls around us as we stand under the little canopy area. His hand is still at my elbow and I want nothing more than to lean into him. My eyes fall to my bus as it pulls away from the curb. Tears pool in my eyes and streak down my face at the thought of my now miserable walk home.

Lucas uses his other hand to pull my chin up to face him. His eyes roam over my face like he's trying to figure out how to fix the white trash ruin that I am, but he has no idea just how impossible that would be. People are staring, and I couldn't give two shits as Lucas locks eyes with me. His flick down to my lips and back up again.

He looks like he's going to kiss me right before he clears his throat, "Hungry?"

"What?" I ask a little hoarse from not talking for so long.

He smiles. "I'm famished. Want to go over to Pete's?"

Pete's is a small diner kind of place that borders our small town and the next one over, which isn't any bigger than ours. It just holds more of the upper-class, white-collar people. It's also about an hour walk from here. Twenty if we take a car. I shake my head.

His face shows defeat, but he still says, "Please. I promise to drive really slow and careful."

The words take me by surprise. "How did you know?"

He shrugs. "I saw you clenching the armrest last night like it was going to fall off. I just assumed you were super pissed or scared of being in the car."

"And you don't think that had anything to do with me being

in a car full of strange boys?" I ask.

Tilting his head back, he laughs, "With the way that you stood up to Mav, that thought never crossed my mind."

I'd be lying if I said I didn't admire the sight of his smile and the sound of his laugh. If he hadn't accused me of being scared and the words hitting home, I may have told him no. So, when I say yes, I'm not sure if it's to prove him wrong or myself.

"Come on," he says, pulling my hand to the crook of his elbow without letting go, almost as if he's scared I'm going to take off running. That's not too far from the truth.

He leads me over to the newest car in the lot, a huge, black pick-up truck. It's raised so high that Lucas gives me a boost up. I'm so nervous that I can't even manage to thank him. Snapping my seatbelt and watching him walk around the front of the hood, I take several deep breaths trying to calm down. This is harder than last night, and I think it's because I was so angry at both the Dicks and Maverick.

I try to distract myself with Lucas. When he comes around the corner, the street lamp catches his hair just right and turns the brown a tinge red. There's a five o'clock shadow across his jawline that makes me wonder what it would feel like under my fingers. It's been so long.

He hops up into his seat and I notice his clothes for the first time. In brand-new jeans and white, long-sleeve shirt underneath a navy vest, he looks like he's ready for prep school. The only thing that argues that is a black, leather jacket lying against the center console.

It takes a minute to catch on to the fact that he is saying something. "What?"

He passes me a knowing smile. "I just asked if you were good."

I nod and he starts the engine.

The ride to Pete's is quiet, but not the awkward kind. Almost like he doesn't want to pressure me into talking. Lucas makes a few turns to take us out of town. This road runs parallel with the train tracks. All I can hope for is one not to pass. The thought has no sooner left my head and I hear a horn behind us.

My throat clenches tight and my breath comes in short gasps. "Pull over."

"What?" he asks with concern.

I reach out for his hand. "Please. Just for a minute. Pull. Over."

True to his word, Lucas has driven more than careful and pulls slowly over to the shoulder. I close my eyes and try to slow my breathing down, so it will slow my racing heart.

When I can no longer hear it, I risk opening my eyes. The last car keeps moving until it's no longer in sight. It's then that I realize that I've been squeezing the shit out of Lucas's hand.

"Sorry," I say, trying to let go.

His fingers tighten around mine. "Nothing to be sorry for."

I'm breathing in through my nose and out my mouth; Lucas doesn't rush me. I'm just thankful he's not asking if I'm okay. I'd probably break down again.

"We can go now," I say quietly.

He clenches my hand and never lets go the rest of the way to the diner.

We walk into Pete's and a few people turn around to stare.

"Hey! What's up, Lucas?" A tall boy says striding up to us. He's dressed in the same uniform style as Lucas, so they must go to the same school.

They do a crazy fist-bump, handshake thing, "What's up bro?"

The stranger all but jumps up and down on his toes, "You

ready to whoop some Eastern ass on Friday?"

Lucas grins. "You already know."

"This is the year we go undefeated, man. I feel it," the stranger says. "Oh and after party is at Kelly's lake house."

He looks over and notices me for the first time. "Hi, I don't think we've met. I'm Henry Edward the third. Most people just call me Eddie."

I take his outstretched hand. "Kendall. Nice to meet you."

He smiles. "Likewise. You should definitely come to the soirée Friday night. It's going to be banging. Especially if our boys take us to state."

Glancing up at Lucas, I see he's watching me. Possibly waiting for the next breakdown. I have half a second to be thankful that the tears have stopped falling and I don't have a bad after-crier's face, other than slightly puffy eyes. Trying to make my face relax, I smile and one side of his mouth quirks up. I turn back to Eddie. "Sounds like fun. I'll be there."

"Most excellent," he says before fist bumping us and making his way back to his booth where several other people dressed the same wait.

Lucas's hand finds my lower back and sends a kaleidoscope of butterflies straight through my belly as he leads us to a booth in the corner. He gives me a little nudge to sit with my back against the wall as he sits to face me.

"Sorry about that. You didn't make any promises that you have to uphold or anything," he says watching my face.

I shrug. "I'm actually off Friday night. Might be nice to do something different for a change."

This earns me a full-on smile and I have to look away before I find myself falling into it. "So, you guys are like some big football stars?"

He looks surprised, "Wow, are we that easy to guess?"

I roll my eyes. "I may be the weird girl from the trailer park, but I do like my football. Just not our team because they fucking suck. Not to mention the players are complete dicks."

There's a quick moment of silence before he bursts out laughing. It's a 'head back' kind of laugh that draws the attention of the people around us, including his schoolmates in the corner. The tiny, blonde girl sitting with them gives me an appreciative nod. I'm not sure I understand why, but it's nice to not be glared at for once. When my eyes move back to Lucas he's smiling enough that the laugh lines are still there around his eyes.

The waitress chooses this moment to walk up, "How are you doing today, Lucas? Where are the other three to the fantastic four?"

His smile turns respectful. "They all had detention after school. So, it's just Kendall and I today, Judy."

Her gaze flicks to me. "He being a proper gentleman?"

If it were Teagan or Maverick in front of me, I wouldn't hesitate to get them in trouble. I'm just not going to do that to Lucas, so instead, I answer, "Yes ma'am."

"Oh, pretty and polite," she says, then moves her hand beside her mouth as she mock whispers to him, "This one's a keeper."

He grins at me again and I feel my face turn red from the attention.

Judy saves me, "Are we ordering the usual?"

"Yes, please," he replies, "And Kendall will have the same."

He winks at me as she says, "Ok, be back in two shakes of a lamb's tail."

"Did you just order for me?" I ask with mock horror.

The grin he shoots me could melt sugar, "I do believe that I just did."

My eyebrow goes up in question, "What if I don't like what you ordered?"

Shrugging he says, "I guess you'll just have to trust me."

This takes me aback. It's been a long time since I trusted anyone other than Gramps. My spine straightens, and I lean back against my seat. I pick at a spot on the table with my fingernail.

"Sorry," he says quietly, "I didn't mean to say anything to upset you again."

I shoot him a sad smile. "It's okay really. I've just had a bad couple of days."

"Does it happen to have anything to do with us?" he asks.

My turn to shrug. "Maybe in an off-hand kind of way, but not really."

Judy runs two waters out to our table and says the food's going to take a little longer before disappearing again.

Lucas takes a long drink of his before he says, "You know, Teagan didn't mean for all of that to go down the way that it did last night. He has never been the super serious type, so sometimes, he comes off as an offensive asshole."

Thinking back on my reaction, my face turns pink. "I may need to be the one apologizing. I overreacted a little. I just didn't feel right taking his money like that."

He lets out a short laugh, "You know, honestly, I think that very reason is why Maverick took a liking to you."

I snort softly, "Right."

"No, it's true. He's rough around the edges and a bit harsh sometimes, but he's a good dude. Trust me when I say that he wouldn't have let just anyone get in the Rover drenched with soda like you were. I'm pretty sure he'd probably go to jail for attempted murder if one of us tried it," he says.

I think on his words for a minute. "Speaking of which. Why am I here? Why did you bother to come to the school, Lucas? Especially after I showed you where I live."

He sighs, "Because you were wrong." My eyebrow goes up again and he says, "What? You think that just because we go to a prep school that we're snobs? That sounds a lot like stereotyping to me."

Shit. I don't want them to be, but his words are true. My actions are no better than Derrik's toward me and I never even thought about it like that. "I'm sorry."

One corner of his mouth quirks up in victory. "No reason to be sorry. I'm sure it's what you're used to at that school and probably in life period."

Before I can say anything, Judy drops plates covered in french fries and two of the biggest burgers I've ever seen in my life in front of us. "Y'all let me know if you want anything else."

Lucas thanks her as I attempt a half-assed thanks. I know my eyes are as big as saucers, "You actually eat all of this?"

He laughs and rolls up the sleeves on his button-down. "At least once a week."

As he eloquently digs into his plate, I admire the way that his muscles flex in his forearms. Tattoos run from his wrists all the way up his arm underneath the rolls in the shirt.

I am completely entranced trying to pick apart the different designs. "How far do those go up?"

Looking up, I see that he's been watching me the whole time as he's taking bites. "Eat some and I might tell you."

Unladylike, I stuff three fries in my mouth at once and look at him expectantly. He almost chokes on a drink of his water and it makes me smile. After wiping it off his mouth and the little specks that landed on his shirt, he says, "These go all the way to my shoulders, but I have more across my back and chest."

I narrow my eyes at him. "Wait, how old are you?"

He points at my food and waits until I take a bite of burger before he answers, "Nineteen."

My mouth falls open in shock. Thankfully, there's no food in it. "But those must have taken hours to do. What do you go and get new ones every weekend?"

Laughing, he says, "No, I actually started some of them when I was sixteen."

"How?" I ask

"Richie from Suburbiaville, remember?" he says with a smile.

Damn, he's never going to let me live those words down and if I'm honest, I don't really deserve to. I try to bring the conversation back to my curiosity. "Can I see the rest of them?"

This earns another laugh. "You better be glad you're asking me that question and not Maverick or Teagan."

"Why?" I ask suspiciously.

"Because," he starts, "they have some that you can't see unless they are fully undressed, and I know for a fact they wouldn't tell you no."

My face turns red and I make it a point to eat and not talk anymore.

After a few minutes, Lucas says, "Want to make a deal?"

Tilting my head to the side, I ask, "What kind of deal?"

"One where I show you the rest of them," he replies.

It sounds sketchy, but what girl in my shoes would say no? "Ok."

He nods as if he expected my answer. "Tell me where you were earlier, and I'll show them to you."

I'm confused, "What do you mean? I went straight from home to school today."

"Not then," he says with a sad smile, "Where you were in your head when I called for you today?"

"Oh," I say, glancing at the table. "I told you. I've just had a shitty couple of days and I'm just mentally exhausted dealing with the bullshit that comes with life."

"Does it have anything to do with those assholes in the car last night?" he asks with a serious tone in his voice. I don't want to lie to him and tell him no, because they have been some of it here lately. "Or is it about the reason why you're scared of cars?"

My eyes flick up to his and I rein in the anger trying to bubble out of my mouth. His voice turns soft again, "My dad died in a car crash when I was two years old. I wasn't even old enough to know anything. He was just there one day and not the next. I don't even remember anything about him. If it hadn't been for my uncle, I'm pretty sure that my mom would have gone insane."

My face scrunches with confusion and he says, "Yeah, my dad's brother is now my step-dad. Trust me. I caught so much shit for that one growing up. People love the incest jokes even though they aren't even close to being the same thing." He pauses and runs a hand across his jaw, "That's how Maverick and I became friends. Seventh grade and he was new, he hadn't heard all of the rumors yet. This kid we called Johnny comes up and started shit with me one day and Maverick threw him to the dirt and beat the hell out of him. We've been best friends ever since."

I mull his words over in my brain before quietly asking, "But what if my story doesn't have a happy ending like yours?"

He leans his arms down on the table and waits until I'm looking straight at him, "With the way that you carry the weight of the world on your shoulders, I assume that it doesn't."

I suck in a shaky breath, "My boyfriends died in a train wreck two years ago."

He doesn't even flinch at the plural use of the word, "They were the guys in that old Camaro?" I nod, and he says, "Yeah, I remember when that happened."

Tears roll down my cheek and there's no stopping them now. "They were my best friends and it'll be exactly two years ago next week. That's where I was today when you called for me. Wishing for the millionth time that I had been in that car with them."

He chews his bottom lip and I close my eyes, not wanting to see any kind of pity or whatever on his face. I hear him shift in the booth and the next thing I know, he is pushing into my side to get me to scoot over. When I oblige him, he sits and takes my hand in his. "Do you think that's what they would've wanted?"

I shake my head and let out a small laugh, "No, if they were here they'd either be pissed or laughing at me right now."

With him sitting this close, when his voice goes quiet, it turns into this smoky sound that sends shivers down my spine, "Kendall, this is probably one of the hardest things that you will ever have to go through, but it will make you a better person for it. You just have to live. If for no other reason than for them. Live life to the fullest, just like you know that they would want you to."

His words make sense and he's right. I don't know why it takes him saying it for it to click in my head, but I do want to live for them. I want to start right now. With Lucas sitting so close, it's nothing to tilt my head up and give him the 'ok' look to kiss me. His eyes flick down to my lips and I close my eyes as I feel his breath on my face. That's the moment his phone decides to go off in his pocket. It's playing the song from Top Gun and I can already guess who it is calling.

Lucas sighs and presses his forehead against mine. "I'm sorry."

He pulls away and answers the phone as I'm left wondering what he's apologizing for, sympathy for my story or the almost kiss.

"Yeah, hang on just a sec," he says to one of the guys on the line. Turning to me, he says, "They got out early and want me to meet them here for food. If you don't want to see them then now's our chance to run. We've got about a five-minute window."

If I'm going to try my hand at this new me, I've got to keep it rolling or I might wimp out and decide it's not worth it after all. "It's okay. We can wait for them."

One side of his mouth pulls up and he puts the phone back to his face. "Already here waiting on you, dude. Yeah, I didn't know you were getting out early and I was fucking starved. Whatever, asshole, see you in a few."

"Let me guess," I say, "Maverick?"

He laughs, "I would say how'd you guess, but it's not even worth the breath it takes."

For the first time in a very long time, I feel a small weight lift from my heart as I laugh with him.

It isn't even the full five minutes later when Teagan, followed by Goose and Maverick, comes strolling in through the door.

Teagan throws Lucas a shit-eating grin right before he catches sight of me sitting next to him. He halts so fast in his tracks that Goose slams into his back and it knocks his phone to the floor.

"What the fuck, T?" he all but yells as he bends to pick up his phone. "You better hope you didn't crack the screen mother fu—" Teagan elbows him in the stomach before he can finish. He follows his line of vision and smiles at me. I could be wrong, but I think Maverick was the first one to see me. I feel his gaze like a sunburn after sitting on the beach all day.

Goose walks around Teagan and slides into the booth opposite us. "You didn't say that you were on a date."

"It's not a date," I say, quickly jumping in to defend Lucas and possibly even my own pride. I don't want to hear Lucas say it. He cuts his eyes over to me in question, but smiles as if he already knows my reasoning. Maverick slides in after Goose and leaves Teagan to grab a random chair to sit at the end of the table.

There's an awkward silence for a few seconds before Lucas breaks it, "You guys get out for good behavior or something?"

The three of them smile, but it's Teagan that answers in that smug tone of his, "It was Ms. K, dude. Just told her we were hungry and growing boys and we needed food."

Wow. These guys really are used to getting their way. "What were you in detention for anyways?"

"The usual," Maverick says then points at Goose and Teagan, "These two were horsing around and talking shit."

"And you just got caught in the middle?" I ask.

He nods. "As always. The staff just assumes now that we're all in on it, even if we're not even close to each other. The only reason Lucas lucked out is because he doesn't have that class with us."

"Yeah, dude," Teagan says, offended, "What the fuck? Why didn't you do something to get locked up with us?"

Lucas laughs, "You're kidding right? I'd say that I spent my time much better than that today."

Maverick's eyes narrow on me and I have to look away as he says, "Yes, I would say that you did."

I could kiss Judy as she chooses this moment to bring out three plates that look exactly like ours did. They dig in just as quickly as Lucas had earlier. It's surprising to watch teenage boys eat hamburgers and fries with such refined table manners.

"What?" Goose asks as he catches me watching him. I just shake my head. I'd rather not insult them by saying they're supposed to be acting like complete slobs.

Teagan is the first to finish. "So, what are we doing this weekend?"

"Well," Lucas starts, "I think we'll be going to Kelly's lake house for the party after the game."

Maverick looks up from under his glasses with a confused look on his face and Teagan laughs, "And why the fuck would we be doing something stupid like that?"

Lucas smiles over at me. "Because Kendall told Eddie that we would."

I cringe down in my seat a little. "I was only trying to be nice and I didn't say that you guys would go. I just told him I would."

Maverick's eyebrows are high on his forehead and he smiles for the first real time since I met them. Goose shakes head and looks at Lucas. "You must not have explained it to her."

Now it's my turn to be confused. "Explain what?"

Teagan smiles at me. "We don't go to anything like that alone. Always as a group."

"It saves us from doing stupid shit," Maverick adds.

I shake my head. "I'm not in your group, though. Besides, I probably won't even go, so it's no big deal."

They all look at each other before Lucas says, "Let's just say you've got a temporary pass and we're going to the party Friday night."

Teagan just about jumps out of his seat. "Does that mean you're coming to the game, too?"

I shrug, "It's been awhile since I've been to one. I always

work on Fridays, plus our team sucks."

The guys laugh like Lucas had earlier and Teagan says, "Yes they do. So, that means you need to come watch how the game is really played." He jumps up from his seat and strolls over to the table in the corner where Eddie and his friends are. My eyes travel across his body and I can't help but admire the swagger that he puts into his step. It makes his jeans hug in all the right places.

When I tear my gaze away, I catch Maverick staring at me. I feel my face heat up in embarrassment. Goose, in my peripheral vision, is watching the two of us and smiling like a lunatic.

"Ok," Teagan says, walking back to the table with the small blonde under his arm, "Kendall, meet Ryleigh, my baby sister. Ryleigh, Kendall."

She holds out her hand across the table. "Nice to meet you."

"Back at you," I respond as I shake her hand.

Teagan throws his arm back around Ryleigh as he talks to her, "Kendall is coming to the game and Kelly's party Friday. She doesn't know anybody from our school. You'll help her out and let her sit with you at the game and stuff, right?"

Her eyes light up like she's happy to do anything and everything he asks, "Yeah, of course." She turns to me. "I can come get you right after school since you get out a little later than we do. We can hang out at our house until the game starts."

I see Lucas stiffen in the seat beside me and even as I answer her, he still doesn't relax. "Sure. Sounds fun," I say.

"Hey, Ryleigh, we're heading out," Eddie says from the door.

She throws up her hand at me. "See you Friday."

I nod at her and Lucas pounces as soon as she's out of earshot, "Are you going to be okay riding with her?" His words are quiet, but the guys still catch it.

"Why would she not be okay?" Maverick asks in that serious tone of his.

Lucas looks at me in question and I shake my head. "No reason, man," he answers Maverick. Then to me he asks, "You ready to go?"

I nod and dig my wallet out of my side pocket of my shirt. Lucas puts his hand on top of mine stopping me. The other three watch the exchange with expressions ranging from curiosity, hurt, and anger. The last coming from Maverick, of course.

Lucas whips out a twenty and tosses it on the table, "I'm going to run Kendall home real quick. Meet you guys at the house in a little while."

They all give me polite goodbyes, but if looks could kill, Lucas would be a dead man. I return Judy's wave on the way out the door. Lucas opens his door for me and once I'm inside and buckled in, I take a tension-relieving breath. It's intense being around the four of them together like that, especially being attracted to all of them. Not to mention the seriousness of the conversation and the almost kiss earlier.

Lucas lets me get lost in my head the entire way back to Sleepy Pines. He goes to pull in and I stop him, "Right here is okay."

He shakes his head. "I thought we were past this. Which one?"

Shame burns hot spots on my cheeks, but it's not really for our place. It's for all of the others around us. They're all in bad shape and no one bothers to keep their tiny spaces clean like Gramps and me. I point to it on the end, "That's me."

He pulls up behind the Malibu and I grab his hand as he goes to throw the truck in park, "Thank you for everything today. I didn't realize how much it would help to talk to someone about all of it. It's not the same when you pay someone to listen. You're much better than my therapist any day of the week."

I feel stupid for saying so much, but he just smiles. "Anytime, Kendall. Truly. If you ever need anything, just call me." He reaches in the glovebox and pulls out a pen and napkin. After he writes down his number, he hands it to me. "Use it if you need to. Or even if you just want to."

I nod and hop down. He shuts off the truck and comes around the side. "Can we go inside real quick? I almost forgot that I owe you something."

My thoughts are jumbled in confusion caught somewhere between what he's talking about and the thought of him coming inside.

His fingers move to the buttons on the front of his shirt. "Or I can just strip down out here."

Then it clicks. His tattoos. "Oh my god, Lucas!" I freak out, "You can't take your clothes off out here."

He undoes the top button and his hands move to the bottom of the vest thing that he's wearing like he's getting ready to pull it over his head. My hands close around his. "Please stop. Save it for another day."

His eyes narrow teasing me. "Are you sure?"

I nod. "I won't let you forget."

He smiles and leans down to press a kiss against the corner of my mouth. It sends tingles all the way to my toes. I watch as he gets back in the truck and winks at me before pulling out of the little driveway. Watching until he's all the way back on the road, I don't go inside until I can't see his lights anymore.

Chapter Six

S'mores

On my way out the door the next morning, I take a hard look at the keys on the hook. After I got home last night, I did a quick run through on all of our bills coming due for the month and was surprised to find that Gramps already paid the electricity bill. When I asked him about it, the only answer I got was 'it's covered until at least December.' I pressed him for more details, but it was like pulling teeth, so I gave up. That means that I've got an extra one fifty in the bank. Teagan's words got me to thinking and why shouldn't I get a cell phone? There are those prepaid things and if I don't have the money that month then I just won't keep service on it. I was so excited last night that I almost went right then to get one, but common sense won me over. It's always best to sleep on big decisions.

I'm pretty sold on it this morning and since I have to work later, it would make more sense to drive. I'll never make it over to the store and into work on time if I'm walking. Snatching the keys down, I walk toward Gramps's door. I knock softly, but there's no answer. I hate to wake him up, but I need to make sure that he isn't going to need them today. It's not like he can drive, but sometimes, the neighbors come over and borrow the car to run errands for him or take him to the doctor when I can't.

"Gramps?" I call out softly, knocking again. I get no answer. One of my biggest fears is that I'm going to come knocking one day and the no answer will mean the worst. I know it's inevitable. We all die at some point. I just don't want it to be right now. There's rustling on the other side of the door and I let out a relieved breath.

I hear him cough before saying, "Kendall? Everything okay?"

Cracking the door, I give him a few seconds warning and then peek my head around the corner. "I was going to take the car today. Would that be okay?"

He tries to hide his shock. "That's perfectly fine. Robert did everything I needed him to do yesterday. Just drive carefully please."

"I will, Gramps, promise. I won't be back after school. I'm going to run to the store before work. Want anything?" I ask.

He shakes his head then stops. "You know, I saw a commercial the other day for some of those white-fudge-covered Oreos. Your Nana would have loved those. Could you pick some up for us?"

I smile. "Of course. How are you feeling?"

"Better than I have all week," he says, smiling.

"Good," I tell him, "I'll be back later tonight. Call me at the school if you need anything or need me to bring the car back."

He nods as he slowly lays back down. "I will, Pea. Drive safe."

His words choke me up and I have to shut the door before I start crying. Gramps and I have never really said that we love each other, but his use of the nickname Pea reminds me that we don't have to. It's enough just to know that he cares, because we both already know. My heart takes a deep stab wound as I think about losing him. Not today, Kendall. Keep your shit together.

I manage to make it all the way through school without running into any trouble, other than Mr. Parker telling me that if I'm going to start driving to school that I'll need a parking pass. I spend my lunch break in the office filling out paperwork and waiting on the secretary to get her ducks in a row, but it pays off. Waiting until last bell, I rush out to put the sticky thing on my window, so I can hurry to the store.

"Goddamn it," I say, getting frustrated. The thing is monstrously huge and super sticky and for some reason keeps trying to crinkle on the window. I'm about ready to give up when a male hand reaches around and takes the sticker from me.

"Here let me help," a voice says. I look up to see Billy Terth, the school's quarterback, smiling back at me. Embarrassingly enough, he flattens the sticker in less than five seconds.

I want to thank him for his help, but my mouth is glued shut. His dirty-blond hair shines in the sun and with his hazel eyes plus a bright-white smile, there's no doubt that he's a looker. He doesn't run in Derrik's circle, but that doesn't mean that I trust him. Call me a stereotype if you want, but I don't put anything past that asshole.

"Thanks," I say finally.

He smiles wider. "You're more than welcome. Those things can be kind of tricky at times."

If I was feeling anything towards him, his next words would have crushed them, "I haven't seen you around before. Are you new here?"

"You're kidding right?" I say, not able to stop myself.

He looks taken aback. "What?"

"Dude, we've been going to school together since the fourth grade," I say, backing up to open my door. "And what's even worse is the fact that we have three classes together right now."

His eyebrows draw down on his face as it scrunches in confusion. When I start the car, he backs away, throwing me a smile and a wave. It's actually a fucking creepy smile. His look is how a runner looks at the finish line. It makes me miss Lucas and the other guys. They may be arrogant prep boys, but at least they are genuine and don't give me the willy nilly's.

I try to shake it off as I go into the store. Conscious of my time frame, I know I don't have a lot to spend picking anything out. Doing the next best thing, I get someone to help point me in the right direction. I manage to make it out of the store with a working smart phone, whatever the fuck that is, and a month's worth of service for less than ninety bucks.

The first thing I do when I get to the car is save Lucas and Teagan's number in the contacts the way that the guy showed me in the store. It takes me about five minutes, but I also figure out how to send them both a text message letting them know that I finally got a phone and giving them my number.

"Shit," I say, glancing at the time. "Shit, shit, shit." I'm going to be late for the first time ever. I've got five minutes to make the fifteen minute drive to the restaurant. After Charles's words the other night, I don't think he'll fire me over it, but it's more than that. Nana and Gramps raised me with a work ethic of knowing better. Early bird gets the worm and all that hoopla.

Unfortunately, it looks like I won't be getting that metaphorical worm today. I'm ten minutes late and have to rush through throwing my uniform on in the bathroom. Trying to make up for being so late, I work my ass off into the night. We are busier than normal and since I'm trying extra hard, tips roll in.

By closing time, there's a fat wad of cash in my pocket. I've been staying so on top of everything that by the time Charles locks the doors, all I've got to do is fold some silverware up into napkins and the dining room will be done.

He walks by and pats me on the shoulder. "You're the best employee I've got, girl."

I smile at his back and he says, "Just don't tell the others."

It makes me proud as stupid as it sounds. It's not much, but I've never really stood out anywhere except here. I'm still ridiculously smiling as I grab my clothes from the back and Charles locks me out. There's a whistle that sounds like a bird and I raise my head to find Teagan sitting on the ass-end of a brand-new hunter-green Jeep Wrangler.

"What are you doing here?" I ask as I make my way to him.

Holding up his phone, he says, "You never messaged back. Just wanted to check and make sure you were okay."

Oh hell. "Sorry, I got here late and had to rush to change my clothes and everything." I dig the phone out of my bag and see that it's got four new little message symbols at the top. When I open the texts, I see that two are replies from Lucas and Teagan and two are from numbers I don't recognize. There's no question who they are, though. Sure enough, when I open them, I see Maverick and Goose's name.

"You gave them my number?" I question.

He looks sheepish. "Technically, it wasn't me. Lucas sent it to them, but only because they threatened to beat him up for it if they didn't."

I laugh. Fucking boys.

"Besides," he adds, "For one, there's never been any secrets between us. And two, what if they needed to get in touch with you while Lucas and I weren't around."

"One of the perks of the temporary pass?" I ask

He nods. "Don't worry, though. If you don't want to talk to them, just tell them to back off."

I smile. "Ok."

There's a few seconds of silence before he asks, "Want a ride home?"

For the first time today, I'm disappointed that I drove, "I

borrowed my Gramps's car today, so I could go get the phone before work."

It only takes half a second for me to see that Lucas told them about our conversation. "Wow, there really are no secrets between you guys, huh?"

I get an apologetic smile in return. "He didn't really mean to. Maverick has a way of dragging shit out of people."

"Oh, and I'm sure that you and Goose had nothing to do with it at all," I lightheartedly accuse.

He places a hand over his heart. "Ouch. Already grouping us together like everyone else does."

My eyebrow goes up. He laughs, "Ok, fine. We might have had a little to do with it. I can make it up to you, though."

"Yeah?" I ask. "And how's that?"

He watches my face. "Well, I was going to see if you wanted to come hang out with me for a little while tonight. We have this fucking awesome fire pit out back and I'll even stop to get stuff for s'mores."

"Isn't it a little late, especially since we've got school tomorrow?" I ask.

Shrugging, he says, "I'm somewhat of an insomniac, so I'm used to working with little to no sleep."

"We definitely don't have that in common then. I turn quite bitchy without sleep," I say, watching disappointment flash in his eyes. I sigh, "But it probably wouldn't hurt to lose a little tonight."

"Hell yes," he says, jumping up.

I laugh, "I just need to go check on my Gramps before we go and change my clothes real quick."

He nods. "We can drop off your car and I'll drive you home when you're ready to leave tonight, if you want."

The thought sounds more appealing than I think it would, "Ok, but I hope you don't mind that I'm taking the long way home."

He grins. "Nope."

I hold up my phone. "Let me just answer them back real quick so they don't think the worst like you did."

"Here, let me see it," he says, reaching for it. It only takes him several presses of the buttons before he hands it back, "Just type in your message and hit send. It'll go to all of us in a group chat."

I do as he says, telling the others what happened and that I'd talk to them later.

"Don't tell them you're with me," he says quickly before I hit the send button.

My eyes narrow. "Why?"

He shrugs and fiddles with his keys. "I just don't want them randomly showing up at the house tonight. I'd rather keep it just us, if that's okay?"

I smile. "Sounds good." When I hit the send button, Teagan's phone beeps and he shows it to me.

"That's pretty cool," I admit. "Saves time."

"Yep, and if you don't delete the message then you won't have to go back in and start a new one," he says.

I nod in understanding. "Thank you."

He grins and one-arm hugs me, "You're welcome. Now, let's go. The night is wasting away. I'm following you."

When I get in the car, Teagan's scent still clings to my shirt. It smells amazing and makes my palms sweat at the same time. I wipe them on my jeans and drive home, with him right on my heels.

All the lights are off in the trailer, so that means that Gramps is already in bed. I tell Teagan to stay in the Jeep and I'll be right back. Making quick time of it, I change clothes and am back out the door with my wallet in one pocket and phone in the other. At the last second, I remember to grab my leather jacket out of the Malibu.

When I jump in with Teagan he smiles at me and asks, "Ready?"

I let out a quiet breath and nod.

He pats my knee before backing out. Driving just as carefully as Lucas had, Teagan takes back roads and we are at his house in roughly thirty minutes. He blares music and sings along never missing a lyric. My fear was absolutely nonexistent the whole drive, because I kept going back and forth between laughing and singing with him.

The house that we pull up to is one of the most stunning places I've ever seen. It looks like it belongs in a painting from the Civil War. Plantation-style columns hold up a wraparound porch on both the top and bottom floor. There are windows everywhere and with the lights on inside, it is a fucking dream house.

"Wow," I say quietly as Teagan comes around to help me down from the Jeep.

He doesn't even bother looking, "I know. It's ostentatious, but it's what Cynthia wanted."

"Who's Cynthia?" I ask.

Throwing his arm around my shoulder, he looks at me and smiles, "My stepmom. Want to meet her?"

I tuck the loose strands of my hair behind my ear nervously, "I didn't know I'd be meeting anyone tonight."

His cheeks lift again, "We don't have to if you don't want to."

Right. I may be trailer trash, but my Nana taught me southern hospitality. "It's okay," I tell him, adjusting the bottom of my shirt to try and hide one of the holes. The last thing I want to do is embarrass him or myself.

"You're beautiful," he assures me.

My heart does a skip pattern at his words. There have only been three people in my life that have said them to me. Even Nana never did. She said that it made people vain. I plaster a fake smile on my face and he pulls me to a stop. "I'm sorry. I didn't mean to say the wrong thing."

"It's not you," I admit quietly. "I've just got a lot of issues."

He looks down at me for so long that it makes me feel a little awkward, so I blurt out, "Look, maybe this was a mistake. You can take me home if you want."

Pulling me in for a hug, his voice rumbles through his chest into my ear, "You're not going to get out of tonight that easy." I want to have some witty comeback, but being this close to his smell has deep fried my brain. I just wrap my arms around him and live in the moment.

"Let's go get the fire started," he finally says. His voice is a little deeper and butterflies take flight in my stomach. Dazed, I walk hand in hand with him through the house until we come to the last room near French doors in the back. I wouldn't be able to describe the inside if my life depended on it. I'm too distracted by Teagan.

He pulls us to a stop before we make it to the doors. There are two people in a sitting room of sorts. The woman is sitting with her feet curled under her and a book in her lap. She's very pretty, but not much older than us. If I had to guess, I'd say twenty-five at the most. The man is just an older version of Teagan with short hair and a leathery sort of face.

"Hey, guys," he says to them.

The woman looks up immediately, but the man finishes whatever he's doing on his gigantic phone-looking thing.

"This is Kendall," he says, pulling me forward a little. "Kendall, that's Cynthia and Steve aka Mom and Dad."

She gets up and comes over with an outstretched hand. "Nice

to meet you, Kendall."

I shake her hand in return. "Nice to meet you, too." She gives me a once over with her eyes and smiles.

"Nice to meet you, Kendall," his dad says. Before I can respond, he continues, "How was practice today, Son?"

Teagan shrugs. "Same as any other day."

His dad makes a tsk noise behind his teeth. "Did the coaches confirm about scouts at the game on Friday?"

Shaking his head, Teagan says, "No, Sir, not yet."

He hrmphs and goes back to what he was doing before.

"We're going to go out back to the fire pit," he tells them as we start toward the door again.

Cynthia follows us, "Do you guys need anything?"

"Shit," Teagan says, turning back around quickly. "We forgot to stop by the store."

"It's okay," I say at the same time Cynthia says, "For what?"

"I told Kendall we could make s'mores and I'm an idiot and forgot to pick up the stuff," he tells her.

She claps her hands and reaches out for my other hand that isn't in Teagan's. "I bet there's some stuff in the kitchen left over from Ryleigh's last little get together." I want to look back at Teagan to see if this is normal behavior for her, but she's pulling me along before I get the chance to.

We walk into a well-lit kitchen that is covered in chrome. It looks expensive and pristine. She finally lets me go and walks into a closet that has shelves as full as a grocery store. I can't help but to stare, even after she's already walked back out.

She notices my attention. "Have to keep a full pantry around here. Never know when all of the boys will be here, and they eat up everything in the house. But here you go." She hands over graham crackers and a Ziploc bag that has individually-wrapped chocolate bars and a bag full of marshmallows in it.

"This is awesome, Cynth. Thanks," Teagan says, coming around me to side-arm hug her.

She blushes a little. "You're welcome. Glad I could help."

Her reaction is strange, but I wait until Teagan has the fire roaring and we are warm and toasty before I ask him about it, "So, Cynthia?"

His eyes watch the fire. "Yeah, my birth mom left us a long time ago, right after Ryleigh was born. Dad has been married four times now. I guess you could say that he's just a hard man to live with. Cynthia is the coolest one out of all of them. She just tries a little too hard sometimes. And I get it, man. It's hard raising kids when they are right behind you in age."

I'm curious. "What's the age difference if you don't mind me asking?"

"You can ask anything." He smiles, turning to look at me. "I like you knowing things about me." Those damn butterflies are back, but he doesn't need to know that. "There's only a five-year gap between us. I'm eighteen and she's twenty-three."

Damn. She's even younger than I thought. "Ok, I have to ask. Is your dad not worried about you guys being so close in age?"

His face scrunches up in disgust and I laugh, "Not like that, but what about your friends or friends of friends?"

He shrugs. "I've never really asked him, so I don't know how he feels about it. No one but the guys have ever spent time over while my parents are here and I'm not worried about them. That would be worse than sleeping with Ryleigh and they know that shit won't fly."

"Yeah, I get that," I say, pulling my eyes away from his.

"Hey, losers, why wasn't I invited to the party?" Ryleigh says from behind us. She catches sight of me and her step picks up. "Oh, hey, Kendall. I didn't realize it was you out here. I thought it was just the boys again."

"Hi," I say in return, "Nope, it's just us tonight."

"Hey, sprout, will you go grab the skewers inside? I forgot them earlier," Teagan asks her.

She laughs, "Well, I would have said yes, but you just added that 'sprout' thing in there." Her butt falls into a chair opposite us.

Teagan smiles and mumbles under his breath about sisters as he gets up, "Don't go anywhere until I get back."

I'm not sure if he's talking to me or her, but we just look at each other and I let out a small laugh when she giggles.

I watch him walk all the way into the house and when I turn back to her it's to find her staring at me. Clearing my throat, I say, "I hope you don't mind that we borrowed your stuff from the kitchen."

She shakes her head. "Not at all." Leaning forward she braces her forearms on her knees, "They like you, you know."

I'm not even going to pretend to not know who this 'they' is she speaks of, but I can't think of anything to say to it. I just keep my mouth shut.

"It's been a really long time since I've seen Lucas laugh like he did with you yesterday. Fully letting go like that. Not to mention, Teagan has never once brought a girl home before," she says.

"Never?" I ask curiously.

She sits back in her chair and shakes her head again. "Nope."

In my state of shock, I stare at the fire and mull over her words. It's only a few seconds before Teagan comes strolling back out with the metal sticks in his hand.

"Are you staying, little sis?" he asks Ryleigh.

She stands up and brushes imaginary dust off her pants, "I

don't know why you do that. I'm not that much younger than you, but no thanks. Beauty sleep and all of that jazz. Bye, Kendall. I'll see you Friday." She throws me a wink. "If not sooner."

A thousand-watt smile from Teagan makes me forget everything for a moment, "S'more?"

I take the gooey mess from him, "Thanks."

I've never had one before, but I'm not going to admit that to him. Taking my first bite is pure heaven on earth. I don't even know if the fudge-covered Oreos I left on the counter for Gramps could even compete. "This is fucking amazing," I say around a mouthful. Not the most elegant thing I've ever done, but it can't be helped.

Teagan looks at me incredulously. "Please tell me that you've had one before. Did I give you your first?"

My face flames as hot as the fire at his innuendo and he throws back his head and laughs. Oh really? As much as I hate the waste of a perfectly good roasted marshmallow, I dip my finger into the goo and wait until the right moment. His head turns at just the right angle and it catches the very tip of his nose. I couldn't have planned that better if I truly tried.

His mouth hangs open in surprise, still half smiling. "Is that so?"

Flashing out in a lightning move, his hand grabs ahold of my wrist of the hand that has the goo still on it. I try pulling it back, but it's no use. My thought process is he's going to use it to smudge it against my face, so I quit fighting. My heart thuds in my chest as he locks eyes with me and slowly lowers his head to take my finger into his mouth. I feel like such a moron for not seeing his intentions beforehand, but I can't bring myself to complain at the situation I've found myself in. His tongue swirls around my finger and as odd as it sounds, it feels so good. My eyes close on their own accord as I savor the feelings that he is stirring inside of me.

A deep hum comes from him as he pops my finger out of his mouth, “That’s so much better than a s’more any day.”

I want to clear the rest of the distance between us and get my own taste. As if reading my mind, he leans into me and presses his lips against mine. When his tongue teases my lips, I open for him. Just when I think that nothing in the world could possibly taste better than the s’more, he proves me wrong. His hand comes up to cup my chin and it’s warm against the chill of my skin. All too soon, he is pulling away and kissing the tip of my nose. He leans in again and I get my hopes up for another kiss. Instead, he rubs his nose against my face and spreads the goo across my cheek.

“Never play with the master,” he says, retreating back into his seat, laughing.

Wiping the marshmallow off my cheek, I can’t help smiling with him. It’s contagious.

He moves his chair as close as he can without sitting in my lap and takes hold of my hand. “I’m sorry if you didn’t want us to know about what you told Lucas. It was an invasion of your privacy and we shouldn’t have pressured him so hard to tell us.”

I sigh, “I’m actually kind of glad that he did. It seems like I might be hanging around for a little while and I’d rather not go through it three more times.”

He nods. “I get it. I’m here if you ever do want to, though.”

“Thanks,” I say, relaxing in my chair.

Squeezing my hand and playing with my fingers, he asks, “Can I just ask one question?”

“You gave me all access, so it’s only fair, right?” I reply.

He hesitates. “I just don’t want you to feel obligated to sate my curiosity. I’ve just been kind of wondering and Lucas wouldn’t tell us."

"What is it?" I ask.

"He told us why you're scared of riding in cars," he says, "and trust me, I completely get it. I can't imagine what it's like going through something like that. Who was it that you lost?"

I take a deep breath and let it out slowly as my hand tightens in his. It will never be easy talking about them, but it seems to be easing some of the weight off my heart to say their names out loud, "Their names were Will, Casey, and Brian VanPelt."

His head jerks toward me. "I knew Brian through the construction place that we volunteered for a few summers ago. He went to lunch with us a couple times and was an alright dude."

I nod. "That he was to say the least."

"So, they were family?" he asks.

"Might as well have been," I say softly. A tear rolls down my cheek, "They were mine."

"Wait, what?" he asks, stunned. "What do you mean yours? Like your boyfriends?"

As I nod again, he whistles under his breath, "Wow."

"I'm not a whore if that's what you're thinking," I say, going on the defensive. "It wasn't conventional, but I loved them, and they loved me. What's so wrong with loving more than one person, huh? Who the hell ever set up those fucked-up rules anyways?"

"Woah," he says, pulling my hand to his lips, "I wasn't judging, babe, and I'm sorry if it came off that way. You just caught me by surprise is all. I tend not to have a filter sometimes, and you are more than welcome to slap me if it ever offends."

He softly says, "Hey." When I don't look away from the fire, he pulls my chin to face him. "There's nothing fucking wrong with the way that you love, and I'll kick anyone's ass who tells you otherwise."

Another tear tracks down my cheek. "It's not like it matters anymore, right?"

"Don't think like that. While you're still breathing, there's always tomorrow and I'll be damned if I let you forget it," he says right before he pulls me in for another kiss that's even more breathtaking than the last.

Chapter Seven

Feeling Dizzy

As my alarm blares at me, I have a moment where I consider just skipping school today. Teagan didn't bring me home until late last night, well early this morning, and I wasn't lying about being a total bitch if I didn't get sleep.

My phone beeps from somewhere under my pants I had shucked as I crawled into bed. "Ugh," I groan, throwing the covers off my body. Fuck, it's cold. I shiver and dig through my pockets. It stops beeping as soon as my hand folds around it. Of course. I take it with me back under my thick quilt. *Screw it, I'll just go in late today.* Just as my eyes close and I feel myself drifting off, the phone starts beeping again.

I look at the screen and see that it's an incoming call from Teagan.

Pressing the green button and holding it up to my ear, I grunt as a hello.

"Good morning, sleepy head. This is your wakeup call," he says sounding chipper as fuck.

I grunt again and think about hanging up on him, "I didn't ask for a wakeup call."

He laughs, "Of course, you did. You just don't remember it." There's noise in the background and even though he pulls away from the phone, I still hear him say, "Dude, shut the fuck up."

It makes me smile, but I say, "Remind me again why I bought one of these things if all you're going to do is wake me up before the crack of dawn, yelling in my ear."

He laughs, and I hear Goose's voice in the background, but I can't understand what he's saying. "Fucking A," Teagan then says, "Hang on just a sec, Kendall."

There's rustling around the phone and I can hear them talking, but all I want to do is just fall back asleep. In the few seconds it takes for him to come back, my eyes close again and I nod off. "Ok, Kendall, you there?"

I half groan, half growl into the phone, "Don't want to be. I just want to go back to sleep."

Maverick's deep voice comes down the line and sends those crazy butterflies into overdrive, "That's what you get for staying out so late. You've got school today just like the rest of us."

"Yeah," Goose says, "Why do you get to play hookie and we don't?"

"Why can everyone hear me?" I ask.

"Oh," Teagan says, "The guys had me put you on the Bluetooth through the Rover."

I'm just going to pretend that I know what that is. I feel like such an idiot when it comes to some of these things, because I've never used them before. If there's no need for them, then there's no need to know about them.

I ask a question that I already know the answer to, possibly just because I just want to hear his voice, "Lucas there, too?"

"I'm here," he says, and I can tell by his tone that there's a smile on his face.

With their voices having stirred feelings inside me, it's going to be impossible to go back to sleep now. That doesn't mean that I can't have a little fun and let them think otherwise. "Ok, is there a point to this conversation, because I really want to get back to sleep." I end it with a huge, genuine yawn.

There's silence on the other end of the line, before I start hearing snickers. Probably Teagan and Goose if I had to guess. The baritone of Maverick's voice turns deeper, "Kendall, don't make us late to class because I will come over there, drag you out, and drive you to school in whatever you're wearing."

"So, I won't even get to put on my pants?" I ask in mock horror. There's dead silence on their end and my face is turning red from holding in my laugh. "Well, guys, this has been awesome, but I'm going back to sleep. Have fun at school."

I push the end button and let out the laugh that I've been fighting. It feels good, too. I can't remember the last time these walls have even heard it. There's been nothing but a black void inside my heart and head for so long that it's going to take a while to learn who I am again. I know I won't be the same person as before, but hopefully, something more than the shadow I've become.

Dragging my ass out of bed, I take a hot shower and brew some coffee while I make my lunch. I don't have a lot of time after that, even if I am driving and want to make it to school on time. My hair hangs in a wet mess around my head, but I don't have time to stop. I'll throw it up when I get to school. Rushing out, I almost forget to grab my shit off the counter.

I rush out into the cold and instantly regret washing my hair this morning. It's cold as fuck. I make it all the way down to the second stair before I realize there's a car parked behind the Malibu. Not just any car, though, a Range Rover and Maverick is leaned against the side with his arms folded across his chest. His pose says he is pissed, but I can see the amusement hiding behind the glasses.

"What are you doing here?" I demand.

"You hung up," he replies.

Trying to keep a straight face, I give him the best sarcastic look I can. "Thanks, Captain Obvious."

The windows are down on our side and I can hear the other guys laughing.

I want to throw myself at his feet and apologize as he shoots me one of the stern looks I've come to associate with him, "You shouldn't ever hang up on someone. It's rude. Plus, what if you're on the phone with someone and something happens, but they're so used to you just hanging up that they'd never know because it wouldn't be out of character."

Call me stupid, but I want to push his buttons. "So, you came by to give me a lesson on manners? My Nana will whip my ass if I ever make it to heaven."

I side step him heading toward the car. He reaches out to grab my arm, but his hand finds my hip opposite him instead. When he pulls slightly, it causes me to lose my balance and topple right over into him.

"Sorry," he says directly into my ear, not sounding it in the least. The hand not holding my hips runs through my hair. "Why is your hair wet? You're going to catch fucking pneumonia out here with wet hair."

There's some kind of cologne on his shirt and it mixes with the smell of him and short circuits my brain for a second. "What?" I ask stupidly.

A smile crosses his lips. "You need a hat." I nod without saying anything. The smile gets wider. "Do you have one?"

I pull myself together, take a step away from him, and clear my throat, "I do, but I don't need it. I'll be fine."

"Just go get your hat, girl," Goose says from the passenger seat. "He's not going to let it go."

Looking up to Maverick's face I say, "It's packed away with

some of my winter stuff. I don't have time to go find it, but I'm putting my hair up anyway, so it doesn't matter."

He ignores me and turns back to the Rover, "We've got an extra somewhere in there, right?"

The guys scramble around looking in the glovebox and seat pockets. I'm just about to say 'fine' when Lucas says, "Got one."

"Me, too," Goose says from the front.

Lucas passes his up to Goose, who hangs them out the window, "Take your pick."

One is a baseball cap with the Atlanta Braves logo on the front and the other is a plain black beanie with faint white lines. I take the latter from his fingers and pull it over my head. "Thanks," I tell them and then look back at Maverick, "Satisfied?"

His face is unreadable as he says, "Yes. Now we can all be late to school."

I walk around to the driver's side door of the Malibu and I turn to see him getting behind the wheel of the Rover. Waving bye to them, I watch them pull out of the drive. Once they're out of view for a few seconds, I sit and wonder the real reason Maverick decided to come by this morning. He can't possibly be worried about me making it to school on time. Why would he?

It's a question that follows me around until lunch time. I'm sure that it would have carried on into the afternoon, but I get distracted at lunch. Sitting at the end of a table in the corner, I never eat with anyone. Normally, I do something constructive like homework or somedays, I'll stare at the wall. Today, I take bites of my sandwich around texting Lucas and Teagan back from this morning. I haven't even thought to check it until now. They both respond back instantly, which makes me smile.

I get so caught up talking to them that I don't even notice

Billy sit down in front of me until he clears his throat, "Care if I sit here?"

Glancing up, I see that it's pointless for him to ask, because he's already sitting down. It's also bringing us lots of unwanted attention.

"Look," I start, "I don't know what you're after, but I don't want any of what you're selling."

He stares at me with a ketchup-covered French fry half-way to his mouth. "I'm not selling anything."

His words are nice, but I just don't feel comfortable enough to be sitting here with him. He's too close in relations with the guy that has spent the past two years torturing me. "No thanks."

"I just want to be friends," he says, "What? You have so many that you don't need one more?"

I cross my arms against my chest and my phone beeps in my lap. Without thinking about it, I open the group chat and say, *Sorry guys. Give me a sec. Some rando won't take no for an answer.* Right after I hit the send button, I realize my mistake and my heart drops into my butt. I count to three in my head before the reply from Maverick comes through followed by one from Goose.

What do you mean won't take no for an answer?

What the fuck?

Shit, I tell them, *Sorry. That was meant for Teagan and Lucas. I accidentally did the group chat thing.*

Maverick's reply is instantaneous, *I don't care who it was meant for. You have less than a minute to tell me what you're talking about before I have to get in trouble leaving class to call you.*

After I explain about Billy, I look up to find said subject watching me. I take a deep breath and think about the fact that I've never seen him sitting with the football crew. "Are you friends with

Derrik?" I ask.

He takes a drink of the sports drink in front of him before responding, "Am I sitting with him?" I shake my head and he says, "Well there's your answer."

My eyes narrow as I try to fight off the suspicions. "Then why are you just now wanting to be friends? As I told you yesterday, we've been going to school together for years. Why are you just now wanting to be friends?"

Propping his elbows up on the table he says, "Yeah, look. I'm sorry about that. I walk through here with a blindfold on most of the time. I wasn't trying to be rude or anything yesterday. I just saw a pretty girl who looked like she needed a little help. But I completely understand if you don't want to be friends."

He starts putting his stuff back on his tray and goes to stand up before I stop him. "I'm sorry that I'm being such a bitch. You can stay."

"You sure?" he asks, still half out of his chair.

I nod. "Yeah, it's fine. I'm just cranky because I didn't get much sleep last night."

"Out late with the boyfriend?" he asks.

If it wasn't for the blasé way he asks, I would worry about ulterior motives. But it does throw me at a loss as to what to say, so I settle for, "Not exactly."

This makes him smile. "Which part? Being out all night or the boyfriend?"

"That's for me to know and you to never find out," I say, looking back down at my phone.

There's been an entire conversation between the four of them that I've missed, so I have to go back and catch up. The bell rings as I type in my opinion on an argument that needed a tie breaker.

Billy stands, "Thanks for letting me sit with you, Kendall. Same time tomorrow?"

"Sure," I say.

He smiles, and I'm left staring in wonder at his retreating form. How is it that I go from being the trailer trash freak to where I am right now in only one week? My text must have ended the fight, because no one has said anything else. There are three other messages in my texts however.

Hey Kendall, I hope u don't mind I stole ur # from Ts phone.

This is Ryleigh. Want to go shopping after school?

KENDALL???

Her impatience makes me smile. I dump my tray and text her back as I walk to class.

Sorry. Walking to class. No work today so I'm free. Want me to meet you there?

She must be waiting on my reply because she answers, *No way. How will we gossip? Pick u up right after school?*

Squinting through my eyes that the smile has caused, I type back, *Sounds good.*

I stuff the phone in my pocket and someone bumps into me from the back. Shoves me from the back would be more accurate. I've been looking down the whole time, so I miss the open locker in front of me. It's one of the top lockers and the push sends my face directly into the corner of the door.

The pain is blinding for a second. My shoulder slams into the lockers beside me and then my ass hits the floor.

"Holy shit. Are you okay?" a little brown-haired girl bends down and asks.

Something warm is running down my face and I put my hand up to catch it before it has a chance to hit my clothes. When I pull it away, I see that it's blood.

A small crowd has gathered around us and I hear one of the teachers trying to cut her way through them. When she makes it to us, I see that it's Mrs. Carpenter, "What happened here?"

"I tripped," I say with the thick liquid still running down my face. The girl in front of me looks at me as if I'm insane for not telling the truth. I know exactly who it was, but I refuse to give the fucker the satisfaction of knowing he got to me.

"Ok hun. Well, let's get you to the nurse," she says, helping me up off the floor.

I stand with her and it makes me a little dizzy, so I grab her arm in support and shift my bag on my shoulder. Derrik is standing two lockers down smirking at me. Yeah, there's no question who did the shoving.

We make it to the nurse's office and her eyes widen in surprise as she gets a full view of my face, "Here, sit down."

I oblige, and she sets about getting bandages.

The late bell rings and Mrs. Carpenter says, "I've got to see to my class, but we need to talk, Ms. Davis."

"Yes, ma'am," I answer around the nurse's hands in my face.

She leaves, and the nurse finally says, "It wasn't too bad. Just a small nick on your nose. Anything on your head tends to bleed more than any other part of your body. You're going to have somewhat of a black eye though, I'm afraid. Are you feeling dizzy or having blurred vision?"

I nod a little. "I got dizzy when we stood up in the hall."

"Ok," she says, "Let me help you to the bathroom here so you can get cleaned up, then I want you to lay down and relax for just a bit."

My first look into the mirror makes me want to throw up on the floor. There's blood all over my face and running down the front of my neck. The wound itself is small, but it's already bruised and swollen. I'm not going to have a black eye. I've already got one.

Chapter Eight

Don't Destroy Them

Someone touches my shoulder softly, "Ms. Davis."

My eyes pop open. I'm still sitting in the nurse's office. I must have fallen asleep. The clock on the wall shows that there's only five minutes until the last bell.

"Oh my god," I say sitting up. "I can't believe I slept that long. Am I going to be in trouble with my last classes?"

The nurse is nowhere to be found. It's just Mrs. Carpenter, "No hun. You're not going to be in trouble. Everything is taken care of. I'm going to need you to tell me what really happened, though."

Raising my hand to the spot on my nose I say, "I already told you. I was texting then tripped and fell into that girl's locker."

Her lips pucker like she's sucking on something sour, "Is that your final answer for me? You know that bullying isn't tolerated in this school."

Psh. Since when? "Yes, ma'am. That's my final answer because it's the only answer," I tell her.

She looks disappointed but nods her head and walks out, leaving the door standing open. I hop down from the table that I'm sitting on just in time for the bell to ring. My face hurts like a motherfucker. I'm counting my lucky stars that I'm off today and can go home, take some Tylenol and pass the fuck out. I wait until the halls clear out before leaving the office. The less people I run into the better.

I'm still careful to keep my head down as I make my way out.

I let out a sigh of relief that's cut short when I hear footsteps behind me. I turn quickly expecting a fight. It's even worse.

"Hey, Kendall, what's up?" Ryleigh starts then catches sight of my face, "Holy fucking hell. What happened to your face?" Her hand goes out to touch it then drops away.

"I tripped today and fell into a locker," I lie.

"It's never a good idea to start a friendship with a lie. You don't expect me to believe that shit, right? Teagan won't," she warns. Damn. I really need to work on my bluff and kick myself in the ass while I'm at it for not calling and canceling our shop date.

I grab her hand and beg, "Don't tell them, Ryleigh. Please."

"One condition," she says. I nod, and she continues, "You tell me what really happened."

What choice do I have? If the guys find out, they'll come over here and get into trouble starting shit. I'm not sure about all of them, but Maverick seems the type for sure.

I sigh and nod. "Can we skip shopping today, though?"

She gives me a smile, "Sure. We can always do that tomorrow."

My laugh is cut short when my smile pushes my cheek up and sends a jolt of pain down the side of my face.

"Want to go to Pete's?" she asks.

"Umm," I start, "That may not be a very good idea. What are the chances the guys would be there or show up?"

Her finger taps her chin. "True, true."

I don't think that the guys have told her where I live yet, and I'd rather keep it that way as long as possible, so my house is out. We can't go to hers because of Teagan. And there's no way in hell I'm going to ask her to go to a fast food restaurant.

That thought process takes less than five seconds, "Fuck it.

Let's just go to the mall."

Clapping her hands in glee, she grabs ahold of my hand and pulls us to her Jeep. Seems like everyone is doing that lately.

"You both have brand new Jeeps?" I ask her as we buckle in.

She sighs dramatically, "Yes. I don't want to sound like a spoiled rich kid, but it wasn't my first choice in cars. Dad is a bit of an overprotective helicopter parent when it comes to me and he seems to think that this was safer than the little Audi that I wanted. Teagan, the traitor, wasn't any help, either. At least I got to pick the color. It's custom. I did good, right?"

"Yeah, definitely," I tell her in truth. The dark purple is pretty and has a weird blackish-blue transition color, depending on the light.

We're already driving down the road, so I'm hoping that she doesn't notice me watching her out of the corner of my eye. Long, blonde hair that matches Teagan's falls around her shoulders and frames a petite face that wears light makeup. Her brother came off as a spoiled brat the first time that I met him, but there's no way that I could think that about Ryleigh. Even from first impression and dressed in new clothes, she is sincere and doesn't seem fake at all.

We make small talk on our way over to the local mall, which is actually only like twenty stores. It's pathetic compared to most, but if you can't find what you need to in those twenty stores or in the super store around the corner, then you really didn't need it in the first place. Ryleigh parks the Jeep, and I pull down the visor to have a look at my face.

"Shit," I say out loud, not meaning to. The bruising is getting worse by the hour.

She digs around in her purse and hands me a small compact. "You can say that again. Try a little of this. It won't cover it up completely, but it'll help you not look like a battered housewife."

I nod and thank her as I put it on. It does as she says, taking away some of the darker coloration. Can't do anything about the little butterfly bandages on the cut, though. Eh, fuck it.

Ryleigh is a single-minded shopper and I love it. We don't have to peruse every single store to find what she's looking for. She tells me that there is one store that she swears by and it's the only place she ever buys clothes.

"Most of the girls that go to my school spend so much money on clothes. It's disgusting," she says, perusing the clearance rack at the back of Forever 21. "Call me a freak if you want, but it's such a waste when there are so many more important things in the world than clothes. I always take an extra fifty bucks off dad's credit card every month and donate it to the Feed the Hungry thing that they do in Brinkley. They need it more than I need a pair of designer jeans."

Her confession knocks me speechless for a long while, until I say, "But don't your friends and stuff say anything about you not wearing designer shit?"

She shakes her head, "No. Rich kids aren't half as bad as the rep that they get. Now, don't get me wrong, some are straight snots, but most everyone at Prim Wood are pretty decent people."

I find a cute skirt and legging set on sale for five bucks. I'm still undecided until Ryleigh's eyes light up and she says, "You're definitely getting that."

"I don't know," I say, still unsure.

A winning grin crosses her face, "Teagan would love it and the others would, too, if I'm being honest."

I sigh, "It's been a really long time since I tried for anyone."

She nods, "Then don't do it for anyone else. Do it for you. I've already seen it on you in my head and you look marvelous." At that, she flips her hair and walks away leaving me with this crazy feeling in my chest.

An hour later, we're sitting in the food court with some delicious Chinese food in front of us. It's been awhile since I splurged any kind of money on myself. There's normally none left after bills, even if I wanted to. Having a little extra money in the bank makes me feel less guilty for buying the skirt. Ryleigh beat me to paying for lunch, but we cut a deal for me to pay next time. So, I'm feeling pretty good as I dig into the food and it almost makes me forget about my face.

She's not going to let me off that easy. "You ready to talk about what really happened today?"

I take a sip of my drink and try to wash down the lump in my throat, "I wasn't lying when I said I hit the corner of a locker. I wasn't really paying attention when I was texting you, got bumped in the back and ran right into this chick's locker."

"Bumped?" she asks skeptically.

I shrug, "More like pushed, but I don't think he meant for me to trip and hit the locker like that. It was my own clumsy feet."

"What?!" she asks loudly, causing people around us to turn and look. Lowering her voice, she says, "I thought we were dealing with some bitch face. It's a guy?"

"Yeah, this guy named Derrik. He's been a pain in my ass since the accident two years ago," I tell her.

Giving me a sympathetic smile, she says, "I'm sorry about what happened. The guys were talking about a train accident and I put two and two together."

"I know I'm supposed to say 'thank you' or 'it's okay,' but it's not. It hasn't been okay for a really long time. Honestly, I feel like I'm waking up out of a coma right now. Everything is still kind of raw."

I'd rather not talk on that subject, so I switch it back to Derrik, "Anyways, I think Derrik has always had a thing for me, because he'd always pick on me and shit in school. Will kicked his ass one day for it and I thought I was in the clear. Then two years ago, after the accident, he started relentlessly torturing me."

She scrunches up her face in confusion, "Something about the whole situation just doesn't sound right to me. I mean, I can already tell that you're an awesome person, and effing gorgeous to boot, but I just don't understand why he would hold on to that much hatred and resentment just for you rejecting him. Have you tried asking him about it?"

I'm not used to getting compliments, so I don't really know what to say. I choose to ignore them, "I never saw the point. He's such a douche hole that I'd rather not even let on that he's bothering me. If I give him the opening, I know that he'll be so much worse."

Ryleigh lowers her voice again, "You're not scared of him, are you? I heard about the way you stood up to Mav and no one ever does that."

Thinking back on that night makes me laugh, "He was being a bossy asshole. To answer your question, no, I'm not afraid of Derrik. I've only got a few months left in high school, then I'll never have to see him again. Those people mean nothing to me and the last thing I want to do is give them any kind of leverage over me."

She nods, "Makes sense I guess. But you can't let him get away with shit like this. You better hope that we can find some phenomenal cover up for your face, because shit is going to hit the fan if the guys see this. He'll get payback whether you want it to happen or not."

"You promised," I remind her.

Letting out a short laugh, she says, "Yes I did, and I'll

probably pay for it later, but they have their ways of finding out shit. No one can have secrets around them for long."

Her familiarity brings a question to mind, "Have you ever wanted to date any of them?"

Coke spews from her mouth and she quickly cleans it up with a napkin, "Please tell me you're kidding. I've known all of them since I was a little kid. I can't even think about them that way. It would be like dating Teagan." When she shudders, I laugh again. Her next question pulls me up short, "Do you want to date any of them?"

Isn't that kind of what I've already by accident been doing? They're all best friends and I've kissed one and almost kissed another. I wonder if they kept that a secret. If it ever came down to choosing one over the other, well let's just say that I have never been great at choosing.

I shake my head at myself, but Ryleigh takes it as an answer to her question. Surprise shows on her face, "You're not interested in any of them like that?"

Putting my face into my palms, I groan.

She giggles, "I knew it." When I look up to her she says, "You don't have to tell me which one or ones, but you have to promise me something."

I nod in reply and she says, "Just don't destroy them. They've got a lot riding on this year and I just don't want to see any of them, or you, for that matter, getting hurt."

Teagan's kiss flashes through my mind. Shit. I may have already fucked this promise before it was even made.

Chapter Nine

Assuming

Friday comes and the school day rushes by. Fortunately, Derrik hasn't bothered me since giving me a face full of locker the other day. Unfortunately, the Prim Wood game is tonight, and my face looks like hammered hell. The bruising looks horror movie bad and no amount of that cover up Ryleigh has is working on it.

She tosses the tiny sponge thing on her bathroom sink, "I give up, Kendall. There's nothing I can do that's going to hide it. Fingers crossed that they'll leave that kid alive when they find out who did it."

Fuck me sideways with a wooden spoon. This is so bad. "Thanks for trying," I tell her.

She laughs, "It'll be a dead giveaway if your face says you're headed to a funeral."

Sucking in her breath, she looks to the floor. It takes me a minute to figure out why she would be acting like that and when it hits, it's not as hard as I thought that it would be. I reach out and one arm hug her, "It's okay."

"I'm such a bird brain sometimes," she says with tears pooling in her eyes, "I didn't think before I said it. I'm so sorry."

I squeeze her, "It's getting a little easier. It took me a minute to figure out why you were reacting like that. Besides, I never went to their funerals."

Of course, that opens a whole new can of worms, and for the first time, I tell someone about right after. The only other person that has ever known is my therapist, but I doubt she remembers any of it.

Not really, anyways. I'm sure it's written down on a notebook somewhere, but she only pretended to care because she was being paid to.

Ryleigh sits on the end of her bed staring at me with a sad frown. Maybe that was too much info for the start of a friendship, "Sorry."

She shakes her head, "No, Kendall, I'm sorry. That's more than any grown person should ever have to go through, let alone someone our age." Standing up, she comes over and wraps me up in a hug.

It takes a minute for me to fight the tears in my eyes from spilling over. When she lets go, I reach for my bag angling myself away from her, "Ok, enough mushy stuff. Should we go ahead and get dressed then head over?" We've been chatting so much that it's already after six, and the game starts a little after seven.

"Yeah, probably. You don't want to be the last one there or you'll end up with a shit seat," she says, pulling on a scarf and cute denim jacket.

I've seen girls wearing them, but I've never owned one. Never had any reason to, but it looks so good on her that I'm rethinking that decision.

She notices me looking, "What? Do I look okay?"

I nod and laugh, "Sorry. I was just admiring the scarf. It's really cute."

"Thanks," she says, walking over to a wardrobe and pulling the door open. There are pegs on the back and something close to about thirty scarves hang from them. "Pick one to wear tonight if you want."

After I bring the time to her attention, Ryleigh rushes us out of the house and gets us to the game by six thirty. "Plenty enough time to find good seats," she says as we are buying our tickets at the gate.

There are a ton of people here and I find myself fidgeting with the soft material of the scarf around my neck. I chose a light-grey one with tiny, black stars. Since I'm wearing the jean skirt with black leggings and a black shirt under my leather jacket, it matches perfectly. My nerves have nothing to do with the crowd, though. It's due to the butterflies in my stomach at the thought of seeing the guys and watching them play. They've been busy all week, so I haven't seen them, or even talked to them much. Only a few texts and phone calls. That's it.

Thankfully, Ryleigh doesn't notice my nervousness as she hooks her arm in mine and we walk toward the bleachers. People call out to her as we pass, and she always throws her hand up and smiles. She leans in to me, "One of the things about being the sister to four of the star players on the team, everyone wants to say hi." If her words the other day at the mall hadn't worked, those seal it in concrete. She really did have brotherly feelings toward them.

Leading us to the middle of the bleachers, she sits in what she says are the best seats in the house. It's funny to watch people give us a wide berth, but then scoot closer after we sit. All of them act like they hope Ryleigh will talk to them.

She does, of course, and tries to invite me into some of the conversations, but my eyes are glued to the small area where the guys are due to walk onto the field shortly, so I just nod and smile. I catch her rolling her eyes dramatically and grinning.

We don't have to wait long before the crowd lets out a roar and the first few helmet-covered heads peek through the little walkway. I had Ryleigh tell me their numbers earlier, but I don't need them. My body tingles as I catch sight of the four of them and it's so hard to look away. None of them are looking at the stands. They are facing forward, and have a look of pure determination on their faces.

"Are there scouts here tonight?" I ask Ryleigh.

Eddie, who arrived at some point, leans around her and says, "They weren't supposed to be here for another two weeks, but they came early."

"How do you know?" I ask.

He puffs out his chest, "Because I know everything."

Ryleigh snorts softly, "Yeah, right." She turns to me, "His older brother is number ninety-seven."

"Damn it, Ryleigh. You're no fun," he says after deflating a bit.

She winks at me and I can't help but to laugh.

The game turns out to be one of the best I've ever been to. Prim Woods wins, of course, but at one point both Maverick and Goose took hard hits, and my heart leapt into my throat. It took them a minute to get up, and I felt like I couldn't breathe until they did. I will say that I don't know how the scouts do it. After watching the team play, I would want them all to play for my school.

People are starting to file out of the stands, which makes it hard to see the guys as they head off the field toward the locker rooms. The only one I see before they all disappear is Goose. He catches my eye and waves as he smiles, which is replaced with a look of confusion as he gets a full view of my face. He says something, but I don't think it's meant for me and then the team is whisked away.

"The team has special parking in the top lot," Ryleigh says. "Cut around the side of concessions and it's up on the hill. Just look for Maverick's Range Rover. Unless you'd rather ride with me, and save the drama for later?"

I shrug, "Might as well get it over now, right?"

She side-arm hugs me, "Just in case."

Jeez. Now I feel like I'm going to war or something. I follow her and Eddie down the stairs. When we get to concessions, they keep walking and I go up the hill. It feels a little weird to be the only one heading this way, but I trust Ryleigh's instructions. As I crest the top, there sits the Rover. I lean against the grill and get lost in my head for a second. I never want to forget this feeling. The excitement of the game and being able to get lost in the moment of just being a fucking teenager.

Without the crush of people from the stands, the cool wind sends goosebumps up my arms. After about twenty minutes, I'm cursing myself for not just riding with Ryleigh. The wind is somehow slipping through the bundle of my jacket, and I'm shivering.

I'm so distracted with trying to keep myself warm that I don't see the shadow that rushes toward me. Before I even have a chance to scream, I'm picked up and spun around in a circle. Teagan sticks his face right into my neck and breathes, "I've missed you."

His words are sweet, but he's hit one of my few tickle spots. I gasp in air while trying not to laugh and push him away at the same time. He smiles and finally pulls away. They must shower before coming out. I can smell the soap on him, and his hair is up in a wet messy bun.

The smile drops into a worried frown, "What happened to your face?"

I try for the most genuine smile I can manage, "I fell into the corner of a locker the other day."

His fingertips trace the bruises and I feel myself leaning further into him. When his lips find the small cut on my nose, I hope wholeheartedly that they'll move to my lips next.

Then I hear Goose and Maverick somewhere behind him and he pulls away.

When he steps to the side, I get to watch as Maverick slows his pace as he takes in my face.

Goose doesn't look surprised, but the closer he gets, the more pissed his face turns.

Neither one of them are the first to speak. Lucas, who has been trailing behind them, has the same kind of reaction that Teagan had. Straight from all smiles to concern, "What happened?"

I ignore the glares coming from both Goose and Maverick, "I fell into the corner of a locker the other day."

"How did you fall?" Goose grinds out.

"Well," I start, "I was texting Ryleigh back and wasn't paying attention to where I was going."

Teagan looks like he halfway believes me, but Maverick folds his arms across his chest, "So, it was an accident?"

"Yes?" I mean to say it as an answer, but it comes out more of a question.

"I'm not trying to overstep boundaries," Goose starts, "But if something needs to be said to your Grandad then we will. Say the word."

It takes a second for his words to register in my brain and then my rage takes over as his accusations hit home.

"Gramps has never once laid a hand on me," I say through gritted teeth. "It's might fine shitty of you guys to think that, too. You don't know him. Hell, you don't know me."

I'm pissed and freezing cold, so I'm not going to stand around and defend Gramps to people who I shouldn't even be messing around with in the first place. I take off back down the hill. Ryleigh is probably long gone by now, but I'm sure I can bum a ride from someone. If not, that's okay, too. It's only an hour walk back home.

"Kendall," Goose's voice follows me down the hill. A warm

hand closes around mine and pulls me to a stop. I shock myself when I realize I'd love nothing more than to punch whoever it is. I'm anything but a violent person normally.

Goose pulls me to face him, "Hey, I'm sorry, okay? I didn't mean to piss you off."

I lock eyes with him, so he can see that I'm not kidding when I say, "Don't ever say anything like that about Gramps again. Even if he was the type to do something like that, which he's not, he couldn't. He's dying from lung cancer, and does his best to even get out of bed in the morning."

"Fuck, Kendall," he says frowning, "I'm sorry. I didn't know. It's just I've been there. On the receiving end, and scared to say anything. I just didn't want that to be the case for you. I guess there's always that old saying about assuming."

"What?" I ask. "That it makes an ass out of you and me?"

He laughs, "Yeah, but mostly just me this time."

I laugh with him, because I refuse to deny that one.

"You still want to go to the party?" he asks. "We can go hang out somewhere else, or take you home if you want to go. Up to you."

I think about it for a second. Now that the bad part is out of the way, having a good time doesn't sound like such a bad idea. "Party?" I ask.

He does a weird bow thing that makes me laugh, and we walk back up the hill. "Fuck, your hands are like ice."

"What do you expect?" I say sarcastically. "I've been out here for like thirty minutes waiting on you guys."

When we make it up the hill, the others are all still hanging around the front of the Rover.

"Mav, you need to leave the keys with Kendall next week," Goose says. "She can warm up the car while she waits on us."

His eyebrow quirks up, but it's Lucas who says, "We good?"

I nod at him and Teagan says, "Well, let's go party then."

Chapter Ten

Lies Are For Cowards

The party is in full swing, and we have to park at least thirty deep on the side of the road leading up to the main house. We get out of the car, and I take an extra few seconds to stretch out the tension in my body. Riding with a silent, semi-pissed Maverick is not good for stress. He didn't speak one word on the way here, and even now, he's already halfway up the road with Lucas right beside him. Teagan and Goose hang back with me.

"What's his problem?" I ask, inclining my head towards Maverick.

Goose follows my eyes, but I know he doesn't need to, "Let's just say that Mav is one of a kind. He's got some anger issues. Maverick is just…"

"Maverick," Teagan finishes for him. They laugh as we start walking.

The bass of the music thumps all the way out of the house and into my chest as we get closer. I know I said I wanted to come to this thing, but if I'm honest, I'd rather not go inside the house at all during the party. Lucky for me, someone is thoughtful enough to have started a bonfire close to the lake. That's where we find Maverick and Lucas already sitting. Goose leaves us to take up the spot beside Maverick. I sit down in the closest spot to the fire and Teagan looks like a lost puppy for a second as he looks from them back to me.

Never in a million years would I want him to choose between

his friends and me, so I say, "You can go sit with them. I just want to be closer to the fire." I'm even nice about it, and don't mention that I'd rather sit on a bed of nails than to go sit next to Mr. Pouty Pants.

He sits down, "Nah. They're okay. I'm a little chilly myself."

"Umm, what was that speech you guys gave me the other day about wet hair in the cold?" I tease. "Shouldn't you be wearing a hat?"

"Well, I would," he retorts, "But someone never gave mine back."

"I'm sorry," I laugh, reaching into the inside pocket of my jacket. I haven't wanted to give it back. Even after me wearing it, it still has the smell of him on it. I'd really hate for him to get sick, though. "Here," I say, handing it back.

His hand brushes against mine as he takes it, "Thanks. I know you haven't found yours yet, so I'll give this one back to you later."

I nod to keep the butterflies from escaping my stomach. The girl beside me passes over a bag of marshmallows and I watch as she skewers hers and begins to roast it over the fire. It brings back memories of the other night, sitting around the fire with Teagan, when he first kissed me. When I look up to him, I can tell he's thinking the same thing. My face flames as hot as the fire and I pass the bag to him without taking any. In my peripheral, I can see that he's still smiling down at me. The bigger problem is that my eyes lift to see Maverick watching us. I could be wrong, but I think that he saw the entire exchange.

He stands up without breaking eye contact with me and heads inside the house. Teagan says he's going to get us a drink, and leaves me with a promise that he'll be back in a minute. Lucas and Goose follow the other two inside quickly thereafter.

Fucking boys. What am I even doing here? I'm restless, and I decide now is as good a time as any to take a stroll down to the dock on the lake. Teagan can find me when he gets back.

Once I'm alone, it's so much easier to breathe. In the darkness, the lake water looks black, and reminds me of a mirror, with the way it reflects the stars in the night sky. Absently, I notice some of the stars are covered by clouds. A storm must be rolling in. Damn, I hope it waits until I get home to rain. I love the sound that it makes as it hits the trailer's tin roof.

"What are the chances I'd find you here, trailer park?" Derrik's voice says from behind me.

I startle so much that I'm scared I'll fall into the lake, but I try not to let it show in my voice, "Pretty good since I'm here, huh, Dick."

His face drops from fake friendliness to pure hatred, "Found you some Prim Wood boys to whore out to I guess. There's no other reason for you to be here. Do they know what you are, white trash?"

He's got me cornered like a cat and mouse. I can't move around him, because I know for a fact that he'll push me in, and I'd rather not go for a swim. So, I do what I should have done a long time ago, and ask, "What's your fucking problem, Derrik? I'm sorry that Will kicked your ass over me, but that was years ago. Why can't you just move on and leave me the fuck alone?"

The laugh that he lets out is rough and it gives me chills. "You're nothing but a fucking whore, trailer park. Why would you ever think that fight was about you?" he sneers.

This throws me for a second, and he inches closer.

"Then why?" I ask. "I've never done anything to you."

"Yes, you have. You lived when it should have been him," he says harshly.

The words strike home harder than I'd like, and I have to put a hand against my heart to make sure that I wasn't actually stabbed.

"He wouldn't have even been out that night if it wasn't for

you," he says, digging the knife a little deeper.

Derrik has moved even closer and I'm sure at this point that my ass is getting wet tonight. I can only hope that he won't try to drown me after I go in. I try to stall him and get a question off my chest at the same time, "Why do you care so much?"

I watch his face as the pain flashes there, and it's in that moment that I know. He must see something on mine, because he makes a quick move to push me in.

"Hey!" a voice yells from behind him. My stomach falls into my butt in relief when I hear Teagan's voice.

Derrik turns around with a smile plastered to his face, "Hey, man, what's up? Killer party."

"What the fuck was just going on here?" he asks. "It looked like you were going to push her in."

The laugh that he lets out is fake and I hope Teagan can read straight through the bullshit. I'm not opening my mouth. If they find out that Derrik was the cause of my bruises, I have no doubt that he would have a rough night afterwards. I should have known that I wouldn't have to say anything.

Derrik opens his mouth and inserts his foot, "Oh, you mean trailer park? She was just offering me sex for money, and I had to be a little forceful in telling her off. Figured a swim might do her some good."

"Is that so?" Teagan asks in a chilly voice I'd yet to hear from him.

Throwing up his hands, Derrik says, "Look, man, I wasn't trying to start any trouble. We were just talking."

"I thought she was offering you sex for money?" Teagan says, crossing his arms. "Can't be both, so which is it, dickhead?"

He laughs and looks at me, "This is who you're whoring

around with now?"

"Don't fucking call her that or it'll be your ass in that lake," Teagan says, taking a step closer to him.

Derrik throws his hands up again, "You're more than welcome to her, dude. I'm out."

We watch as he makes his way to the end of the dock. I breathe a sigh of relief. Only, it's short-lived when he turns around and walks backwards as he says, "See you around." It would have been fine if he hadn't reached up and tapped the side of his nose.

Teagan, who had come to stand at my side, stiffens as Derrik's laughter echoes back to us, "Kendall?"

I look up to his face, only to see a fury that I associate with Maverick not him. "Please tell me that he didn't just mean what I think he did," he says, barely containing the rage.

Refusing to answer him is enough of an answer, apparently. He storms down the dock as he yells, "Mother fucker!"

"Wait, Teagan," I say, catching up, and trying to pull him to a stop, "It's not as bad as it sounds."

He stops and turns around to look down at me, "Tell me that prick has nothing to do with the bruises on your face." When I say nothing, he nods, "Thought so."

Fuck. Fuck. Fuck.

If he makes it to the guys before Derrik leaves, it's going to turn into a bloodbath. I'm way the fuck out of my element, and I have no idea how to stop them. Ryleigh. I've got to find Ryleigh.

By the time that I find her, I almost cry in relief. She's sitting in Eddie's lap inside the house. Just as I motion for her to come outside with me, one of the guys' teammates runs through the middle of the room, "Fight!!!"

Forgetting Ryleigh, I rush out with the rest of the crowd to the front yard. What I see turns my stomach. Maverick has Derrik on the ground pounding fist after fist into his face. Goose tries to pull him off the bloody mess that's Derrik, but Maverick just pushes him away. So, of course, I do the stupidest thing I can think of.

Pushing my way through the crowd, I get in Maverick's face, "Stop it! Maverick! Look at him! Stop!"

There's so much anger when he looks at me that I know some of it is meant for me. He jerks up away from Derrik, who is moaning on the ground.

I want to say something to him, but he's gone before I get the chance to.

Ryleigh comes up and yanks on my arm, pulling me away from the scene. She walks us back to Eddie, "Go find my brother and tell him that I'm taking Kendall home." He nods and gives her a quick kiss on the cheek.

Once we're out of earshot of everyone, she starts grilling me. It takes me all the way to her car to get it all out and when I do, she says nothing. She just stares at me, open-mouthed. At least I think she's staring at me, until I realize that she's actually been staring right over my shoulder.

"Why did you lie to me?" Maverick's voice growls in my ear.

Since I don't want to turn around and face him, I find a spot on Ryleigh's tire to stare at, "I technically didn't lie about anything."

His palm smacks the Jeep beside me, "Omitting the truth is the same fucking thing. Lies are for cowards. Lies are also for people who don't want any friends." The last is whispered so close to my ear that I feel his breath fan over my neck.

He pulls away from me and I don't watch as he walks away this time. It's all I can do to fight the tears threatening to spill down my cheeks.

Chapter Eleven

Twunt

I go the rest of the weekend without hearing from any of them. The only person who is still talking to me is Ryleigh. I've not tried to text the guys, though, so maybe it's just as much my fault as it is theirs. Possibly more mine, since I've yet to apologize. I work my feelings away at the restaurant, and get banging tips in return for it. Doesn't really make that much of a difference to me, I just drop it in the bank and move on. It'll be there when I need it.

Gramps hasn't really been up to moving around much the past couple of days, so I've been making sure that he doesn't need anything while I've been home. Sunday night is particularly bad when he goes into a coughing fit that scares the shit out of me.

Needless to say, as I wake up Monday morning, I feel worse than hammered ass from not having any sleep. I get assurances from Robert that he's going to take Gramps to the doctor before I catch the bus for school. I want to stay and take him myself, but Gramps spills some bullshit about a good education. Right, because that's going to get me out of here.

I fall asleep in half of my classes and just grunt in reply to everything that Billy says to me at lunch. I'm not in a social mood. At least not with anyone at this school.

I'm super cranky as I make my way into the bathroom. Sitting down to do my business, I hear the door open and close.

"Did you hear that trailer park got Derrik beat up over the

weekend?" Stacey says loud enough to echo around the bathroom. They had to have followed me in here.

"Come on, Stace. I heard her grandpa is really sick," the new girl says.

Stacey huffs and then laughs, "Yeah, her grandma died a couple years ago, too. Must be the trailer trash plague. Best stay away or you'll catch it, too."

I've had about all I can take for the day. I yank the door open so hard that it smacks against the wall loud enough to sound like a gunshot, "Shut. The. Fuck. Up. Stacey."

She whips around, "What's wrong, trash? Grandma a soft subject for you? I'd bet that's where you learned how to be a whore."

Adrenaline courses through my body, and I move faster than I ever have before. My fist connects with Stacey's face with a loud crunch. She screams, and her two friends take off running.

"Say what you want about me, but you keep your fucking mouth shut about her," I say through my teeth.

"What's going on in here, Ms. Davis?" Mrs. Carpenter demands as she stalks through the door. The pod squad is right on her heels, but she yells at them to go back to class.

She helps Stacey to her feet, "Let's go, you two."

Stacey squeaks, "She attacked me Mrs. C, I was just trying to use the bathroom."

"You can tell your lies to Mr. Brooks," she tells a horrified Stacey.

I've never once been sent to the principal's office. There wouldn't be a better reason than this. I'll accept the consequences of my actions, and maybe, next time, Stacey will know better than to use my family against me.

Mrs. Carpenter drops a still bleeding Stacey off at the nurse, and then herds me into Mr. Brooks's office. She shuts the door behind herself as she talks to him, "Found these ladies fighting in the bathroom. The other one is over at the nurse's office." The nurse's office? Why can't she just call her by her name? I know that the two of them are good buddies outside of school. For some reason this strikes me as hilarious, and it cracks me up. I'm in one of those delirious moods from not getting enough sleep, one of those where you get the giggles, and can't stop.

"You think this is funny, Ms. Davis?" Mr. Brooks asks.

I shake my head instead of answering out loud. I'm scared the giggles will break free again and that won't do anything good for my current situation.

"Why were you fighting?" he asks as he's filling out paperwork on his desk.

Biting back what I really want to say, instead I tell him, "She's been saying shit that she shouldn't."

His eyes flick up to mine, "Language."

I shrug, and Mrs. Carpenter comes into my line of vision, "Was she the person you covered for the other day?"

Staring her right in the eye, I tell her the truth, "No."

She sighs, and Mr. Brooks takes over again, "Well, god forbid there be a next time, but if there is, it's best to tell someone instead of fighting amongst yourselves. Violence is never the answer. You of all people should know that, Ms. Davis."

What the actual fuck?

"Are you serious right now?" I ground out before I can stop myself. "And why me of all people, Mr. Brooks? Because of where I live? Because both of my parents are in jail?"

"Stop blowing things way out of proportion, Ms. Davis," he replies in a monotone voice as if he hears the same teenage bullshit day in and day out.

I sigh, "Can I please just have my punishment, so I can go back to class?"

He shakes his head and hands me a pink slip of paper, "You need to gather your belongings and leave school grounds. You're suspended for three days for fighting."

Feeling the shock on my face, I try to maneuver it into a more neutral, 'don't give a fuck' stare.

"Is there someone we can call to come pick you up, Kendall?" Mrs. Carpenter asks softly.

Staring at her for a second, I finally say, "No, ma'am. My Gramps is probably at the doctor right now. I'll be fine."

She nods, and I gather up my stuff that I was smart enough to bring with me from the bathroom. When I walk out of the office, it's with my head held high. That only lasts so long, because it's drizzling rain outside. I take a deep breath of fresh air and steel my nerves.

Pulling out my phone, I send out a group text to the guys.

I'm sorry.

Kind of like the pot calling the kettle black if I stay pissed at Maverick for overreacting, when I just did the same exact thing. I'm not in the mood for their responses, so I turn the phone on vibrate and stuff it in my pocket. Thankfully, I'm not carrying much today that it will hurt to get wet. I tighten the leather jacket around my body and step out into the rain.

It's a long walk home and I'm soaked to the bone when I get there. The Malibu is missing from the driveway, so Robert must still have Gramps at the doctor. I'm worried fucking sick over his health. I know he doesn't have much longer left, but he's giving it every fighting chance. Any thought of it makes me want to puke.

I let myself into the house and head straight to the shower. I need to get my temperature up pronto, and chase these chills away, or I'm going to end up sick as a dog. After my shower, I don't bother doing anything other than crawling underneath my covers and falling right to sleep.

It feels like it's only been a few minutes when I hear Gramps calling out for me. I groan and twist myself up further into my blankets like a burrito.

"Kendall?" he calls again.

If I don't get my ass up, he'll have to come get me or what if something is wrong? I jerk up so fast that I go tumbling back to the floor again with an 'oomph'. Unwrapping from my blanket, I stumble to the doorway where I promptly crack my pinky toe on the corner of the wall.

"Fuck. Shit. Fuck," I try to keep it quiet since Gramps isn't a huge fan of cussing.

I hop on one foot down the short hallway, "What is it Gramps? Are you okay?"

For the first time in years, an actual smile passes over his face. "Everything is fine, but you may want to go put some more clothes on. We have company."

I'd been so focused on making sure that he was okay, that I completely missed Goose sitting on the couch across from Gramps's chair.

"Shit," I say, backtracking down the hallway, but not before I watch him get an eyeful of me head to toe. I'm in my usual sleep stuff, a tank top and pair of boy shorts, so he doesn't see more than if I was in a one-piece swimsuit, but still.

Gramps is laughing too hard to correct me, even though wheezing and trying not to cough is more like it. I throw on the first thing that my fingers land on, an old Metallica shirt with holes all in it and a pair of cutoff jeans that I normally mow grass in. Fuck it. He knows I'm not rich, so why should I pretend to be? My hair probably looks like I have a whole family of rats living in it from not brushing after the shower, but I don't care about that either. Having Goose in the house is making me anxious and I just want to rush him off as soon as I can.

When I make it back to the living room, Goose is helping Gramps up from his chair. I stick out my arm on the other side to help.

"Thank you," he says out of breath from just standing up. "I'm going to go lie down for a bit, Kendall. You and your young man are welcome to stay here in the living room." I take that to mean that I'm not allowed to have him in my bedroom, so I nod that I understand.

"Need help getting there?" I ask.

He smiles sadly at me and shakes his head. "No, but I would like to know why you were home from school early today. Were you sick?"

I hate to disappoint him, but I have to tell him the truth, "No, sir. I got suspended for three days, because I punched Stacey Marsh in the face."

In most cases parents would chastise a child for fighting. Gramps looks like he's fighting a smile. "Did she deserve it?"

I nod. "She's a dirty twunt and wouldn't quit saying bad shit about Nana."

He looks proud for a moment, then confused. "What's a twunt?"

My face turns red. There's no way I'm going to explain that it's a mix between twat and cunt, since I refuse to say either word. Goose has, apparently, put them together, because he's fighting a smile. "It's just a new-age insult."

He shrugs and ambles his way to the bedroom, mumbling

about kids these days. Stopping at his door, he looks at me over his shoulder. "Proud of you for sticking up for her, Pea."

My sad smile follows him the rest of the way in the room, and then I turn to Goose to ask, "What are you doing here?"

The grin he throws me could rival any of the other guys any day of the week. "Now that's not very hospitable of you."

I fold my arms across my chest. "You could have at least called first. I don't like anyone coming in here, because he's not feeling too well."

"Ok, one," he starts, "I did call. Not even an hour after you sent the text. And for two, he was feeling well enough to grill me on my intentions for about thirty minutes before he woke you up."

My mouth drops open in horror. "You're kidding. I'm so freaking sorry."

He half shrugs and sends me another grin. "It's okay. I was expecting it before I came over, because you weren't answering your phone."

"Yeah, that's another thing," I say. "He doesn't need to be moving around too much. It's hard for him to breathe right now."

"I'm truly sorry," he repents. "I'll make sure that I follow all the rules next time."

Next time? He plans on repeating this?

"Thank you," I say nicely. "Now what are you doing here?"

He throws his head back and laughs and it brings a smile to my face.

"This weekend sucked balls, so I just wanted to see if you'd like to hang out for a little while," he admits.

I take a second to think about it. I'm off work and if he leaves right now, the only thing I'm going to do is go back to sleep. "Only if there's a promise of food," I say, causing him to laugh again.

"I'm sure we can find something to whip up here," he says, then notices my reaction, "Or we can go to my house. The folks are out of town, so it's pretty quiet around there."

My hands motion to my clothes. "Ok, but give me a few minutes to change."

He does that crazy bowing thing again and I roll my eyes at him when he smiles up at me. I walk back toward my room and I'm almost there when I realize that he's followed me down the hall. He's scanning the pictures on the wall. Somehow that seems more personal to me than him seeing me half naked.

"This was your Nana?" he asks softly.

When I move to stand next to him, he shifts, and our arms brush against each other. I ignore the tingles that jolt down into my fingertips. "Yep. That's her and Gramps right before I came to live with them." I point to one of the smaller ones next to it. "That was my first birthday with them."

His eyebrows crease. "Why do you look so sad?"

I smile as the memory washes over me. "Because I had just finished crying. I'd never had a real birthday before, so Nana wanted it to be perfect, and she forgot the candles for the cake. You would have thought it was the end of the world with the way that she cried. Something not a lot of people know about me is that I'm a sympathy crier. It set me off, and of course that made her cry even harder. Gramps probably thought we were insane that day, but he was a good sport about it."

"I feel for him just hearing the story," he says with a fake shudder.

I elbow his arm. "I'm going to get dressed. Be right back."

One arm is propping up the other on his chest as he admires the rest of the photos. "Mmm hmm."

I roll my eyes again and go to find some clothes. I need to do laundry since I was a fucking bum all weekend, and haven't done any in about four days. That's about the extent of my pants. I'm down to my least favorite pair that's shoved in the back of my drawer. Oh well, beggars can't be choosers. I throw them on and search for a decent shirt without any holes. I find a school shirt from when we had to buy them for gym. It doesn't have any holes, because I wasn't stupid enough to wear it outside of school.

Just as I strip my Metallica shirt off, I hear a small half-choking, half-coughing sound behind me. I turn to find Goose standing there with his eyes wandering my exposed body.

It puts chill bumps on the surface of my skin. "Do you mind?"

"Not at all." He smiles.

I raise my eyebrow and he says, "What? I've already seen everything now. What's the point in turning around?"

My heart pounds almost out my chest and I don't know what makes me say it, but I do, "Not everything."

I can't help the laugh that springs from my chest at the look on his face, and I yank the shirt over my head.

His expression quickly turns to disgust as he sees the name of my school on the front. "Yeah, we're going to have to get you a new shirt."

I can't help where I go to school, so I just shrug. He walks around the small space of my room, checking out what little there is to see. There are only a few pictures of Nana, Gramps, and me. Plus, the one of me and the VanPelt brothers before the accident. Goose doesn't comment on that one, though. The rest are ones I took a while ago when my camera still worked. "Gramps would shit bricks if he saw you in here right now," I tell him.

He ignores me as he leans over to examine my water collage. “Did you take all of these?”

“Yep,” I confirm. “A long time ago.”

“Are there any recent ones?” he asks.

I shake my head, “My camera broke a few years ago, and I just haven’t had a chance to get it fixed or replaced yet.”

“Hmm,” he says. “You’ve really got an eye for detail. Are you going to major in photography in college?”

I laugh, “You’re kidding right?” When he just looks at me in confusion, I throw my arms out. “I’m not going to college. I’ll be right here working and taking care of Gramps.”

I’m not bitter about it, not really. I’ve always known what my fate would be, and the best I can hope for is to make good grades, get a small scholarship or loan through financial aid, and take a few night classes at the community college.

He doesn’t say anything for a long while, and even though he’s not looking at me, it makes me anxious. “Are you ready to go?”

After nodding, he leads the way to the door. I check on Gramps before we leave, and find him asleep. Once we get outside, my steps falter. Sitting in our driveway is an old Ford truck, completely restored down to its teeth.

“Holy shit, that’s a nice truck,” I tell him.

“You like it?” he asks. “I don’t know if you know this yet or not, but Lucas is from a family of mechanics. He and his four older brothers restore cars in their spare time. For fun.” He says the last like it’s the most horrid thing someone could do with free time. “But anyways, they finished this one last year and I bought it off of them.”

It’s a cherry red in color and it shines in the sun. “Did they do the paint, too?” I ask, reaching to run my finger down the side.

He shakes his head. “Nah, they paid someone for that.”

"Well, she's beautiful," I say still in awe, not just over the truck, but to find out that Lucas works on cars. I could picture Goose doing it and possibly even Maverick, but not sweet Lucas.

Goose comes around me and opens the door as he gestures for me to get in. I smile in thanks, and get one in return that makes my heart skip about three beats before it picks back up again.

Chapter Twelve

Life Isn't Fair

Goose is nice enough to swing by the restaurant to let me talk to Charles before we head over to his house. I am hoping that he'll let me pick up an extra shift during the day since I won't be at school, but I'm disappointed to find out that not only will he not give me the shift but he won't let me work while suspended from school, either. Something about state laws for school kids, even if I am eighteen. He doesn't want to get in any trouble and I get that. I just don't know what I'm supposed to do with myself for the next two days.

When I get back in the truck, Goose notices that my mood has deflated a little, "Everything go okay?"

I shrug. "Charles says he can't work me if I'm suspended from school, which I understand. Just sucks."

"At least you get some free time now," he says with a smile.

I take a second to appreciate how attractive he is. Standing in the quad, he may have a tendency to get overlooked. Yeah, definitely calling them the quad from now on. But, between Maverick and Teagan's strong personalities, and Lucas taking on the nice guy role, Goose doesn't really stand out at first glance. That face makes up for it. He's what I've always called a pretty boy. Everything about his face is perfect, from the green eyes framed with long, light-brown lashes, to a full set of lips, and on to a squarish jawline. All of the guys are on the bigger side to be in high school, but Goose seems even a little bigger yet. That might be because he's taller than the rest. I'm five-five and he probably clears six foot four, easy.

"Is there something on my face?" he asks, as he catches me staring.

"Nope," I say, scrambling; trying to cover up my weirdness. "I was just wondering what your real name is."

He laughs, "How do you know Goose isn't my real name?"

I tick the numbers off on my hand. "Ok, for one, your parents would really have to hate you to name you Goose, and, two, I'm not too savvy with movies, but I've seen bits and pieces of some of them."

Putting his hand to his heart, he says, "Now, that just hurts me right here. How can you not like movies?"

"I didn't say I don't like them," I retort, smiling. "I just never seem to have the time."

He grins wickedly at me. "Seems to me that you've got the next couple days free. Nowhere near enough time to catch up, but you can squeeze some of the good ones in."

I don't think that I'm coming away from this without at least agreeing. If I watch them or not, now that's another matter by itself. "Ok, fine," I say dramatically. "But only if you'll tell me what your real name is."

"See if you can guess," he teases.

There's a million names that it could be. "Don't I get a hint?"

He pretends to think on it for a second. "Ok. It starts with the same letter as Goose."

"Hmmm," I watch his face as I start guessing, "Greg. Gerald. Gus." I say the last one as a joke, and get the pleasure of watching his nose turn up at it. He definitely doesn't look like a Gus. "Can I have another hint?" I beg.

Laughing, he says, "There's a pretty famous actor that has my name as his last."

"That's not fair," I complain. "I don't watch enough movies to know that."

He shrugs. "Keep guessing then."

Squeezing my eyes shut, I think really hard on G names. When I open them, I find Goose watching me with a look that says he wishes he wasn't driving. Fidgeting, I tuck loose strands of my hair behind my ear. Shit. I forgot to brush it and put it up. I try to smooth it down and hope like hell there's a brush somewhere in his bathroom.

"Do you give up?" he asks.

I narrow my eyes at him, "Never. I was just thinking. Gabriel. George. Glenn. Grant. Gordon." One of the last ones makes him smile. Score! "Is it Gordon?" I ask.

He shakes his head, and I try again, "Grant?"

This makes him smile. "Yep."

"That's pretty cool. I like that name," I confess.

He winks at me, and it makes the butterflies go crazy in my stomach. "I was named after my dad and he was named after my grandfather, so I'm Grant Michaels the third."

"Well, you do it justice," I say without thinking.

We come to a stop, and he turns to look at me. "Is that so?"

I feel my cheeks get warm, "Well yeah, you're a big football star, and I'm sure you'll be giving the other guys in college a run for their money."

He grins over at me, and puts the truck in park. "We're here."

'Here,' turns out to be a massive house right smack in the middle of the suburbs. I wasn't too far off with my assumptions, even though I feel bad for that now. His house isn't as big as Teagan's, but it's got this antique look about it that makes it just as impressive. It looks like one of those old Dutch Colonial houses.

"Your house is beautiful," I say, meeting him at the front of the truck.

He glances at it, and then turns back to me. "Yeah, it's nice. I'm just ready to get out of it."

I know my face must show the confusion that I feel, and he sighs, "Sorry. I'm not trying to come off as this spoiled, rich dick. There's just a story behind it that I'll tell you someday."

"We have time today, if you want," I offer as we walk up the steps.

He's one step up from me when he stops and looks down to me. "We'll save it. I want today to be a good day."

I can understand that, so I nod, and we make our way into the house. With the way that the outside looked, I fully expect it to be stuffed full of 'rich people' junk. I'm surprised to find that I'm wrong. The furniture is very scarce, and everything is pure white. The living room to the left has two little loveseat-looking things in front of a fireplace, and over to the right is a dining room, complete with white carpets and a light-wood table. As I look around, I see that there aren't any family pictures hanging up or sitting anywhere. I find that odd, but don't comment.

"Want something to drink?" he asks, and I nod.

We walk into the kitchen, and it's the same as the other rooms. Pure white, everywhere you look. I couldn't even imagine cooking in here. I'd be too scared that I'd stain something.

Goose walks over to the white fridge, "Ok, we've got water, soda, or these little juice things."

He holds up a silver can that says something about tomato juice on the side and makes a face at it before sticking it back.

I try not to laugh. "I'll take a soda."

"Soda it is then," he says, walking it over to me. "Now, on to the best room in the house. Mine."

I smile at his back as he walks away. His eagerness makes me think of Teagan, which reminds me that I never checked my phone. Pulling it out, I see three different messages from them and a missed call from Goose. The only name I don't see is Maverick's. Whatever. He can keep being pissed at me if he wants.

Texting Teagan and Lucas back, I stuff the phone in my pocket and follow Goose down the stairs. As we make it to the bottom, I'm thankful that no one is walking behind me, because I stop so fast that we would have gone tumbling down to the floor.

"This is your room?" I ask in awe.

He turns around and smiles at the look on my face. "Yep. This is it."

"Holy shit," I say, looking around. It spans the entire length of the house. There's a bed pushed against the far-right wall with a few movie and football posters surrounding it on the walls. On the same side, there's a door that must lead to the bathroom or something. It's the left side of the room that shocks me more than anything. There's a massive flat screen hanging up in the middle of a crazy system of bookshelves that look like they are built into the wall. Every inch of the surface is taken up with some form of entertainment, but as I move closer I see that most of them are DVDs.

"Is it safe to assume that you're a big fan of movies?" I ask.

His voice comes from directly behind me, "Maybe." He leans so close that I can feel the heat from him radiating onto my back and when his next words are said, his breath tickles the hair on my neck and sends chill bumps down my arms, "You want to pick or should I?"

Turning slowly until we're face to face, I look up to him. "Can I trust you?"

The playful smile turns wicked, and before I take my next breath, we are chest to chest as he pushes me back against the media shelves and crushes his lips against mine. My heart beats out of my chest as I open my mouth for him and his tongue sweeps in pure domination. Having a mind of their own, my hands find the rock-hard abs of his stomach. It's been so long since I had skin to skin contact that I find myself craving it. Slipping my hands underneath his shirt, I let them roam all over his body. When I get to his back, I pull him even closer and he lets out a soft groan into my mouth before he deepens the kiss.

When he finally pulls away, I reach up lightly and kiss him on the column of his throat.

We're both breathing hard and I can tell that I'm flushed from my face down to my chest.

Using his thumb, Goose brushes a loose piece of hair behind my ear. "I'm sorry. I wasn't expecting that to happen. I just haven't been able to get you out of my head this weekend. The way that you stood up to Maverick Friday night, it was like you lit a fire underneath my skin and I haven't been able to put it out."

Wow, I never would have guessed that he would be the poet of the quad, or maybe that was just a movie line. With my heart still trying to get back to normal pace, I try to keep my voice from shaking, "It's okay."

Narrowing his eyes playfully, he says, "Just okay?"

I shake my head and can't help the smile that crosses my lips.

He grins in return. "I'll take that answer." Reaching behind me, he pulls a movie down from the shelf. "You can trust me," he says with a wink and I get the feeling that he's talking about more than just the movie. A pang goes through my chest. I don't know why these guys are getting to me the way that they are. I never wanted this to happen. After the accident, I swore to myself that I would never allow another person into my heart that wasn't Gramps. If I could see it as a physical thing, my heart would have stitches running through it right now trying to mend. Only I see those stitches in three different colors and I'm not so sure that's a good thing.

"Kendall?" Goose asks softly from one of the big, black chairs in front of the screen.

I walk over to the chair next to him and sit. "Sorry."

"It's okay. I'm totally cool with my kisses causing a momentary lapse of awareness." He winks over at me. Damn. I'm in so much trouble.

We spend the next few hours watching some of what he calls 'The Classics.' It's funny, because every one of them is actually really good. He may be onto something with this.

"I would love to major in film studies next year," he tells me during one of the breaks.

I'm confused. His family is rich and he's going to college. Why wouldn't he be able to major in whatever he wants? So, I ask.

He frowns. "Father doesn't think that any career that could come from it is good enough for a Michaels." Shrugging, he says, "So I'll be majoring in Economics with business management as a minor."

I catch how he says 'father,' and not 'my father.' Grabbing his hand, I say, "I'm sorry. At least you get to go to college."

He looks at our intertwined fingers. "You're really not planning on going next year?"

"I don't know," I say honestly. "If I do, it will just be a few classes over at MCC. I don't want to leave Gramps alone."

Nodding, he says, "Yeah, I get that."

After a few seconds of silence, he officially closes the subject, "I'm starving. Oh shit, Kendall. I forgot that I promised you food earlier. I was so damn excited having you in my house and all to myself that it slipped my mind. Want to order pizza?"

My stomach growls in response. It's been forever since I had a good pizza. Those little dollar pizzas from the frozen foods just aren't the same. I nod to him and he whips out his phone. He mumbles as he's typing, and I catch something like five large, wings, and bread should be enough.

"Did you just say five large?" I ask in shock. "How much do you think we'll actually eat of that?"

He looks at me a little sheepishly. "There's kind of something that I didn't tell you."

I tilt my head. "And what's that?"

"You'll see in approximately twenty-two minutes," he answers vaguely.

Giving him the benefit of the doubt doesn't help my nerves as I wonder what he could possibly be talking about. Twenty minutes later, I jump when the doorbell rings.

Goose laughs and heads upstairs, "It's just the pizza, babe."

I'm floored by his pet name and it takes me longer than it should to get up and follow him.

He's shutting the door with his foot as I make it to the top of the stairs. "Need any help?"

"Nope," he says, and I follow him into the kitchen.

I go to get drinks out of the fridge as he sets the boxes on the counter. "What do you want?"

When he doesn't answer, I turn to find him right behind me. His hands find my ass and he lifts me to the counter. He kisses me like a man possessed, and I take advantage of our height being level for once. My palms rub against the sides of his hair where it's cut short before they find the back of his neck, and I pull him closer.

I feel his fingers on my knees before they make their way up the outsides of my thighs. I'd be lying if I said it didn't feel just as good as his lips against mine.

The doorbell rings, and Goose pulls away. "I wanted to get that in before they got here."

"Before who got here?" I ask, even though I should have already known.

It rings again, and he sighs against my lips as he sets me back down on the floor, "Plates are up here in the cabinet. Go ahead and make yours. We tend to act like animals around food."

"Speak for yourself," Lucas says, strolling through the doorway like he owns the place.

Goose jumps away from me like he doesn't want us to get caught. It stings a little, but I've kissed Teagan and Lucas, too. Feelings are going to get hurt if I don't go ahead and put a stop to all of this and just be friends with each of them.

Lucas walks over and pulls me into a hug. I catch Goose turning away at the last second. Yeah, I'm a shit person. Just because I was lucky enough to have what I did with the VanPelt brothers, doesn't mean that I will ever find that again. I'd rather not test the quad's friendship trying.

Even if Lucas does look and smell amazing. The tips of his brown hair are wet making them darker. When he pulls away and smiles down at me, it crinkles the skin around his blue eyes. That smile would melt the panties off a nun.

"I didn't know you were going to be here," he says, lingering by my side.

I laugh, "I could say the same thing to you."

A new voice echoes down the hall and it freezes me to the spot, "Goddamn it, Lucas. Why did you take off like that?"

Maverick rounds the corner and I want to say that my palms aren't sweating at the sight of him, but I'd be lying. He's only a tad bit shorter than Lucas and Teagan, but his presence is more commanding, making him seem that much larger.

No one says a word as we stare at each other. I already apologized, so I'm not backing down. Apparently, neither is he. The front door opens and closes again. There's no need to guess as to who it could be; there's only one person missing from this scene. Teagan rips around Maverick and his eyes lock on to me. Not giving a shit about the tension in the room being thick enough to slice with a knife, his face lights up and he runs over to pick me up.

I'm swung around in a circle as he says, "Kendall! I'm glad you're here." His blond hair tickles my face as he sets me back down and whispers in my ear, "I missed you."

I try not to let my red face be a dead giveaway to his words. Instead, I focus back on Maverick. He's moved to one of the bar stools and is loading a plate full of pizza beside the other two. "I hope you know that doesn't mean that you won or anything," I tell him.

There's absolute silence in the room before Goose busts out laughing, quickly followed by Lucas.

"What did I miss?" Teagan asks, confusion pulling his brows down.

Lucas shoots me a smile. "Kendall not losing at a staring match with Mav."

"Hey," I say defensively, "That wasn't fair."

Maverick's eyes seem to turn even darker blue behind his glasses as his dark eyebrow shoots up, "Life isn't fair, little girl."

This raises my hackles as much as it makes me sad, "One, you're preaching to the choir. Two, I'm older than you are. Little boy."

Goose's mouth hangs open and Lucas looks stiff, like he's ready to stop a fight. Teagan stands beside me stuffing his mouth with a slice of pizza while watching us. Maverick just glares. I watch his mouth twitch like he's having to fight whatever it is that he wants to say. I could be the bigger person and have Goose take me home, but I was here first tonight. I'm pretty sure that Goose didn't invite them, so he's more than welcome to leave. Instead, he shrugs and goes back to eating his pizza, relieving some of the tension in the room at the same time.

Jeez, this is going to be a fun night.

Chapter Thirteen

Rollercoaster

After our stomachs are full, Goose drags us back downstairs for another movie.

"We should be working out instead of sitting on our asses," Maverick complains once we're down here and settled in. Goose gives up his chair for me and sits between my legs on the floor. I see Teagan throw him a look out of the corner of my eye, but Lucas just shakes his head with a smile.

Goose turns to Maverick, "Dude, we lifted after school. Won't hurt to take a break and relax for a bit."

Maverick mumbles, but quietens down when the credits start. I haven't heard of the movie that Goose put in, but it turns out to be pretty decent, and has lots of action. There's a slow part in the middle, and I find myself nodding off. With a belly full of the best pizza I've ever had, and hardly any sleep, it's no wonder really.

The next thing I know, Lucas is shaking me awake, "Kendall. Come on, let's get you home."

It takes me a minute to fully wake up and I yawn. "Sorry I fell asleep. I didn't get much sleep this weekend."

He smiles. "No need to apologize. Teagan didn't make it through, either." I look over, and sure enough, he's asleep. His long blond hair hangs around his face since his head has fallen forward. That can't be very comfortable. Lucas goes to the rescue, and wakes him up, too, but Teagan just curls up into a ball in the chair and doesn't say a word. It's not until I laugh that he shows any kind of reaction. He glances over his shoulder and smiles sleepily at me.

"If you want a ride home, you better come on," Maverick says. At first, I think he's talking to Teagan, but when I turn to look at him, he's staring at me.

"You're taking me home?" I ask, trying to hide my disappointment.

I must not do a very good job, because he narrows his eyes, "You can walk home. Your choice."

He makes his way up the stairs, and I glare daggers in his back in hopes that he can feel them. I turn to Lucas. "Do I really have to ride with him?"

Lucas smiles, "One of us could run you home, but it'll take longer since Teagan is already on my way. Maverick just lives across the street, so he won't have to double back around."

"That's how you knew that we had ordered pizza," I say.

He shrugs. "Goose knows better than to order from our favorite pizza place and have us not show up." Makes sense. That's why he went ahead and ordered so much food.

Goose comes racing down the stairs, "Kendall and Maverick haven't left yet, have they?" He sees me standing beside Lucas, and a relieved look passes over his face.

"We haven't left," I tell him, "but you better hurry up, or I have a feeling I'm going to be walking home."

He finds an old messenger bag thing in the corner and shoves a laptop inside followed by a power cord. He comes over and drops it across my shoulders, "This is for your free time tomorrow. There's a ton of movies on there. I left the file open for you. It's got the first ten you should watch, and I'll come over after practice to watch some of them with you."

Teagan jumps up. “Hey, count me in.”

I laugh at his enthusiasm and Lucas says, “Yep, me, too.”

Shaking my head, I say, “Why don’t we just meet back over here then. It’ll be a tight squeeze in my room, plus I don’t know how Gramps will be feeling, either.”

Goose wraps me up in a hug. “Sounds good to me.”

“I get to pick Kendall up tomorrow,” Lucas says. The other two look like they want to argue, but finally agree.

Maverick honks the horn outside. “God, he’s such an impatient prick,” I mumble.

Lucas pulls me from Goose and throws his arms around me. “Go easy on him.”

I go to nod, but Teagan comes up from behind me and squishes me against Lucas, “Kendall sandwich!”

I try to laugh, but it comes out muffled against Lucas’s chest.

“Okay, okay,” Goose says, “Mav’s going to murder us all if she doesn’t get up there.”

Reluctantly, I step away from them and wave bye as I make my way up the stairs.

My hand has just closed around the doorknob when Teagan’s voice calls out, “Hey, wait a second.”

When I turn around, he pulls the beanie that we’ve been trading back and forth out of his pocket and puts it on my head. I smile up at him and he leans down to press his lips against mine. It’s just a quick stolen moment, but it’s still sweet. My eyes catch movement by the stairs. Lucas. He’s standing with a curious expression on his face, but he doesn’t look angry like someone typically would in this situation.

His face is front and foremost in my mind for half the trip home. Maverick ruins it by opening his mouth, “Heard you punched some girl in the face.”

I roll my eyes. "Maybe. What's it to you?"

"Just sounds kind of hypocritical if you ask me," he says. "You stopped me from giving that guy what he deserved the other day and then turn around and start punching people at school."

I turn my head to look out the window. "You have no idea what you're talking about."

He sighs with exasperation and I look back to him. "Stacey was talking shit about Nana. It was just the last straw. She's been in cahoots with Derrik, and trying to make my life as miserable as possible. Gramps had a bad weekend and I got no sleep, so when she started running her mouth, I warned her. As you can see, she didn't listen. I stopped you with Derrik because it looked like you were going to kill him. I didn't stop you from giving him what he deserves. In my opinion, they both got what was coming to them. I apologized, because I brought drama to the party, and because I'm sure that I embarrassed you guys."

By the end, I'm looking away from him again, but his next words have me whipping my head back around. "I'm sorry I'm being such a dick, Kendall. You didn't embarrass us at the party. I was more pissed at myself than I was you or even that guy. I see how the guys are with you. They like you and that could turn out to be a very bad thing. When Teagan told us what had gone down, at first I got pissed at the guy, then I was furious with myself for how much I cared."

"Why would it be such a bad thing if you guys cared for me? Because I don't come from the right family?" I ask carefully.

Maverick looks like he gets pissed for a second, but then his face settles back down. "That has nothing to do with it, and you know it. Do the math, Kendall. There's four of us and only one of you. How exactly do you see this ending? I'm going to speak for myself when I say that I don't share well with others."

"I'm not asking you to," I say quietly. "It's just nice to have friends again."

His eyes cut over to me. "Think things will stay that way?"

That's not exactly something that I can answer honestly. I've kissed two out of four of them and have partially kissed one of the others. I didn't set out for any of this to happen, but it's like being on a rollercoaster. Once you're strapped in and the chain is pulling you up, there's no turning back. You can't do anything but crest the hill, fall over, and pray to all that is holy that nothing will go wrong before you make it back to the loading dock.

Everything in the Rover is quiet for the next few minutes before he says, "What happened to your hair? Goose make you ride with your head out the window of the truck or something?"

If it wasn't for the barely contained smile on his face, I would have probably smacked him. Who would have thought Maverick had it in him to hand out a joke?

By the time that we make it to Sleepy Pines, things with him are better than they've been since the first day that we met.

We pull up outside of the trailer and I grab Goose's bag as I hop out. "Thanks for the ride, Mav."

The smile that he throws me before pulling off leaves me with sweaty palms, a racing heart, and my mouth gaping like a fish.

Chapter Fourteen

A Million Other Excuses

After apologies are made, and bridges are rebuilt with the quad, the next month or so flies by. Almost every day is spent with at least one of them, but I have taken Maverick's words to heart and haven't let any of them kiss me. I haven't even given them the opportunity to do so. I'd rather have them as friends than not at all.

Thanksgiving comes and goes just as it has every other year. The guys invite me to Lucas's house and even extend it to Gramps, too, which I find super sweet. There's no guarantee to how many I have left with him, so I decline, and Gramps and I spend the day together. I even cook some of Nana's favorite recipes. He doesn't eat much, but I can tell that he at least appreciates that I take the time to do it. I see more smiles out of him that day than I have in a full year.

School doesn't even suck as bad as normal either. Neither Derrik nor Stacey bother me in the least. I just have to fend off advances from Billy at least once a week. It's not all bad, truly. The genuine attention is nice for a change. He just doesn't do it for me. It might partially have something to do with there being no room left anywhere inside of me for him. Brain or heart.

Today is the first official day of winter break from school, and I'm more excited about sleeping in than anything. I should have known that the guys would have other plans. Around seven-thirty, my phone starts going off. I let it go to voicemail the first time, but then it starts ringing again right after.

I swear under my breath as I dig it out of my jacket. Waiting until I'm back under the covers, I answer with a mumbled, "Hello."

"Wakey-wakey, eggs and bakey," Ryleigh's voice calls out to me in a chipper tone that makes me want to throw my phone.

I grunt, "Dude it's not even eight yet. You do realize that this is called vacation for a reason. That means that normal people sleep in."

"Well, we aren't exactly normal, are we?" she asks.

"Do I have to?" I whine.

She laughs, "Yep. We're going shopping."

"Oh. My. God. Ryleigh. You woke me up this early to go shopping?" I growl.

I hear her trying to contain her giggles, "Well yeah. We have to drive up to Riceville to the good stores. None of these around here have good snow stuff."

Snow stuff? "Ryleigh, it never snows here. Why the F would we need snow shit?"

A gasp comes over the line, "The guys didn't tell you?"

I'm wide awake now and sitting up in bed, "Tell me what, Ry?"

"Oh, this is too great," she says a little too gleefully. "Get up and get dressed. I'll be there in thirty."

It takes less than fifteen for me to get ready, and then I spend the other fifteen minutes nervously fidgeting and biting my nails while I wonder what she's talking about. I do a double check in the mirror at least four times. My brown hair fans out from under Teagan's hat that I've taken to wearing more often than not. The usual minimal makeup covers my face. A blue shirt that reads Prim Woods Football underneath my leather jacket, is the only new addition. Goose made me take it a few days after he expressed his disgust with the maroon one from my own school. It's a little big, but I don't like tight fitting clothes anyways, and it's easy enough just to tuck into my pants without looking like trash.

My phone pings, letting me know that Ryleigh is outside. I run and check on Gramps real quick and find him still asleep in bed. He's been doing so good lately that it's kind of given him a little life back as far as getting around. I leave him a note on the counter letting him know where I've gone and when I'll be back. I put my number down at the bottom just in case. I always do lately.

Making sure that I have everything, I race out to the Jeep. It might not ever snow around here, but it still gets pretty cold, and I'm a fucking wimp when it comes to being cold.

The door has barely shut before I start grilling her, "Ok, now what am I supposed to know and why are we up at the ass crack of dawn to go shopping three hours away?"

She can hide her toothy grin all she wants, but I can still tell that she's beyond herself with being the one to tell me, "Well, for the past two years, the guys have been taking a long trip to a ski lodge up in the mountains during Christmas break. Normally, it's just them, but this year, Teagan asked me if I wanted to go. I said yes only if I could bring Eddie."

"Sounds like fun," I tell her, matching her enthusiasm.

This time she lets out a loud laugh and I can't help but to join in. "They're probably going to kill me, but I can't help it if they were supposed to talk to you and didn't. You know you're coming with us, right?"

My mouth hangs open in shock before I sputter, "I can't, Ry. I've got work and Gramps and—"

"And a million other excuses," she finishes for me, "that aren't going to work. You said that Gramps is doing better. Plus, it's only for three days and I hope you're not mad, but I talked to Charles.

He's already given you the time off. I told him it was for a surprise and not to tell you." For the first time, she looks a little guilty.

"I'm not mad," I say honestly. "I just can't afford to go. I don't have clothes or jackets or whatever else I would need."

She looks at me like I've grown two heads, "Why do you think we're going shopping? I may have eavesdropped a little on the guys talking and they were trying to figure out the best way to drop the bomb on you about getting stuff. They knew you'd be difficult in letting any of them pay for anything, so I figured I'd help." I open my mouth to tell her that I just can't when she says, "Please don't tell me no, Kendall. I couldn't decide what to get you for Christmas anyways, so this is like the two birds with one stone thing."

Trying to choose the best phrasing I can think of, I say, "It's really nice of you guys to think of me and all, but won't your parents be pissed that you'd be spending their money on me?"

I'm relieved that she doesn't seem pissed, "It's my money we're spending actually. I didn't tell you before, but Teagan and I both have this trust fund thing that we're allocated money from every month. My brother, believe it or not, is a wiz with numbers. He's got us both invested in a few things that turn a profit every month on top of that. I still use dad's money sometimes. I stopped for a little while about a year ago, but he got upset about it. Something about not providing enough for his children or some crazy bullshit. That's why I still swipe his credit card from time to time. If that's what it takes for him to feel better, then screw it."

I take a few minutes to absorb what she's told me, "Will you let me pay you back?"

She shakes her head no and I can't say that I'm surprised, "Let me do it as a Christmas gift if you must. Please."

After a pause, I finally nod my head. Who can say no to her

pleading like that. She just about jumps out of her seat and it makes me laugh. The music cuts off suddenly and her Bluetooth lets her know there's a call coming through. Yes, I finally understand the purpose, and how to work it for the most part.

Ryleigh cuts her eyes over to me, makes a shh motion with her hand, and grins as she sing-song answers, "Heellllooo."

Teagan's voice comes across the speaker and makes it sound like he's in the car with us, "Hey, sis, have you talked to Kendall? I was thinking about riding over there today, but I haven't been able to get her to answer."

"Shit," I say without thinking, automatically going on the search for my cell.

"Kendall?" he asks curiously.

Ryleigh rolls her eyes and smiles as I mouth 'sorry.' "Yeah, it's me. Sorry. We had the radio going and I didn't hear my phone."

"It's cool," he says. "What are you ladies up to today?"

We look at each other in question, and I answer, "Ummm, shopping."

There's rustling on his end of the line like he's moving around, "You guys heading over to the square? We can meet up for lunch if you want."

"Actually," Ryleigh starts and then runs her words together really fast, "We're going to Riceville."

She makes an 'uh-oh' face at me, and I try to fight the laugh in my chest. It takes a few seconds before Teagan finally answers, "Sprout, what did you do?"

"Nothing. We're just going shopping like Kendall said." She smiles.

"Yeah right. Because I believe that for a second," he says into the phone. "Knew we should have waited until the last second to tell you."

Jumping on the defensive, she sasses, "We are leaving in a week and Kendall has nothing to wear up there. Besides, she's my best friend and I tell her everything."

Wow. I knew we were good friends, but her words almost bring a tear to my eyes.

He sighs, and I can tell he's smiling when he says, "Whatever, sprout. So, you're in, Kendall?"

Ry's face turns red at his drop of the dreaded nickname yet again, so I save him, "I need to talk to Gramps about it, but I don't think Ryleigh's taking no for answer."

"We aren't either," Goose says.

They must already be together in the Rover, because Maverick says, "We're going to meet you guys up there in Riceville."

"So much for a girls' shopping day," Ry says in fake dramatics.

"Well, you should have waited on us to talk to Kendall and then you could have had your girls' day," he chastises.

She makes a face toward the hood of the Jeep, "Whatever."

I laugh, and she ends the call.

I'm not getting a lecture again, so I unlock my phone and text a quick goodbye in the group chat and laugh again as I hit send.

Chapter Fifteen

Blinding As The Snow

I managed to survive the shopping expedition. It ate at me to let Ryleigh pay for everything, but I'm pretty sure that once the guys got there a few of their cards were replacing hers. She managed to set a rule, even though she had to talk me into it to begin with. The rule was 'no looking at price tags.' Maybe she got the impression that I would try to pay her back anyways, and that's not too far from the truth. Between Ryleigh and the guys, they pulled all of the tags off of everything before the bags made it to my house. They're all cheaters, but it's not like I could ask for them back.

Gramps gives me the all clear to go. He says he's feeling better, and I can tell by how much he's moving around and not wheezing that he's not lying. I'll only be gone for three days, and Robert's already promised to stop by and check on him during the day while I'm gone. Plus, they will both have my cell phone number just in case. Gramps just warns me to be safe and not get into any trouble.

When the guys show up Friday morning, I'm packed and ready to go. Goose and Lucas meet me at the door to take all of my stuff out to the Rover. Gramps is already up and sitting in his chair, so I go to hug him.

"Remember what I said now," he reminds me. "Don't be getting into any trouble up there and have fun. Lord knows you deserve to after the past few years."

I throw my arms around his neck and kiss the bald spot on his head, "Thanks Gramps. I promise, no trouble. You don't cause any trouble for Robert here, either."

He laughs and ends up in a fit of coughs that doesn't sound too good. When I try to say something about it, he just waves me off, saying that he's fine and not to worry.

When I start to pull away, he hugs me back and says, "I love you, Pea."

"I love you, too, Gramps," I say, not wanting to let go.

It takes a minute, but I do. When I look back, he's lighting up a cigarette, and it makes me smile. Same ole Gramps.

The guys already have my stuff loaded up, but Maverick is standing at the back, "Have anything else that needs to go in?"

"Nope, good to go," I assure him.

He reaches into a corner and pulls out a heavy-looking black bag. Unzipping the top part, he pulls out an expensive camera, "Goose said something happened to yours and I never use this one anymore." When I start to tell him that there's no way in hell that I'm taking that camera he says, "It's a loaner for now. You can't tell me that you won't take it if I'm not giving it to you and simply asking you to take the pictures for me."

Leaving no room for argument, he hands the camera over to me. "I've never had one this nice. I don't know how to use it," I tell him honestly.

"Goose can give you a run down on the way up there," he says, shutting the back, "but for now. Spin this little knob right here to turn it on and press that button to take one. You'll hear the shutter and if you did it right, it'll pop up on the screen."

I do as he says, and the ready symbol shows up in the top corner. Backing up a little, I aim it at Mav. He's a good sport, and even smiles for me. When it snaps, I know that I'm going to have trouble taking a new favorite this weekend.

With the trip to the cabin set to take several hours of driving, the guys give me the choice of riding in the middle in the back between two of them, or riding with Ryleigh and Eddie. That's not even a true choice. Even if it wasn't for the fact that I would love nothing more than to be stuck in a car with the quad, I don't want to be a third wheel and crash Ry's alone time with Eddie.

The only thing I didn't account for is how hot it would get squished between two huge males. Handing the camera up to Goose for a second, I strip off the thick jacket that they forced me to buy on the shopping trip, managing to elbow Lucas in the side and smack Teagan in the face with the sleeve in the process, "I am so freaking sorry." And I am, but my insides are complete mush at being so close to all of them and it's given me the giggles.

I start laughing and Goose turns around to snap a picture of us with a smile on his face. Meeting Mav's eyes in the mirror, I can tell that he's smiling, too.

Teagan stuffs my jacket over the seat, and when everything settles back down, I'm surprised to realize just how much room that thing was taking up. We're still brushing arms, but the guys aren't squished against the doors anymore. It makes me giggle again thinking about them being too nice to say anything.

Lucas smiles at me, "Someone's in a good mood today."

I shrug, "This is the first time that I've ever really been on a trip like this, and Gramps is feeling better. Plus, I'm pretty sure you guys mentioned snow."

"Lots and lots of snow," Teagan whispers in my ear, giving me chill bumps on my arms. "Good for building snowmen, snowboarding, and snowball fights."

My eyebrow goes up on the last one and Lucas, who couldn't

have helped but to overhear, laughs, "Don't worry. I'll protect you if war breaks out."

"Thanks," I tell him as I pull the sleeves of my shirt up to match his. "It's so hot back here between you guys."

"Hey," Teagan complains, "We're not the only ones generating body heat."

"Yeah," I argue, "but I'm not my own personal heater like you two, either."

The four of them laugh and Goose adjusts the temperature.

"Are Ryleigh and Eddie meeting us up there?" I ask.

Teagan nods and pulls out his phone. He hits a few buttons and after a minute or so it beeps at him. "She says they left a few minutes after we did to come get you, so they'll probably beat us up there."

With the heat at a normal level, and the motion of the car, I find myself trying to fall asleep. I nudge Teagan with my arm. "Don't let me fall asleep. I don't want to miss anything."

He smiles down at me as he takes my hand and kisses the back of it. "I won't."

After I return his smile, I look back to the front to see both Lucas and Goose watching us. Neither says a word, but they don't look pissed. It's the same kind of expression Lucas wore when he saw us kiss before.

It's at least three hours before we even start to see snow, and another two before we're at the cabin. The first thing that comes to mind as I step out of the car and someone wraps my jacket around my shoulders is how absolutely fucking beautiful it is. It's a little after midday, and the sun shining off the white of snow is almost blinding. There are tiny ice crystals dripping down from the barren trees that surround the cabin. I snap a picture of a tiny bird on one of the branches. It takes off mid-click, so I'm not sure if that one will turn out to be any good.

I go to take another, and something smacks into my side. With the wet sound that it makes against my jacket, I'm pretty sure that I know what it was. Sure enough, when I look to my right, Goose is bending down to gather more snow for his second assault.

Shaking my head at him, I warn, "You better not. You'll get the camera wet."

He laughs and launches it anyway. I turn sideways hoping to catch it in the back, but it turns out that I don't even need to. Lucas takes the hit straight in the chest that was aimed for me. We look over our shoulders at each other.

"You're my hero," I whisper.

The smile he throws me is just as blinding as the snow, and my heart skips a beat. "Run behind the Rover on my word. I'll lay down cover."

When he shouts to run, I take off, laughing the whole way. Maverick is, thankfully, still standing at the back waiting on us to get our bags out. I slip on a small patch of ice, and would have hit my ass if he hadn't reached out and caught me by the arm.

I smile up at him, "Thanks."

The cold has turned his cheeks and nose a tad pink and it looks good on him. I'm beginning to think that there's no bad look on any of the quad. His eyes go wide, and he jerks me to him. My face is buried inside his unzipped jacket as his face nuzzles the side of my neck. Less than a second later, I feel impact from the snowball hitting my back. That, however, is the last thing on my mind. This is the first time I've been within true touching distance of Mav and dear all that is holy, he smells so fucking good. It takes him longer than I would have expected to pull away, and it leaves my heart hurting. He's closer to my height than any of the other guys, but he still has to look down at me. The look that he shoots me could melt the snow around us. For half a second, the agreement between us doesn't exist, and I lean into him. His hand comes so close to my face that I can feel the heat coming from it. Then, as fast as it came on, that mask drops back into place and he's back to being the same old Maverick.

He puts as much distance as he can between us by joining the other three in their impromptu war. My emotions are all over the place as I watch them. That one small moment with Mav has my heart hurting. Maybe I lied a little when I said all I wanted was new friends. I'm trying so damn hard, but it seems to get harder and harder every day. I just have to keep reminding myself that the sacrifices wouldn't be worth it. Even as I watch Lucas and Mav lob snowballs at each other as Teagan and Goose wrestle on the ground trying to see who can stuff more snow in the other's pants faster. I can't think of anything that could possibly be any fucking sexier than the four of them.

Taking advantage of the situation, I get some good shots of them acting goofy before Goose tries to pull me back into the war zone. I keep the camera in front of me as an excuse to not engage.

Mav comes to the rescue again, "Guys, we need to stop messing around. We've still got to go back into town for food and shit." When Teagan grumbles, he adds, "Plus, someone didn't put on their gloves. Kendall is going to get frostbite on her fingers if we keep her out here too much longer."

Goose is still within arm's distance. He reaches out and wraps my hands up in his before I can pull away. His warm breath goes a long way in thawing my fingers out when he blows on them.

"You've got to remember to put your gloves on up here, babe," he says quietly.

He's been using the pet name more and more lately, almost

like he hopes that I'll let him back in romantically. It makes me sick to my stomach to ignore it, but if Mav were to hear it, he'd probably go ballistic. Smiling at Goose, I make my way to the back of the Rover. When I reach to take my bag, Lucas snatches it right out from under me.

"I can get my stuff," I tell him.

He winks. "I've already got it. You better go claim a room before Teagan beats you inside, otherwise you won't get the best one."

"I heard that," Teagan calls out from behind us.

Goose comes from our left side as we make our way up the stairs. "Don't let him fool you. It's true."

"Oh, thank god," Ryleigh says, walking out of the kitchen. "I was beginning to think that you guys had gotten lost."

I shake my head. "Nope. Not lost. The boys just had a little too much fun in the snow."

She rolls her eyes. "No. Not them."

"Where's Eddie?" I ask, looking around.

"Laying down in the day room," she sighs. "I may be doing more babysitting than anything this weekend. Apparently, Eddie is sensitive to high altitudes."

"Oh, that sucks," I tell her.

Lucas puts his hand against my back, "We'll be back in just a minute. We're trying to beat Teagan to a room."

She walks away and talks over her shoulder, "I guess we've got dibs on the downstairs room. I'd hate to add to his sickness."

"Come on, Kendall," he says, guiding me up the steps.

The inside of the cabin is rustic and homey. I expected nothing less. There's a runner leading down a long hallway on the second level. It's a hunter-green color that goes well with the hardwood floors and dark-tan walls. There are five doors leading off the hallway.

"You can look through each room if you want to, but this room back here is the best," he says, leading me to the door straight across from the stairs.

"What makes this one better than the others?" I ask.

He smiles. "You'll see."

There's nothing spectacular that I can see about the room. It looks like the basic inside of a cabin with brown wood walls and the same dark hardwood floor of the hallway. Black bears cover the rug, quilt and in the couple of pictures on the walls. My favorite thing is the lamp. It's a small bear holding up the post part of it and the shade matches the quilt.

Lucas grabs my hand and pulls me to the double doors across the room. He moves behind me and covers my eyes as he whispers in my ear, "This is the best part."

A blast of cold air hits me in the face as he crowds my space and moves us forward. He uncovers my eyes and my breath leaves me in a whoosh of a white smoke. Due to the downslope behind the house, I can see straight over the bare trees surrounding the cabin. For miles and miles, all that's visible is mountains and snow.

When I feel that I can speak again, I turn around to tell him thanks for pointing me in the right direction. Only, he's standing so much closer than I expect him to be. His lips slant down across mine and I'm too stunned to do anything other than kiss him back. Anything my imagination could have conjured up would never compare to the real thing. The feel of his hands on each side of my face makes it oh so much sweeter. Lucas acts as if we have all of the time in the world as he takes his time exploring every inch of me that he can. It's a sobering thought to think that it's just the opposite. I pull away with a sad smile and look anywhere but him.

He lifts my chin so that I have no choice but to lock eyes with him. "I know what you're trying to do and it's not going to work." I try to shake my head, but he stops me, "You can't deny it. I don't know what's changed in the past month, but you're keeping us at a distance. I'm telling you right now that it's not going to work."

My voice comes out in barely a whisper as I try to fight back the tightness in my chest, "I can't."

Goose's voice rings out from right outside my door, "Hey, you guys in here?"

I step away from Lucas just as Goose opens the door. He meets us out on the balcony and throws his arm around my shoulder opposite Lucas, "So, what do you think of the view, babe? Best room in the house or what?"

When I glance up at Lucas he winks at me. Whatever. I don't know what they're up to, but I'll play along for now. "It's fucking perfect. Think Teagan's going to be pissed?"

"I would be if it was anyone but you," Teagan says from behind us. I look over my shoulder just in time to see him looking away from Goose's arm around me.

I step out of reach of any of them and lean my back against the rail. "Well, I feel special right now, so seriously. Thank you."

He smiles, and Goose reaches out to me. "Can I see the camera just a second?"

My eyebrow lifts in question, but I hand it over.

"Say cheese," he tells me.

I cross my eyes and stick out my tongue just as I hear the small clicking noise. The three of them look at the picture and crack up. It's contagious and I can't help the laugh that comes out of my mouth. Then the camera goes off again. Oh, sneaky bastard. He might have actually got that one.

"Ok, give it back," I demand.

"Only if you promise not to delete those," he says, holding the camera up where I can't snatch it from him.

I sigh, "I don't even know how to delete them." There's no way I'm playing with that button either. I don't want to risk losing the ones I've already taken.

"Give it back to her," Mav says, walking into the room. "I want to get into town and make it back as soon as we can. It's supposed to start snowing again soon and I don't want to get stuck in town."

The others may have missed the hard look that he throws me, but I feel it like a dagger straight through the heart.

Chapter Sixteen

Silence Of The Night

The quaint little town that we go to for food is just that. Quaint and little. There can't be but a few shops that look like they've survived the last century at the base of the mountain. The grocery store is the most up to date out of all of them. It's very modern, and has everything that we'd have back home.

We make a quick run through as the guys grab everything that they think we'll need. You'd think that we were staying the month with how much food they load up in the buggy. When I comment on it, they remind me that they are still growing. Which of course, makes me laugh, because if some of them get any bigger they'd be the size of a fucking house.

By the time that we leave, the snow has started to fall. It comes down in tiny flakes at first and within a matter of minutes, they turn into fat blobs that don't disappear when they land on you. Maverick rushes us back into the car, and this time, I'm grateful for the space heaters in the back. It feels like the temperature has dropped at least fifteen degrees. There are crazy amounts of salt on the road, but the snow is just coming down too fast. Even with Mav driving super slow, we still slide around a bit.

My anxiety spikes and I have trouble breathing at one point, but Lucas and Teagan grab my hands to keep me grounded. Once we make it back to the cabin, I could literally puke in relief.

"I thought you said you checked the weather," Teagan

accuses Goose.

Goose automatically jumps on the defensive, “Hey, I did check it. This is some of that crazy mountain weather. They aren’t always right about that shit, you know.”

We all grab some bags and haul ass inside. It’s even colder up here. Ryleigh comes out to eat dinner with us then goes back to nursing Eddie with an apology.

“So, what’s there to do if we get snowed in?” I ask them as we settle in the living room. Mav and Goose sit on the couch with Teagan in a chair to my left and Lucas on the floor with me to my right. The fireplace blazes behind me and it feels fucking amazing.

Goose winks at me, and I feel my face go red.

Mav, watching us, says, “There’s a fuck-ton of board games in the closet.”

“I call Monopoly,” Lucas calls out to Mav as he moves to the closet.

“No way, man. You got to choose last time,” Teagan complains. “Get the cards out and let’s play some poker or rummy.”

“Strip poker?” Goose suggests with a grin at me.

Mav and Teagan are raiding the closet and aren’t close enough to hear, but Lucas is. “I second that.”

I shake my head and laugh, “Not happening.”

“What’s not happening?” Mav asks, coming to sit back down.

I jump in quickly, “Nothing.” Lucas and Goose laugh.

His eyes narrow like he doesn’t believe me, but he doesn’t say anything. “Your choice in what we play, Kendall.”

I rub my hands together as I look over my options. There’s a bunch that I haven’t ever heard of, but I know Monopoly and how to play, “Can we do Monopoly and then play cards?” That way it keeps everyone happy.

Mav looks at me like he knows what I'm doing, but says yes anyways. It's an hour or so later when we're neck deep in fake money with Teagan and Mav arguing that I hear the click of the camera. I look over to see Ry standing over by the huge Christmas tree with the camera in her hand. She winks at me.

"Hey, guys," she calls out. She snaps another picture when they all look over. Their faces make me smile. That's definitely going to make for a good one.

A few hours later, as I'm lying alone in bed, I find that I'm having trouble falling asleep. Mav's words from before are on repeat in my head, but I can't seem to stop replaying what happened today between not only us, but Lucas as well. If I can just hold out until the end of the school year, they'll all be off to some ridiculously expensive college and I'll still be in Sleepy Pines. The thought makes my chest hurt, but it's for the best.

I toss and turn for the next hour or so until my phone reads one in the morning. No missed calls or anything from Robert or Gramps either, thankfully, but I'm never going to get any sleep like this. Sighing, I toss the covers back and go in search of something to drink in the kitchen. The house is eerily silent, with only the sound of the heater and fridge in the kitchen to break it. Grabbing a water, I make my way out into the day room. It's a room of mostly windows from floor to ceiling. Since its pitch black, I can see all the way out to the tree line. The moon is so bright that it's visible even through the clouds still spitting little puffs of snow. It's so peaceful that I wish I could live in this one moment forever. Nothing else exists.

"Can't sleep?" a voice asks in a hush from behind me. He can try to be quiet all that he wants, but I'd recognize that deep tone anywhere. Maverick.

I don't bother turning around. "Not really. Just have a lot

stuck in my head right now."

He doesn't say anything for so long that I think that he's left me to my weirdness. Then I hear the air stir behind me. His hand lifts the hair off my shoulder and his lips find that spot between my neck and shoulder. Sighing, I lean into him, taking a risk that it'll make him pull away. He does the exact opposite by wrapping an arm around my middle. I feel his fingers playing with the hem of my shirt right before they slip underneath to rest palm flat on my stomach.

He kisses that spot on my shoulder again and pulls me tight. When I turn my face to him, his lips come down on mine and he wastes no time in begging me to open for him. I'm not given the option. There's so much dominance in his kiss that my skin feels like it's on fire. Without breaking away from him, I turn my whole body in his arms and wrap my fingers into his hair as I pull him even closer to me. He, no joke, growls into my mouth, and I let out this pathetic whimper, almost like a submissive wolf to its alpha. This flips some kind of switch in him, because I'm lifted in his arms as he walks us across the room before I even know what's happening.

My back hits a soft material as he drops us onto a makeshift bed. This must be where he was sleeping tonight. I would apologize for waking him up if I knew I could do it and mean it. As it stands, I'm glad I did.

His hands roam over every inch of skin that's not covered by my clothes and since I'm in nothing other than a light off the shoulder sweater and a pair of boy shorts, there's quite a bit. Not exactly fair with him in a t-shirt and sleep pants. Reaching down, I make a move to pull off his shirt and he freezes. He sits back on his heels and stares down at me. I'm scared to make any moves, because I know he could instantly turn back into his usual distant self, even if it would be hard to come back from this.

Whatever is going on in his brain, he must decide, because his arms go behind him right before he yanks his shirt off and tosses it to the floor. Even in the half light from the moon, there are no actual words to express how fucking sexy he looks. Mav may be a touch smaller in the muscle department, but he's still just as defined and chiseled as the others.

My hands roam all across his bare skin and his head falls back with a look of pure bliss. He's got a few tattoos spattered across his chest, but they're hard to make out from the angle we're in. The scorpion right on his hip bone stands out more clearly than the others. When my fingers go to trace it, he jerks away. I'm pressed into the soft mattress as his body collides with mine.

He starts with my mouth and leaves a burning trail behind as his lips make their way down my neck and collar bone. When his teeth graze my raised nipple through my shirt, my gasp is loud in the silence of the room.

It isn't until I feel his tongue on the bare skin of my stomach that I come to my senses. "Wait," I whisper.

Mav looks up at me. He's ditched the glasses at some point and I'm rewarded with my first glimpse of his eyes without anything in the way. The dark blue is close to being lost in the dark. I almost forget why I stopped him. Using my fingers underneath his chin, I pull him up to level with me again. There are reasons that he's been keeping his distance from me and it would destroy me more for anything to happen tonight then him pull away again. Doing the dumbest thing ever in my life, I place a soft kiss against his lips. He can tell right away that things aren't going any further, because he isn't overbearingly dominant the way that he was before.

As he pulls away this time, he lies down on his side and positions us so my back is against his chest. I've never slept the night with anyone before, so this may turn out to be a more sleepless night than if I'd have stayed in my own room. Mav's hand grips my stomach and hugs me tight. With the snow still falling in the silence of the night, I don't even remember my last thought as I drift away.

Chapter Seventeen

One Of Her And Four Of Us

Waking up the next morning, I feel more rested than I have in months, but that's quickly crushed when I realize that Mav left me alone at some point in the night. Pulling myself together, I shake off the ominous feeling sitting in my gut. I don't hear anything in the house still, so I'm hoping to make it up to my room without getting caught. This feels too much like a walk of shame, even though nothing happened. Have I mentioned just how un-fucking-lucky I am?

As I round the corner of the kitchen, Lucas and I almost run straight into each other. He smiles down at me until his eyes do a once over my body then look over my shoulder from the room that I just came from. There couldn't possibly be more shock showing on his face. I know what he's thinking and my face flames. It automatically puts me on the defensive. Tapping the bottom of his chin, I try to get him to shut his mouth that had popped open and walk around him.

I don't see any of the other guys and I take my time getting ready. When I finally make it down, they are waiting for me in the living room area. Mav avoids my eyes and I'm not going to lie, it stings. Lucas must see something on my face, because his usual smile turns into a frown and he glares at Maverick.

Trying to break the tension, I ask, "So, what are we doing today?"

Teagan is completely oblivious, "Well, that's what we were sitting here trying to decide."

Goose looks at the floor and it sets off my radar, "What is it?"

Maverick meets my eyes for the first time with his mask back into place. All traces of the person he was last night are gone, "It snowed all night, so it might be a rough ride up to the resort where we're supposed to be going."

It takes a second for it to click, "Would you guys make the trip if I wasn't here?"

I'm looking toward Mav and Goose on the couch. Goose shrugs trying not to answer as Mav simply says, "Yes."

"Problem solved then," I say. "Go without me."

Lucas stands up. "No, now wait a minute. We would be gone all day, and we're not just going to leave you up here by yourself."

His gentlemanly attitude makes me smile. "As much as I love the snow, I truly despise being cold." I hold my hands palm up and act as if I'm weighing things, "Falling on my ass and freezing all day, trying to keep up with you guys on the slopes compared to being comfy and warm in front of the fireplace. Not even a competition. Besides, I'm not exactly alone. Ryleigh and Eddie are here."

"Are you sure?" he asks warily.

When I nod, Teagan's blond hair bobs as he jumps up. "Yes!"

I try not to laugh, but it's impossible. They get up to leave and Maverick walks out without a word or look behind him. Teagan picks me up and swings me around before kissing me on the cheek. "You're the best."

Goose waits until he follows Mav out the door before coming to me and placing his hands on either side of my face. "If you change your mind, just let us know and one of us will come get you." I nod, and he kisses my forehead.

Lucas takes my hand and pulls me straight from Goose into his arms. He leans down and kisses my cheek close to my ear before they follow the other two out.

I go to the window and watch them go down the short driveway. Waiting until I don't see them anymore, I go into the kitchen to make some breakfast. While I eat, I check my phone again to make sure that I haven't heard from Gramps. Nothing. No news is good news, right?

It isn't until after I'm done with breakfast that I start to wonder what the actual fuck I'm going to do with my day. I try to read for a little while, but it can't hold my attention. Plus, whoever this cabin belongs to, apparently, isn't a big reader. There are no good books here. The cable picks up pretty good surprisingly, but after a few hours, my attention is elsewhere again. Ryleigh comes out once to heat up some soup for Eddie and promises to return. That was over an hour ago, and I'm starting to go stir crazy.

I'm exploring the rooms of the cabin when I find a map of the area. There's some hiking and horseback trails right off the side of the house. If nothing else, maybe I can get some good pictures in. Plus, I'll be close enough to the cabin to run back if I start getting really cold.

I bundle up, and decide that I look like a fluffed-up marshmallow once I've got all my gear on. I wrap the camera around my neck and stuff it underneath my jacket. I'd feel horrible if I fell or it got wet somehow and got broken, even if Mav is being an ass.

I put a bottle of water in one of the front pockets of my jacket and the map in the other. Contemplating leaving a note for the guys, I decide against it. I'll be back long before they will. I give my phone another once over before tucking it in the same pocket as the map.

Once I'm outside, I take a deep breath of the cold, crisp air. Makes no sense, but it's almost as if I can taste the mountain in that one breath. It's invigorating. The trail isn't hard to find and from there, I just follow the carvings on the trees, stopping every so often to take a picture or two. There's supposed to be a small stream around here somewhere. I'm sure that it's frozen in these temperatures, but my curiosity has the best of me. When I do finally find it, I'm surprised to see that the water is still flowing. It may be slow and filled with ice and snow, but it's still beautiful all the same. I want to follow it up to see if there's a waterfall somewhere close, but I'm not stupid enough to leave the trail.

I take my time walking around the area and putting Mav's camera to use, trying my best not to think about the hole that I've dug myself with the quad. After a while, my stomach starts growling and I realize that I forgot to bring food. Even with me as cold as I am, I haven't wanted to turn back, but I'm fucking starved. Walking around in twenty pounds of extra clothes must require extra fuel.

The trip back to the cabin seems shorter than earlier. Walking out of the tree line, I find the Rover back in its place. I wasn't expecting the guys to beat me home, but I'm definitely not going to complain about it. I've missed them today.

"Thank fucking god," Teagan says from the porch as I round the house.

I don't even have time to say anything before he jumps the railing and lands in front of me. He rushes me and when I lose my footing, we hit the snow hard. A laugh bubbles from my lips, but it's quickly swallowed by his.

It's an amazing feeling to have someone miss me so much. However, Mav's voice ruins the moment, "Glad to see that you're fucking alive."

I jerk as far away from Teagan as I can as I try to sit up, "Mav?"

He shakes his head and walks away.

After last night and doing his best to avoid me today, I'm

pretty pissed. Stomping after him, I yank him to a stop just inside the door. “Wait.”

I didn’t purposely use the same word as last night, but there’s a flicker of something there before anger takes over again. “Just leave it, Kendall.”

He starts to walk away again and it’s Teagan that pulls him back this time. “Dude, what the fuck is your problem?”

Maverick stops mid-step and turns back around. “My problem? *My* fucking problem?”

Goose and Lucas come around the side of the living room. They must have been in the kitchen.

“I’ll tell you what my problem is,” he says, stalking back over. I back up away from him and run straight into Teagan. Mav points at me. “She’s my fucking problem. She’s been nothing but a fucking problem since you fucktards lost your shit over her a couple months ago.”

Lucas, always the peacekeeper, steps up to the side of us, “That’s not true and you know it.”

Maverick laughs in his face, “You can’t sell me that shit, man. The three of you have fallen all over yourselves for her. All she has to say is jump and you’ll ask how high.”

“I’ve never asked anything of you guys,” I whisper, trying to fight the tears threatening to pour down my face.

He sneers at me, “You never have to. They do it anyway. You even had me going last night.” Looking at Teagan over my shoulder, he says, “That’s right. The girl that you’ve been stuck on for months, the same one you were about to fuck in the snow outside, shared a bed with me last night.”

My face gets hot at what he’s suggesting, and I lose the fight against the tears as they roll down my face.

Goose steps up behind Lucas. "You need to chill the fuck out, dude."

"Or what?" Mav asks him. "You going to fight me? Whatever happened to bros before hoes?"

Lucas shoves him back and he crashes into the long table behind him. "Stop fucking talking about her like that!"

Mav's fists ball up like he's getting ready to punch something or someone. "You're kidding me, right? Look at this bullshit. Prime example. I don't know why any of you would even bother anyways. You going to sit here and honestly say that any of your families would be okay with you dating a girl from the fucking trailer park?"

He could have said anything else and it wouldn't have hurt as bad as the knife that cut through my chest at that. The only thing that could have softened the blow would have been one of them disagreeing with him, but they don't. That says all that it needs to right there in that one moment.

Pulling away from Teagan, I make my way up the stairs, ignoring their voices calling me back. I haven't even made it all the way up before I hear the front door open and slam shut. Once I'm safely behind my locked door, I let out the anguish that's sitting on my chest and suffocating me.

Hours later, out of tears and numb inside, I walk out onto the balcony. The guys must be out on the back porch of the cabin, because their voices travel up to me.

"We made this pact at the beginning of the year," Maverick is saying. "The only way to get the fuck away from our parents is by getting into a good school. One that they don't have to pay for. No fucking girls, remember? We all agreed that we'd focus on school and football to get our fucking scholarships. Girls are too much of a distraction. I can't believe that any of us made it this long, but this is an even bigger mess. Coming to fucking blows over the same girl, it's stupid and all kinds of fucked up. I talked to her, and she said that she just wanted friends, so I gave her the benefit of the doubt. My mistake."

I have to place a hand over my mouth to cover the sound of my sobbing.

Someone says something, but it's so low that I can't make out who said it.

Maverick sighs, "The best thing we can do is just put distance between us when we get home. You know what I said before was true anyways. Nothing would ever come from it. That's not to even mention the math in the equation. One of her and four of us. Like I said, it's best just to go ahead and cut ties now."

I can't listen to any more. Each word is like a new open wound in my chest. Sneaking quietly back in, I lay back on the bed and ponder my options as leftover tears roll down the side of my face. I knew this shit was going to happen. I'm just as much as a dumbfuck as they are for even thinking about it. Even though I told myself that nothing was serious with any of them, it doesn't help the clenching of my stomach anytime that I think about it.

My sadness eventually wears off, and anger replaces it. That old saying comes to mind, it takes two to tango, and how fucking true that shit is. I didn't push to be friends. I never made the first move with any of them. And I damn sure didn't ask for this shit. After what I've already been through, this should be a cakewalk. They don't go to my school, so I never have to see their faces again if that's what I choose.

In full rage mode, I'm on autopilot as I pack what little was taken out of my bag. I'm not even sure what all goes in or if I get everything. I just need to get out of here before I say things that I won't be able to take back. I pace the floor waiting for them to go to bed. Luck is on my side for once, they're in bed before nine. I hear all of their doors shut and I count in my head. I'm going to try Ryleigh first, because I doubt any cabs would run up here.

I open the door to my room and almost scream. Ryleigh is standing there with her hand raised to knock. She yanks me into a hug as she keeps repeating that she's sorry. So, I guess it's a safe bet to say that she overheard everything today.

"Can you take me home?" I ask, trying not to beg.

She nods. "We're already packed and ready to go. I figured you'd want to get out of here as soon as possible."

Still on autopilot, I return her nod. "I was just waiting til they went to bed. I don't think I can handle any more of them tonight."

"Come on then. Let's go," she says sadly.

I grab my bag off the bed and follow her out. Waiting in the Jeep for her and Eddie to grab the bags is like pure torture. A sigh escapes me as they finally get in the car, even if Eddie is green-faced and looking like he's going to puke in the front seat. As we pull off, I see a shadow in the window on the front of the cabin. My brain wants to wonder who it could be, but I shut that shit down. Making it to the bottom of the mountain, it's a few more miles before the sound of Ryleigh and Eddie talking in the front seat puts me to sleep.

Chapter Eighteen

Stolen Time

It's a few hours before we get home. I feel really bad about falling asleep when they were nice enough to leave early and drive through the wee hours of the night just to bring me back, but I just can't help it. Crying always leaves me feeling exhausted.

"Thanks," I tell Ryleigh as I unload my bag from the Jeep.

She gets out and comes around the side. Her long, blonde hair whips me in the face as she pulls me into a hug. The blonde locks remind me so much of Teagan that it sends a pang right through my chest.

"Don't give up on them," she tells me. "They're being grade-A assholes right now and I want to throat punch every last one of them, but they'll come around."

I nod, even though I have absolutely no intention of doing it. She smiles at me, and my heart breaks a little more as I watch her drive away. Pretty soon, she'll see what they do, and I'll lose my best friend, too.

Feeling fucking shitty, I sneak into the trailer. The last thing I want to do is wake up Gramps and have to explain why I'm back early. I doubt I could even come up with something good to tell him without breaking down into a stupid, sobbing mess again. Dropping my bag on the floor, I fall face-first into my bed that smells like home. It's funny how just a few months ago the smell made me want to puke, and now it's all the comfort I need to lull me back into sleep.

BANG. BANG. BANG.

Loud beating on the front door has me jumping up with my heart about to burst out of my chest. Glancing at the clock on the dresser, I see that it's only six. I've only been asleep for a couple hours. The little bit of sleep that I managed to get was just not enough and add that to the fact that I just lost about five years of my life being scared like that, let's just say I'm not all fucking rainbows and cupcakes when I throw the door open hard enough to slam against the side of the trailer.

"Damn girl, what happened to you?" Robert asks.

"None of your business. What do you want this early on a Sunday?" I snap.

He rubs the back of his neck like he's nervous, "Lia said she saw you come in late this morning and I wanted to come over to explain before you found out by yourself."

If I wasn't fully awake before, I am now, "Explain what, Robert?"

"Can we go inside?" he asks.

At my breaking point, I yell, "Explain what, Robert?!"

"I came by yesterday to check on your Gramps," he starts. Whatever he says next is lost as I take off towards Gramps's room. Opening the door is like being electrocuted and not being able to move.

Robert comes up from behind me, "Like I was saying, he's at the hospital, Kendall. They say he had some sort of stroke, and on top of the cancer, it isn't looking hopeful."

All I hear is that he's still alive, "Why didn't you call me?"

He throws his hands up in the air, "Hey, I tried that number that you left. It kept saying that you weren't accepting calls. Maybe you didn't have service up there or something."

Thankfully, I fell asleep in my clothes, so all I need to do is throw on my shoes and grab my wallet and keys. Robert is still standing in the middle of the living room when I come out of mine fully dressed and ready to run out the door.

I throw on my leather jacket, "I'm going to the hospital."

He nods, and we walk out, "Don't forget to lock your door and for what it's worth, I'm sorry, kiddo."

Doing as he reminds me, I grind out, "He's not dead, Robert."

When I make it to the hospital, it takes me forty-five minutes just to find him. It's not a big building, but the nurses tried giving me shit about letting me in to see him. I'm getting ready to throw one of the biggest fits of my life when a nurse walks by that recognizes me. She's one of the ones that was always here when we brought Nana for her chemo. Vouching for me, she leads me down to the ICU and explains what she knows as we walk, "He was brought in last night. It was a severe stroke. There's no telling how long he sat there before his friend found him. As of right now, he's unresponsive."

We make it to the room and she stops me before I can go inside. "It's Kendall, right? Listen, I'm not going to lie to you. It was bad. There is a very low chance that he's going to pull out of this and if he does, he'll need lots of hospice care. He won't be the same."

Fat tears roll down my face and there's no stopping them. I thank her the best that I can and steel my nerves to walk into his room. Even the best of circumstances couldn't have prepared me for what I see. Gramps looks as pale as the white wall behind him and has all kinds of tubes running into and out of his body. I go over and take his hand into mine. "I'm so sorry I wasn't there, Gramps. It's my fault."

My chest hurts so bad that I feel like I'm having a heart attack and my breath comes out in short gasps. It's the only sound in the room other than the steady beat of his heart on the machine. I don't know how long it takes to get myself calmed down, but when I do eventually manage, I make a promise to him that I'm not leaving him again. Not for anything. I find a chair in the corner of the room and pull it up next to his bed and take his hand in mine.

That chair becomes my home for the next several weeks. Never once does Gramps wake up, but that doesn't stop me from trying. For the first couple of days, I talk to him nonstop about anything and everything, but mostly about Nana. I try to keep my selfish reasons for wanting him to stay with me out of the conversations both for his benefit and mine. Thinking too much on losing the one person left that cares about me is too much. I can't imagine a life without Gramps. After a week or so, I stop talking. If I don't, all of those fears and emotions are going to start leaking into my words.

His doctor is really nice, but never has any different news. Each day is too much like the last and I feel as if I'm being dragged further and further into the black void of nothing that is just waiting to swallow me up.

Christmas and New Year's come and go without any change. Never once do I hear from Ryleigh or any of the guys. It's not all too shocking considering I left my phone somewhere at home and didn't bother to ask Robert to bring it to me when he brought my bag of clothes from my room. There's nothing that I have to say to any of them anyways, even if they have tried. Which, I doubt.

I'm surprised when Mrs. Carpenter stops by one day somewhere in the third week. She says she came to check on me when I didn't show up back at school. I listen to her sympathies and her lecture on not falling behind or dropping out. Wordlessly promising, I agree to do all of my school work if she brings it to me at the end of the week. I'll have to go back to take all of my tests, but at least this will keep me from having to repeat my senior year if I miss too much work, or so she says. I don't really care, but I know what Gramps would want me to do. He'd smack me silly if I even thought about not finishing school. So, when she brings me the stuff, I do it without complaint.

It's in the middle of one of those assignments that Gramps's doctor walks in with an older guy in a suit right on his heels, "Kendall, this is your grandfather's attorney, Mr. Bishop. He wanted to talk to you about a few things today."

I just stare at them and Mr. Bishop shifts, looks at the doctor, and clears his throat, "Ms. Davis, your grandfather came in to see me a few months ago. He wanted to go ahead and file a will and set up some other precautionary measures just in case something like this was to happen." I still don't respond, and this seems to make him even more nervous.

He shifts again, "I'm sorry it took me so long to get here. I just now heard about your grandfather being hospitalized. There are some forms that I need you to look over with me and sign."

He walks over and sets a packet of paperwork down in front of me, and then looks over his shoulder at the doctor, almost as if asking for help.

The doc looks at me sadly as he comes over to me and squats down to put us on the same level, "Kendall. Your grandfather signed a do not resuscitate order at the same time that he filed his will with Mr. Bishop." My confusion must show on my face, because he reaches out and takes my hand, "What that means is, were he to fall ill and have to be placed on life support, there's a specified time frame to keep him on it, then we have to take him off. If he passes when he comes off of it, we can't try to revive him."

I shake my head and tears fall down my face. Gramps wouldn't do that. Closing my eyes, I feel in my heart that I'm wrong. We went through this with Nana and it was absolute torture to him. He wouldn't want me to watch him the way that we had to watch Nana go. I want to fight it and tell them that they are wrong, or that he wasn't in his right mind to sign that paper, but all the fight I have left inside of me is gone, and I know that I'd be in the wrong. Still, I hold my hand out for the paper.

Mr. Bishop reaches into the packet and pulls out a thin, white paper. It's crazy to think that something so small could carry so much weight. Looking it over, I see that what they have said is true. Gramps had it written in for three days, and we've already bypassed that by far. I guess I should consider myself lucky that I got in the stolen time with him that I have. It damn sure doesn't help the pain in my chest go away.

"Kendall, would you like some time to say goodbye?" the doc asks.

Of course, I don't. Saying goodbye makes it final and I don't know if I'm strong enough for that. This is harder than the accident. Gramps was there every step of the way after. I'll have no one now. I'll be alone from here on out. I'm not letting anyone in again. All they do is leave in the end. One way or another, they always leave.

He stands and places his hand on Mr. Bishop's shoulder, "Let's go get some coffee." I watch their retreating backs in a trance.

Getting up, I go to Gramps's side. The nurses weren't too quiet a few weeks ago, and I heard them saying that he's officially been declared brain dead. He wouldn't be able to hear me even if I were to talk to him. It doesn't stop me from leaning down and pressing my lips against his head just like the last time before I left. My tears leave streaks down his face that I have to wipe away with my hand.

I know how much pain you were in, and I only want to keep you here for selfish reasons. When you see Nana, tell her that I love her and that I miss her. I'm going to miss you so much, Gramps. You've always been there and always had my back, even when I made stupid decisions. I'm going to survive this for you, and I don't care what I have to do, I will make you proud to have claimed me as yours. You can rest now, Gramps, and not be in pain anymore. I love you.

Even though I don't say the words out loud, it makes me feel better having thought them. Maybe somewhere, in some other universe, he hears them. I sit on the edge of his bed and hold his hand until the doctor and Mr. Bishop come back.

"Ms. Davis, I'm going to leave this packet with you. I have the originals at my office," Mr. Bishop says. "I don't expect you'll want to go through the whole thing right now, but I left your grandfather's life insurance information on the top. I labeled the one that you'll need to take to the funeral home with you."

I know what's about to happen, but his lawyer attitude comes off as unsympathetic. I can't think about anything other than the fact that Gramps will no longer be here. When the tears start flowing, the doctor pushes Mr. Bishop out the door and a nurse takes his place.

"Kendall, are you ready?" he asks.

How am I supposed to be ready for this? No, I'm not ready. I'd give anything to have Gramps open his eyes and look at me.

He takes my silence as an okay and motions for the nurse to flip the switch on the ventilator. They remove the tube running into Gramps's mouth. His heart gives it one last oorah and then stops altogether. In the silence, the doctor reads a time from his watch before patting me on the shoulder and walking out.

With Gramps's hand in mine, I sit with him until the very last second that I can.

Chapter Nineteen

A Hole Where My Heart Should Be

My brain goes straight to auto pilot as I leave the hospital. I end up at home on the small couch with my bags in front of me not remembering how I got here. Staring at Gramps's chair brings a fresh wave of grief, and it's staggering. I have to close my eyes just to keep from passing out with dizziness. That might also be due to the fact that I can't remember the last time I ate anything. The last full meal that I can remember was on Christmas when one of the nurses brought me dinner and I didn't want to be rude and not eat it. Otherwise, I've been living off of what few things I've been scrounging from the vending machines.

The house phone rings off the hook, but I never answer it. There are also numerous knocks on the front door, but I don't move to open it. I've never wanted to be anything other than human, but right now I truly envy hermit crabs. I wish I had a shell that I could crawl up into, and stay forever without coming out if I don't want to.

When I signed the last of the paperwork for the hospital, they informed me that I would have to wait until tomorrow to contact the funeral home. So, I curl up on the couch and sleep the day away.

My dreams make me restless, and I eventually have to get up to take one of my old sleeping pills. I stopped taking them, because they turned me into a zombie the next day. Right now, I don't give a shit. I just want to sleep the pain away.

The medicine does its job, and I don't wake up until after

noon the next day. My body aches, and feels like it's been run over by a Mack truck. I'm still not ready to face life, but I don't have a choice. I have to do it for Gramps.

I shower and throw on some random clothes before I grab the paperwork and head over to the funeral home that Gramps used for Nana. Fortunately for me, they still remember me, and I'm not required to talk at all as we go through the motions of planning everything out. Whatever life insurance plan that he had is taking care of all expenses for the funeral. My gut twists painfully thinking about if he wouldn't have had that plan. I don't know what I would have done. When it's all said and done, they give me their deepest condolences and say that they'll see me in two days' time.

Something hit me in the shower this morning; I have nothing to wear. There's no way I'm going to disrespect Gramps and wear jeans to his funeral. I head over to the local thrift store. Sitting at the hospital with him for almost a month means I wasn't working. I'm sure I've lost my job by now, but I don't care. If Charles can't understand the circumstances, then fuck him. Those jobs are a dime a dozen anyways, but that also means that my funds are limited. I don't need anything fancy, just something to not embarrass us.

The first rack I come to has a dress in my size. It doesn't have any holes or smell funny, so I buy it without even trying it on. As I make it home and walk in, I realize that all of the lights and the heater are off. Shit. I must have forgotten to pay the power. Oh, fucking well. I don't care.

Hanging the dress up so the wrinkles will fall out, I down another one of those pills and crawl under the covers on my bed. I sleep all through the next day, since all I do is take a pill, sleep for eight hours, and repeat the process. By the time the day of the funeral rolls around, I'm good and numb.

My brain wakes way before I want to, and add that to the cold shower from not having the hot water heater, I'm fully awake hours before I need to be at the funeral home. I know that I promised Gramps that I would do my best to make him proud, but I'll have to start tomorrow. For now, I want to keep living in the black abyss. As I'm digging through my bag, that I still haven't unpacked, a familiar sight tumbles out onto the bed. Mav's camera. A glutton for punishment, I sit down on the side of the bed and turn it on. The first picture steals my breath and takes a stab at the bubble of numb that I have wrapped myself in. I click to move it along faster. Each picture of the guys puts even more pressure on my chest. When I make it to the one of all of us sitting around the table, it's too much. I shut it down, take the batteries out and throw them across the room. I hope they roll somewhere it'll take forever to find. I need the numbness to stay, and it hurts too fucking bad to think about them on top of putting Gramps in the ground today. My leather jacket settles across my shoulders, and I take a deep breath of the leather. It doesn't smell like Brian anymore, but it's comforting nonetheless. It makes me feel almost like Brian, Casey, and Will are here with me today.

We worked it out so that there wouldn't be a viewing. Gramps always said that he hated having one for Nana, and when he passed, he wanted people to remember him the way he was before, not as a cold body lying in a casket. There is a small service inside the funeral home that more people than I thought knew Gramps show up to. They all give me their sympathies and condolences with tears in their eyes. I feel like I've got cotton balls jammed down in my ears, so I just nod whenever someone speaks to me. At the end, I'm loaded into the family car, and we make our way over to the cemetery.

Gramps and Nana are going to be buried side by side. The headstone that was put in for Nana also has his name on the other side.

Someone will have to add his death date to it, so I'll have to try to remember to call about that, too. I've handled as many people as I can today, and the numbness is trying to wear off. I'm going to need them to hurry.

It doesn't take long for a few words to be said over him. Everyone starts to drift away back to their cars as the casket is lowered into the ground. One of the funeral home employees walks over to me. "Are you riding back with someone?"

Not taking my eyes from the box that holds what's left of my grandfather, I nod to him.

"Ok, great. We'll see you back there," he says, walking away.

The two guys standing off to the side are watching me as they begin to push dirt back into the hole, successfully severing the one tie that I had left in this world. I stand there long after they finish and stare at the space on the ground between Gramps and Nana. They didn't have to take me in when my parents decided to be complete shitheads, but they did. The two of them raised me better than I ever would have been otherwise. I wish I could crawl right there between them. If it wasn't for my promise to myself and Gramps, there's no guarantee that I wouldn't try. I'm doing what I can, but I just don't know if I'm strong enough for this. My chest hurts again, and no matter how hard I try, I can't get the numbness to come back, except in my fingers and toes. That has more to do with the sun going down and the wind whipping around me. Tears make warm tracks down my cheeks. My knees hit the frozen ground, but if it hurts, I don't feel it. Nothing could beat the pain that sits in the middle of my body right now. *I just...I just can't...*

Sobs rack my body and I can't stop it. Pressing hands to my stomach and chest where it hurts does nothing to obliterate the pain.

A voice cuts across the grass, but I don't care if anyone sees me like this. Who are they to judge how I grieve? Another voice closer than the last one means they're probably heading my way. Please. Oh, fucking please, just leave me alone.

"Kendall?" I recognize the face in front of me, but the pain in my chest is just too much.

The owner of the second voice comes around the side where I can see them and drops to their knees in front of me. Hands reach out to take mine and the difference in temperature between the two of us burns. "Jesus Christ, baby. You're fucking freezing."

Lucas shrugs off his jacket and throws it around my shoulders. He and Teagan both are in expensive-looking black suits. Sitting on the ground with me is going to ruin them. I want to tell them not to bother, but I can't think around the pain.

"Can we take you home?" Teagan asks softly.

I can't even bring myself to look at either of them. I'm just an empty shell of a person right now, and I'd be more than happy to burst into flames and have my ashes scattered on the wind.

Gentle hands lift me from the ground. Goose puts his hands behind my back and knees as he picks me up, "Come on, babe."

I'm jostled as he walks us down the small hill. Someone says something beside us. The one voice I wasn't expecting to hear and one that makes the tears flow even harder. Maverick.

Goose sighs, "I don't know, man. She's so fucking skinny. Looks like she's lost at least fifty pounds."

Let them talk about me like I'm not here. I stare into the darkening sky as I count the stars between my tears.

Never putting me down, Goose loads us into the backseat of the Rover. Lucas sits in the back with us and I feel his hands trying to rub some feeling back into my legs. The whole ride to Sleepy Pines, Goose talks to me. Repeatedly telling me how sorry and stupid he is. I want to respond to him, to soothe his guilt. I just can't. There's a hole where my heart should be, and if I open my mouth to speak, it's going to cave in on itself.

When we make it home, I'm carried up the few steps to our porch.

"Door's locked," Teagan says.

Standing in front of us, Lucas turns around, "Do you have your key?" I rake my eyes over him. His shaggy hair is lying all over the place like he's been running his hand through it. I meet his blue eyes and I see so much regret and sorrow there that it breaks my heart all over again. Sobs rack my body and I can do nothing but watch as his own tears begin to fall.

"I'm going to search your jacket for the keys, baby," he tells me quietly.

They find the keys that I must have stashed in my pocket at some point. When we walk in, Maverick swears under his breath, "Why's it so fucking cold in here?"

"Lights aren't working, either," Lucas says, flipping a switch on and off.

Teagan's face is illuminated from the screen of his phone, "Already on it."

Goose shifts underneath me, "Can you stand if I put you down?" When I don't answer, he tries anyway. I reach out and grab the counter for support. With him hovering, I make my way around the counter to the sink. The one thing I need right now is sitting right where I left it. Popping the lid on the medicine bottle, I toss back one of the little white pills without anything to even wash it down. Doesn't matter, it's only going to take a few minutes to kick in and I'll have the security blanket of numbness back.

"What was that?" Teagan asks, coming around the counter and picking up the bottle from the counter. With Lucas standing over his shoulder, he reads the label and his eyes go wide. Maverick comes from the side and rips the bottle from his hands. The fury on his face would scare the hardest of criminals. He takes a quick second to read it then steps into my space so that I have no choice but to watch as he takes the lid off and pours the pills down the drain. Dropping the bottle and lid in the sink, he turns to stalk away.

That will matter later, but right now, I don't give a fuck. I push my way through the three of them crowded in the small kitchen and make my way over to the couch. Laying down, I face the back and tuck my arms in on myself. I fall asleep wrapped in the smell of leather and Lucas.

My head is foggy the next morning as I wake up. There are voices in the house and I know there's not supposed to be. It all comes back in a rush, and the pain comes back with it. Everything hurts. I'm just physically and mentally exhausted. Today was the day I said I would start new, but I'm not ready. Sitting up, I realize that I'm bundled up with blankets and my head had been lying in Teagan's lap. Unrolling myself from the cocoon of blankets, I ignore the voices as I make my way into the kitchen. The empty pill bottle in the sink is like a kick in the stomach. Turning around, I find Maverick leaned against the wall with his arms crossed against his chest. He's still in his suit from yesterday, only he lost the jacket, and the sleeves of his white button up are rolled up his forearms. I'm torn between wanting to punch him in his smug, rich-boy face and begging him to take me right here on the counter.

Instead, I narrow my eyes and walk back toward my bathroom. What he doesn't know won't hurt him. I dig through the medicine cabinet and just as my hand closes around the bottle that I'm looking for, I feel him come up behind me. It could be any of them, honestly, but there's something about Mav's presence that refuses to go unnoticed. His hand whips out and snatches it from my fingers. I turn just in time to see him stuff it in his pocket.

You don't get to tell me what to do. Especially after what you did, I want to scream. Splaying my palms against his chest, I shove him back as hard as I can. If he would have known it was coming, I probably wouldn't have been able to make him budge. As it stands, I caught him off guard and he slams into the bathroom wall. His nostrils flare and he lunges, pressing me back against the sink. Fists down on the counter top on either side of my hips, his face is only inches from mine when Teagan comes around the corner.

Maverick doesn't flinch or take his eyes off my face as Teagan says, "There's some guy here to see Kendall. Something about the lot for the house."

With the way that Mav is standing, I'm trapped until he decides that he wants to let me move. It's almost as if Teagan and I both are holding our breath waiting to see what he's going to do. He makes me meet his eyes before pulling away, only far enough for me to have to squeeze by him. Teagan puts his hand at the small of my back and guides me through the hallway. By the time that I've made my way into the living room, I've had time to wipe my sweaty palms against my dress.

The property manager stands up from the couch where he was sitting glaring at Goose in Gramps's chair. When he sees me, he plasters a fake smile on his face, "Kendall. Good to see you, kiddo." I watch his eyes glance down to Teagan's hand still on my back and then over our shoulder to where I can hear Mav leaving the bathroom. His smile turns disapproving, but he doesn't say anything about it.

He motions to some papers and a casserole dish laid out on the counter, "I'm sorry to hear about your grandpa and I know it's only been a day, but we've got to cover some legalities of the property. Do you happen to have his will?" They might be in that packet Mr. Bishop gave me, but the thought of this weasel putting his grubby fingers on it makes me want to puke. When I don't say anything, he points back to the papers, "We need to know who the property is passing to after someone dies. If we don't have his will or have you sign this paper right here saying that you'll take over then we'll need you to pack your stuff and leave the premises no later than thirty days from now."

"May I see that?" Tegan asks him. I remember from one of our conversations months ago that Teagan's dad is a lawyer of some sort.

The manager scoffs at him and snatches the papers off the counter, "This is no concern of yours, boy, and you, missy," he says, turning to me. "Your grandparents are probably turning over in their graves right now knowing that you've got all these men in their house. It's so disrespectful with your grandpa barely cold in his grave yet."

My chest feels like someone stabbed me right in the heart, but I'm not longing for the numbness this time. I'm so angry I feel as though my blood is boiling underneath my skin.

"Don't fucking talk to her like that," Goose says, stepping into the man's space. He isn't naturally the leader of the quad, but he is the most intimidating physically. Point proven by the manager almost pissing himself.

He backs away from Goose. "You better not threaten me, boy. I'll call the law out here and have you arrested for taking advantage of such a young girl."

"Get. Out," I grind out. It's the first words I've said in over a month out loud, and it makes my throat feel funny.

Holding up the papers, he starts, "Listen here, girl…"

"I SAID GET THE FUCK OUT!!!" I scream. I know it sounds manic and with my eyes closed, I can only imagine the faces on the five of them.

I hear him scrambling around Goose, "Thirty days and I'll be needing that dish back, too."

He runs out the door, slamming it behind him. *He needs the fucking dish back?* I grab both sides of it and sling it across the counter. Glass and whatever nasty concoction inside is slung all over the room as it shatters against the wall. It makes a mess that I'll have to clean up later, but between that and screaming at him, I'm feeling so good that when Goose touches me on the shoulder, I wheel around on him.

His palms fly up in front of him in surrender. It doesn't matter. I feel like a fucking crazy person. I swing and hit him right in the chest with the bottom of my fist. "I said get out!"

Shock and sadness war on his face as I hit him again. "I don't need your fucking pity."

I hit him again. "You didn't even stand up to Mav when he said all of that horrible shit about me!"

My next swing lands in Maverick's hand instead of on Goose. I jerk it free and shove him again like in the bathroom. He sees it coming this time and only rocks back a little. Half a second later, my back connects with the wall. Hard. I see spots dance across my vision right before Mav's lips come down on mine. I yank at his dark hair and even bite his lip hard enough to draw blood, but it still isn't enough to stop him. He kisses me until my anger fades into pure fucking want. I'm not sure where he starts, and I end, but even more, I don't care. I know the other three are standing there, and if they haven't worked out the shit between them, then I can't help that, either. All I know is that I need this. I need them.

A sob rips from my throat, and I cling to Mav for dear life. He pulls me away from the wall and squeezes me tight against his body. My face is turned to the left and I open my eyes to see the others' eyes wet from what they just witnessed. Goose is looking at the floor with a devastated look on his face. I reach out and grab a handful of his shirt and pull him to us. Mav never lets go as I pull Goose's lips to mine. It's not a kiss like what just happened between Mav and I just now, but I need it all the same. He wraps his arms around the two of us, and before I know it, Teagan and Lucas are on the other sides of me. They hold me together as I fall apart.

Chapter Twenty

The What Ifs In Life

Somehow, we end up as a heaped mess on the floor. I sit between Goose and Teagan with our backs against the wall facing the kitchen. Mav and Lucas sit across from us with their backs against the counter. The middle space is nothing but legs everywhere.

I've got my eyes closed with my head back against the wall when Mav starts talking, "I know this isn't the best of times, but I need to tell you that I'm sorry, Kendall." When I look over to him, he has his glasses off and is twirling them in his fingers. "There are a lot of things that you don't know about me. I want you to, but that's something that we can save for later. Let's just say that I don't let people into my life that can walk out just as easily. These guys are my brothers and I love them as such. I saw how fast they latched onto you, and I was jealous." He huffs out a small laugh, "And believe it or not, it wasn't just for them. Every time I saw the way that any of them would look at you or vice versa it would piss me off to the point that I acted like a complete asshole. That's why I told you the truth about not sharing. Honestly, I was hoping you would choose one and the rest would have to accept it and move on. I never expected my brothers to fall in love with you."

Teagan shifts a little beside me as if the 'L' word makes him nervous. Goose squeezes my hand, and Lucas winks when our eyes meet.

Putting his glasses back on his face, he runs a hand through his hair that isn't laid back in its usual style. "I never expected to fall for you. In the few months that we've known you, you've turned our lives upside down, and not in a bad way."

Goose kisses the hand that he's holding before saying, "This past month was absolute torture. You're the first thing that I thought of when I woke up, and right before I went to sleep. I even tried calling and texting you a few times. When I didn't hear anything back, I just figured that our actions were unforgivable, and I can't really say I blame you if you feel that way. 'I'm sorry' doesn't even begin to cover it."

"He crossed a few boundaries when he said some of what he did," Teagan says, pulling my attention to him. His hair must have been pulled back behind his neck since he's playing with a hair tie and all those long, blond strands hide his face. They don't, however, hide those chocolate eyes when they turn to me, "But some of what he said is true. None of us give half a shit about what our parents say. They didn't exactly set the bar too high with examples of healthy relationships. Well, except for Lucas's parents."

I look over to him and he winks at me again and Teagan fidgets with the hair tie again. "I don't get the dynamics of how this is supposed to work. I don't get crazy jealous like Mav does, but what if I've had a bad day and want you to myself, but you're with one of them instead? Can you sit there and honestly say that there's enough of you to go around the four of us?"

He's so right. It was so easy with Will, Casey, and Brian. Everything just was, and nothing felt forced. The same way that the quad felt before things exploded on the mountain, but I'd tried to keep it strictly platonic. I can't help that the four of them broke down walls that were made of concrete. The tears that come this time make my face hurt from trying to hold them in.

Lucas taps my leg with his foot and when I look up to him he smiles at me. "It's not going to be easy. There's going to be jealousy." He motions around the group as he says that, "There's no doubt in my mind that there will be judgment for it, and even more so outside of our families."

He leans up and grabs my toes. "But that's a risk that I'm willing to take. Like Mav said, this is way beyond the appropriate time for us to be talking about all of this, but you need us right now." When I don't deny it, he continues, "And I, for one, am not going anywhere, even when you feel like you don't need us anymore. In all the years that we've known each other, we've never fought over anything, and I'm not saying that you're not worth it, because baby you are and so much more. But there's no reason to start now. If Kendall thinks she can handle all of us, then it's at least worth a shot, right?"

For the first time in well over a month, I feel my lips pull up into a smile. Only Lucas could have pulled off a speech like that. My brain wants to tell them no. I don't want to have to deal with it when they leave again, but my heart isn't going to give me a say on the matter. With me not using it for so long and then screaming, my voice is scratchy, "How did you know where to find me?"

Teagan knocks his shoulder with mine and when I look up to him, he bends down and kisses the tip of my nose. "Ryleigh. She misses you, you know. She tried to call you for a few days, and when you didn't answer, she gave up, thinking you wouldn't want to have anything to do with her because of me. Then she saw the obituary from dad's paper yesterday. She wanted to come with us, but she doesn't think you want her around."

I shake my head. "It didn't have anything to do with her. I left my phone here when I went to the hospital and I don't remember too much in between."

"Do they know exactly what happened?" Mav asks in his

quiet, deep tone.

Thinking about it makes my chest and stomach constrict. Goose squeezes my hand again and it gives me the courage to tell them, "They say it was a stroke. He, umm..." I choke back tears. "he was here for a few hours before our neighbor found him."

Letting go of his hand, I dig the heels of my hands into my eyes as I whisper the thought that has been in my head for weeks, "He was here alone. If I had been here, I could have done something. But I wasn't. I wasn't here." A sob racks my chest.

I feel Teagan shift beside me before he pulls me into his lap like a fucking baby, "Did they tell you that you being here would have helped?" I shake my head as he rubs a hand up and down my spine, "Do you honestly feel like you being here would have made a difference?"

His questions are so logical and serious, highly unusual for his normal laid-back fun-loving self.

"I don't know," I tell him, "But now I'll always have to wonder, what if. What if he fell and it somehow caused the stroke? What if someone was here to call 911 and it would have saved him?" By the time I get to the last 'what if,' I'm in full-blown hysterics, "What if he laid right there on the floor and called for me until he couldn't anymore?"

He tucks me underneath his chin and rocks me back and forth as they let me purge the guilt that's sitting heavy in my heart.

Maverick waits until my loud crying turns to sniffles, "Come here, Kendall." He uses that tone that leaves no room for argument. Teagan releases me, and I crawl the little bit of space over to sit between his legs. I feel like I'm going insane, because I can't help but to notice how fucking sexy he is in this moment. The black pants of his suit are in a tighter style, so it shows off just how well-built his long legs are. And holy fucking suspenders. I never thought that such a small thing could be so attractive. Taking a second to look at the others, I see that Mav is the only one with them. Doesn't make them look any less appealing, though. Teagan's shirt is unbuttoned and untucked making him look very much the carefree spirit he is. Lucas's sleeves are pushed up like Goose's showing off his tattoos and I find myself wondering when I'll get the chance to see the others like he promised. Glancing up, I find his blue eyes studying me. He's got one of those half smiles on his face, like he already knows what's been floating around in my psychotic brain. My eyes flick back to Mav to see that he's watching me as well. It makes me nervous, because there's no way in hell that he missed me checking out the others just now. Right after I just bawled my eyes out, nonetheless. Goddamn it. I'm such a fucking wreck.

I close my eyes and shake my head. The sides of my face are surrounded by his hands and I feel him lean into the space between us. His lips cover mine for one quick moment, "You can't worry yourself sick over the what ifs in life. That's no way to live. Everything happens for a reason, and you'll look back on this one day after you've forgiven yourself, and you'll know that there was nothing that you could do, even if you would have been here."

As his lips come down on mine again, I can only hope that he's right.

Chapter Twenty One

Soft Smiles

After a few more hours of sitting on the floor talking, all of our asses are numb, and the guys start to get hungry. They give me shit for a few minutes about how much weight that I've lost. I don't really care about how much I weigh. Skinny or fat, I'm still the same person. Albeit a little less on the inside now, but they are doing what they can to help fill that void. I'm not going to lie and say that it's going to be rainbows and fucking cupcakes overnight. It's going to take time, and I'll never fully heal. There are still days when I think about Casey, Brian, and Will, or Nana, and it makes me want to hide myself away. Gramps and I had each other after Nana, and he tried his best to be there for me after the accident. Even with the guys here, it hurts worse than words could ever express. I can't even imagine what it would be like without them right now. If they would have come back and offered nothing but their friendship, I would have taken it. I just need that lifeline to keep me from falling into that nothingness again.

Mav and Teagan are talking about going to get clothes, so they can get out of their suits, and stopping for pizza on the way back. Lucas throws that option out there, walking out of the hallway, because he knows it's my favorite and I won't turn it down. Goose stands to my left, propped against the counter with me, his arms crossed against his chest. He's got a blond shadow on his face where he hasn't shaved in a couple days. The other guys do, too, but his and Mav's are the worst. It's easy enough to turn my body to where we're chest to chest. His arms instantly unfold, and wrap around me as he places a kiss on the top of my head. Between the sound of his heartbeat underneath my ear and the warmth that radiates from him into my body, I let out a breath that I feel I've been holding in for weeks.

When I look up to him it's to find him already looking down at me. "I'm sorry I hit you."

His smile is soft, and I love the way that it crinkles the skin around his green eyes. Damn, I didn't realize just how much I've missed it. How much I've missed him. "It's okay, babe. No worse than taking a hit from a toddler really," he teases, then laughs at my expression. The rumble of it through his chest hits me in places that it probably shouldn't be right now.

Reaching my hand up to run my fingers across the stubble, I find I like the way it feels against my skin. "Why don't you keep this?" He's got that natural pretty boy look about him, but facial hair makes him look older, and dare I say, fucking sexier. That's when I feel it. I know for sure, without meaning to, I've fallen so hard for them.

The next words that leave his lips are just one of the reminders why. He shrugs, "I've just always shaved it. I'll keep it if you like it, though. Does it make me look more rugged?"

With me still in his arms, he pulls off a pose with his body and it makes me laugh, "Definitely yes. But you don't need it. You're hot with or without it."

"Mmm," his voice rumbles through his chest, "is that so?"

I nod, and he leans down like he's going to kiss me, only Teagan interrupts, "We're going to head over to get the stuff real quick. You guys will be okay til we get back?" I'm not sure if he's asking me or the guys or both, but I nod anyway.

Stepping up behind me and hugging me from the back causes me to be squished between him and Goose, who makes me laugh again when he wiggles his eyebrows at me.

Teagan, at my ear, whisper-sings a few lines from a soft song that sends chill bumps down my arms. He pulls me from Goose and moves my body with him before twirling my hand into a spin move, successfully sending me straight into Mav's waiting arms.

"Hi," I say a little breathless.

A rare smile crosses his face, "Hi. Want anything while we're gone?"

You. It almost slips out, but I catch it in time and shake my head instead.

"If you change your mind, just call one of us and let us know," he says before adding, "I'll even have them put those disgusting olives on your pizza like you like."

From sitting on the arm of the couch, Lucas comes to my defense, "Hey, I like those disgusting olives, too."

This causes a debate about pizza toppings between the four of them. The familiar sound lifts some of the weight off my chest.

"Let's go, man. I'm ready to get this fucking suit off. It itches," Teagan whines to Mav.

"That's not the suit, dude. That's you being allergic to anything other than jeans and a t-shirt," Goose corrects. This gets a full laugh from Mav and my inside voice says, *down girl.*

Lifting my face with his finger under my chin, he presses his lips against mine before he and Teagan walk out the door. I watch all the way until the door clicks shut, I then turn to Goose and Lucas. The latter stands and takes me by the hand to pull me through the hallway.

He leads me into the bathroom and has me stand in front of the sink, "Bath or shower?"

"Bath," I answer without thinking on it. Not only have I not had one in forever, but I know that it'll help loosen some of the muscles in my body right now. Plus, I don't think I've got the stamina to stand for even that long. I can't remember the last time I ate anything and I'm feeling dizzy.

While he runs the water, it gives me a second to ponder on the fact that all of them have kissed me or shown me some kind of affection in front of the others today. It's not like I'm complaining, I just don't understand how it's changed so fast. Exhausted just from standing, I scoot up on the counter. If any of them would talk to me without holding back or being straight alpha dick, it would be Lucas.

"What's changed, Lucas?" I ask while I still have the nerve to.

Watching me over his shoulder, he asks, "With what?"

I motion between us, "With this. With all of you. I can't tell you how much I appreciate you guys being here, because I'd probably still be sitting where you found me if you weren't. I'm just really confused. Only a month ago, Mav refused to even consider any of you guys being with me, because of my circumstances, not having money and such. I heard you guys out on the back porch of the cabin. I didn't mean to, but it was eye opening, to say the least. What I'm trying to say is I'm okay with us just being friends. I don't want you to feel like you have to be anything more out of pity or anything."

"Is that what you honestly think?" he asks, standing and turning to face me. "You think that we want to be with you because we feel sorry for you?"

I shrug, and that's all that it takes. He is in front of me in less time than it takes to blink, "You are wrong, baby." His lips capture mine and all I can do is grab fistfuls of his shirt and hang on for dear life.

We're both breathing hard when he pulls away, "There have been other girls in my life, but I can now honestly say that I didn't love them in any way. I know that now, because I can't ever see myself being with anyone else. You had me from that first look that you gave me in the restaurant. You had me when you stood up to T and Mav the way that you did, and the way that you're so gentle and patient with Goose. You had me then, and you have me now. You're down right now and I'll be here to pick you back up every step of the way if you'll let me."

Tears are running down my face and I feel bad for leaning my face into his shoulder and getting his shirt wet, but I can't help it. I need to be closer. Staying there for a minute or so before pulling away, I lock eyes with him as I unbutton the top one to his dress shirt. He doesn't stop me, so I make slow work of the rest of them. When I get to the last one, he stands like a sexy fucking statue as I slip the hem from his pants where it's still tucked in. Working my way up his abs, I push the sides of the collar over his shoulders. The white material drifts to the floor as he shrugs the rest of the way out of it and I make quick work of his undershirt.

As it hits the floor on top of the other, I'm left with wide eyes and a small fire in my belly. Lucas's tattoos run all the way from his wrists to his shoulders. There are empty places like he's trying to save room for more. The only one that I can see on his chest is way below leading into the top of his pants. What really gets me are the silver bars running through both of his nipples. Who would have ever thought that my sweet Lucas would willingly want so much pain. In the past few months, I've surprisingly only managed to see Mav without his shirt on, and that was in the dark. Looking at Lucas now is intense. He's a happy medium between Goose and Mav in the muscle department, with a broad chest and shoulders, and tapered waist. I finally fully understand the phrase 'washboard abs.'

I can't stop myself from reaching out to touch him. As my

hands roam his body, he leans in to my touch and closes his eyes. Curiosity wins out over logic as I lean down to see what those bars feel like against my tongue. Doing this gives me a clear view of the tub between his arm and side, "Lucas!"

He must hear the panic in my voice and realizes what I'm talking about, because he jerks around and shuts off the water, right as it's only centimeters from spilling over the edge.

"Fuck that was close," he sputters.

The look on his face is priceless, and it starts me on one of those laughing binges. You know, the semi-psychotic, stomach-grabbing laughs that you can't stop even when you try.

There's a knock at the door and Goose sticks his head in, "Heard some yelling. Everything okay in here?" I watch as his eyes roam over a half-naked Lucas up to his elbow in bath water trying to unplug the drain over to me still sitting on the counter. I haven't moved since Lucas left, so my legs are open far enough for him to fit between them. Which, in turn, hikes my dress up to my upper thighs. His face turns pink as he realizes what he almost walked in on.

Of course, all I can do is laugh like a fucking crazy person as I try to spit out, "Lucas is making us an indoor swimming pool."

Replugging the drain, he turns around and flicks the water off his fingers at me, "I turned on the bath, got distracted, and had to rescue us from drowning."

Goose's eyes light up and I know that look. It means he's about to hit us with a movie quote, "It's interesting. The young lady slipped so suddenly, and you still had time to remove your jacket and your shoes."

"Hey! I actually know this one," I say excitedly. "Titanic?"

He winks at me, "You got it, babe. I'm gonna head back in here so you guys can ummm...yeah I'm going back in here."

That reaction causes my laughter to give way to curiosity again, "Hey, Lucas, why don't you and Goose get jealous like the others do?"

He comes to stand between my knees again, "It's not because we care any less if that's what you're thinking."

Shaking my head, I say, "No, I know you don't. It's just, well, take Mav's rage at the cabin and that was just because he saw me kissing Teagan. Does it not bother you watching me kiss them?"

"I can't speak for Goose, but for me, when I see them with you, all I see is you guys making each other happy. I know you both have enough room in here for me, too," he answers, touching his chest. "And as long as we're all happy then it shouldn't matter how many of us you're with."

"You're pretty fucking awesome, you know," I say, leaning in to him.

He kisses the corner of my mouth, "I guess that's why we make such a good team, huh? Now, come on. We didn't almost drown just for your water to get cold."

He helps me down from the counter, but I'm still dizzy. I lean on him for support, "I think I need to eat something."

"Well, come on, baby. They'll be back with the pizza soon and we'll get some food in your system, even though we're already shit at this boyfriend thing. We should be feeding you something healthier since it's been so long since you ate," he says, beating himself up.

I successfully close the conversation with a kiss. "Thank you for everything you've done, and just for being here."

He presses a kiss against my forehead. "Anytime."

Walking out, he shoots me a wink before closing the door. I have a moment of panic where my heart feels like it's going to beat out of my chest and my palms get sweaty. Taking a deep breath, I remind myself that I'm not one of those stage-five clingers. It will be okay. I may not be strong enough on my own and I may need them for a crutch for a little while, but it will get better.

I can't tell you how long I sit in the bath for. I know it's long enough that my fingers turn to prunes and the water gets chilly. It takes me a minute to stand on my own, but I finally manage and wrap one of our shitty towels around myself, which brings me to the next problem. We didn't think to bring me any clothes in here. I'll run naked around the trailer park before I put that black dress on again. Out of the corner of my eye, I see that Lucas forgot his shirts on the floor. The thought of him walking around the house without a shirt because he's too chivalrous to come back in and get it, makes me giggle. Oh well, you know what they say, finders keepers.

I wrap his dress shirt around my body and do up the buttons. Thankfully, it hangs past my thighs and hides the fact that I'm not wearing panties. I set the dress and his undershirt on the sink before walking out toward my room. I'm hoping that I can get some clothes on before anyone sees me.

Not a chance.

Goose is propped against the wall in my full-size bed with Mav's camera in his hand. He's lost the dress shirt and shoes, so sitting there in nothing but a white shirt and suit pants with his blond hair looking like he just rolled out of the bed, he's making it really hard to stay focused.

"These are really good," he says without looking up. "We need to get these…" Those green eyes finally find me, and he loses his train of thought for a second before he finishes, "printed."

"I forgot to take any clothes in with me. It was on the floor. Think he'll mind?" I ask, tugging at the bottom hem.

Goose shakes his head slowly as he starts with my toes and

works his way up. "He'd be an idiot if he did."

Trying to hide my red face, I turn to my drawers. Shit. Now I've got to make the decision of grabbing my panties and making a run for it, or just sucking it up and putting them on in front of him. *Oh, excuse me. I need to go put my panties on while I'm in your buddy's shirt.* Yeah, fuck it. I try not to look at him, but I still see him out of the corner of my eye watching me as I slide a pair of boyshorts up my legs.

"Sorry," I say, turning around and making my way over to the bed.

He gives me that golden-boy smile. "I'm not. That was the hottest thing I've ever seen in my life."

I roll my eyes as I crawl up next to him. He scoots down until he's lying flat and lifts his arm for me. Putting my head on his chest, I let out a sigh as he wraps his arms around me. The camera sitting abandoned beside him. I doze off with the beat of his heart in my ear and the smell of him and Lucas filling my nose.

The next thing I know, I open my eyes to find Maverick standing in the doorway. Goose and I are in the same position we were in before except he must have fallen asleep, too. Lucas is pressed against my back with his arm thrown over my hip. This probably looks so fucking bad. I watch Maverick's face as I wait for him to explode.

I want to cry as a soft smile crosses his face. "Hungry?"

Chapter Twenty Two

Love and Desire

I take the next week off from school. There are still a lot of things to get done, and I'm just not ready to get back to normal everyday life, no matter how much the guys say it'll help. Which is another problem, I've yet to sleep alone at the trailer. It's mostly Goose who spends the night, because his parents are never home anyways. He says we can stay at his, but I don't want to risk the chance that they may make a surprise visit.

There's a ton of stuff on my list to do. First being the trip to see Mr. Bishop. I've put it off as long as I can, but he's called me every day since the funeral. I was going to go around lunch time, but Lucas made me promise to wait on him. After he gets out of school, he drives me over to the office and sits in the waiting room while I talk to Mr. Bishop. I'd love to have him in here with me, but this is one step closer to getting back on my feet.

"I'm glad to finally have you here, Ms. Davis," he tells me once all of the pleasantries are out of the way.

"Yeah, I'm sorry about that. I haven't felt up to doing much in the past week," I admit.

He nods. "That's completely understandable, and again, I'm sorry for your loss."

It feels awkward when people say that, because you're supposed to say 'thank you,' or 'it's okay,' and it's neither one of those. Instead, I plaster a small smile on my face, "You said there was stuff that we needed to discuss?"

Shifting some papers around on his desk, he says, "Yes, yes. I need you to sign some documents for your grandfather's life insurance policy. They went ahead and took care of everything with the funeral home, but I need your signature on a few things."

I shift in my seat. "Are you sure that Gramps had a policy? He never talked about one, and I know that Nana didn't have one when she passed away."

He nods. "Oh yes. I'm sure. When he came to see me, he was very detailed with everything. It was an expensive policy, because he was so sick. I'm sure you understand."

Yeah, I understand alright. That's why we never had any money, because he spent so much on life insurance. Tears well up in my eyes and threaten to spill over at the thought of him trying to take care of me even after he's gone. We suffered pretty bad when Nana died. If it hadn't been for one of the local churches that Nana had often volunteered for, we would have been up shit creek without a paddle. They did some kind of candlelight offering service for her and raised enough to help us. Gramps was too prideful at first to take it, but he had no choice.

Mr. Bishop brings my attention back to him, "Ms. Davis?"

"Sorry," I say, trying to dislodge the rando thoughts bouncing through my head. "How much was the policy for?"

He shuffles the papers around on his desk. "I don't have the figures right here in front of me, but I can get them for you."

I shake my head. "That's okay. I was just curious."

"Well, everything has run smoothly thus far, so just as soon as I have your signature right here, it shouldn't take any more than thirty days for the claim to be processed. Your grandfather gave us an account that he said was a joint account with you. I'll need you to confirm that when you sign."

Doing a once over on the sheets of paper in front of me, and verifying the account number, I sign my name at the bottom.

In less than five minutes after that, I'm walking out with another envelope and Lucas at my side.

"Everything go okay?" he asks as we're getting into the truck.

I buckle up before, still in shock, I say, "Better than okay. Gramps, apparently, had been spending all of his checks on a life insurance policy, and they've paid everything for the funeral and everything." The weight of admitting the words out loud rips a sob from my chest. It's been sitting there for more time than I can even remember and it's such a relief to know that I won't have to struggle like we did with Nana.

Thankfully, Lucas hasn't pulled away from the curb yet as he reaches over and pulls me into the best hug my seatbelt will allow. He wipes the tears off my face and kisses me once on the lips, "Want to go somewhere with me?"

When I nod, the smile that breaks out over his face scares me. How could I possibly ever say no to that? We spend the next hour in the local grocery store with Lucas picking out stuff and putting it in one of those reusable shopping bags. I try to keep up with what's going in there, but I'm so lost in my head that I'm lucky to even know where we are right now. It's not until we're in the truck and heading out of town that I ask, "Where are we going anyways?"

He looks over and throws me a sideways grin. "Technically, my house, but not really."

My palms get sweaty at the thought of meeting anyone today. I dressed nice to see Mr. Bishop, but after the emotions that came from that, I really don't think I can handle any more people today.

"Can we just go to my house?" I ask him.

It doesn't take him long to catch on. "We're not going to my actual house. I don't want my brothers scaring you away, so we are most definitely not going there."

That piques my curiosity, "How many brothers do you have?"

His smile when he talks about his family shows how much he loves them and it makes me smile right along with him, "I've got four older brothers. All but two of them are living on the farm right now. We probably owe them some big thanks. I'd say that my sharing comes easily because of them."

Yeah, because that doesn't open a new can of worms. "Ok, for one, holy hell. Your mom must be Wonder Woman raising that many boys. Is she still sane?"

He laughs, and I feel it like tingles under my skin, "She survived. Mom wears the pants in the family. It's dad that's the pushover."

"Wow," I say, still in shock.

"And two?" he reminds me.

"You live on a farm?" I ask.

He nods. "Right on the outskirts here. We don't actually do any farming. Dad and two of my brothers run a car shop, but Mom loves the space. I guess we kind of needed it, too. Five boys and all. Growing up, we had plenty of space for four wheeling and dirt bikes and everything else you can think of."

The five boys thing is still surprising to me, but I can't seem to stop the image of Lucas on a dirt bike from popping into my head. "Do you still ride?"

Shrugging, he says, "Sometimes. Not as much anymore, because I just don't have the time."

"Would you show me some day?" I ask.

That blinding smile comes back over his face, and he cuts his eyes over to me. "If it makes you happy, of course I will. I'll even teach you to drive it, too. Lincoln and I spent most of last summer restoring a couple old motorcycles. We sold one, but I could take you for a ride on the other, if you want."

I take a minute to ponder his words. I don't know if I'll ever be able to drive one, but riding with Lucas would be sexy as hell. Just the thought puts those tingles underneath my skin again. "Maybe."

He chuckles and reaches out to take my hand. We turn onto a dirt road that leads back off into the woods. I want to ask where we're going again, but I trust him enough not to. The woods break into a clearing. With it still being winter, sunset happens way before it's supposed to. It's so dark that it's hard to make out what's around us, but I can see where the tree line stops.

Lucas throws the truck into park and turns it off. He jumps out then turns around. "Wait here. I'll be right back."

I'm skeptical, but I nod. When he shuts the door, it throws everything into complete darkness. I'd feel bad for anyone who has a fear of the dark. It's completely pitch black and silent out here. I've just counted to fifty-six in my head when the little clearing is lit up. I know Lucas said to wait, but it's so beautiful that I hop out of the truck and walk over. I look up to hundreds of twinkle lights above me. Someone has built little posts to keep them strung up and the soft glow lights up all of the space around the little area.

"What do you think?" Lucas asks, stepping out of the trees.

I look at him like he's lost his mind. "It's absolutely fucking amazing! Did you do this?"

"As much as I would love to have been the one to put that wonder on your face, I have to say no," he admits. "Logan built this out here and used to have parties back when he was in high school. I used to sneak out here, but he'd always send me sulking back home, saying I was too young." He's standing in front of me by this point and looking up to his face, the lights make the best backdrop behind him. Lucas couldn't possibly be any more wonderful if he tried.

My heart thumps wildly in my chest as he smiles down to me. "Hold that thought," he whispers and disappears back into the truck.

It only takes a few seconds before his windows are rolled down and that Ed Sheeran song "Perfect" comes from the speakers. It doesn't have to be very loud to be heard, because the sound echoes around the clearing.

Lucas walks back over to me and holds out his hand. "Dance with me?"

Now we're back at the point I mentioned earlier. 'How could I possibly say no.' So, I don't. I place my hand in his and he pulls us together. He takes over the steps and leads us around the little space. The sound of our breathing and leather jackets rubbing together are the only sound other than the music. Our breath mingles in clouds of white from the cold, even as he puts his mouth to my ear and sings the lyrics softly. His hands are warm at my hips and I love the feel of his shoulders flexing under mine. I move them down, underneath his shirt. The feel of his skin on my fingertips starts a fire in my belly that no one other than Lucas can put out. When I move my face to his, I find him waiting as he presses his lips against mine.

There has never been a more perfect moment in my life than this one. I don't care if we are in the middle of nowhere or that it's mid-winter and cold as fuck outside. It doesn't matter that I'll have to face reality sooner than I'd like. No. I'm taking tonight to live in this dream as long as I can.

Before he can stop me, I have both of our jackets lying in a heap on the ground. As if I weigh nothing, he picks me up and carries me to the back of the truck without taking his lips from mine. I gasp into his mouth as my back meets the cold steel.

He pulls away and in a deep voice that could rival Mav's, he says, "I never meant for this to happen. I just wanted to get you away for a little while. I brought some blankets just in case we stayed out here longer and got cold."

It only takes half a second for his words to click in my head and I pull his lips back to mine. Like I said, I'm going to live in this dream for as long as I can. "Get the blankets," I whisper.

"We still have that food, too, if you're hungry," he reminds me.

The last thing I'm thinking about in this moment in my life is food, so I shake my head.

He kisses me lightly and sets me down. Opening the back door, he pulls out a fluffy looking comforter and a giant sleeping bag lined with flannel, "I wasn't sure which one you'd want, so I brought both."

I reach up on my toes and kiss him on the cheek before he heads around the back of the truck. That fire comes back as I watch his muscles flex as he jumps into the bed. He reaches down and lifts me like a sack of potatoes. I can't help when my lips find his again. There's just no stopping it.

He lets me pull off his shirt, and as before, I'm awarded the sight of that tan, tattooed, and pierced skin. Without the overflowing bathtub here with us, there aren't any distractions as my mouth closes around one of the little silver bars. Lucas groans and grabs the back of my head to keep me from moving. Letting me take my time, it isn't until I pull away that he helps me out of my shirt and bra. His hands roam over the outside of my breasts before he places them against my naked back and pulls us together. The feel of our skin connecting satisfies some small part of me and yearns for more at the same time.

Bending his head down, he presses his lips to that small spot underneath my ear. "Lucas," I whisper.

"Hmm," he says, the sound vibrating through me.

"Please," I say even more quietly.

That one little word is all that it takes for him. He opens the sleeping bag and spreads it out in the bed before helping me lay down on top of it. Getting to his knees, he goes on all fours and presses a kiss against my belly button. In the next few seconds, he removes the rest of my clothes, and then just sits back to look at me. Normally, I'd be uncomfortable in this position, but there's nothing there but love and desire.

"You're fucking beautiful, baby," he says. "I'm one of four of the luckiest guys in the world."

I rise up on one of my elbows and use my other hand to crook a finger at him. He crawls back up my body and braces himself on his forearms, keeping his weight off me. That is the last thing that I want. I wrap my legs around his waist at the same time my arms go underneath his to hold onto his back. When I pull him down, he doesn't resist. It grinds my back into the bed of the truck, and I'll probably have bruises from it later, but they'll be worth it.

Lucas acts like he wants to go gentle and slow. I think that we both know that it isn't what the other wants, so I reach up and nip him on the neck right before I lick it to soothe the sting. His hips drive into me and the denim still covering his legs rubs against me in all the right places. After seeing all of his tattoos and the bars in his nipples, I figured Lucas would be one for a little pain and I'm not wrong. When my teeth find his shoulder, he groans in my ear before rising up to strip the rest of his clothes off. The sight of Lucas bare chested is mouth-watering. Completely naked, he leaves me with a brain full of mush. He is absolutely fucking glorious, with tattoos on his lower stomach and wrap arounds on his thighs. Noticing me checking him out, he grins down at me as he opens a condom and slips it on. The last thing any of us need right now are any little babies running around, so the more protection the better.

He braces himself back on his forearms over me. When he opens his mouth to say something, I cover it with my hand and lift my hips to meet him. That's all it takes for him to enter me in one swift movement. We both groan into the night air. As he moves above me, my breath catches for a second. Giving this piece of myself over to him means that I am moving on from the VanPelt brothers. Not that I'll miss them any less, just accepting that there may be something left for me after all.

"You okay?" Lucas asks.

I nod as much as I can. "Better than."

He smiles down at me and sets a pace that has us coming apart together in no time at all. Scooting us to the edge of the sleeping bag, he zips us up in it. I'm pretty sure that it's meant for only one person, but I don't take up that much room, even around his size. We lay on our sides facing each other.

Wanting to stay here forever, I'm disappointed when I feel myself falling asleep. Lucas props the other blanket under his head for a pillow and I use his arm. His body heat trapped inside the sleeping bag is better than any heater I've ever seen.

When I look up to him, his eyes are closed like he's right on the edge, too. A smile crosses his lips as I reach up and kiss his chin. "I love you, Lucas."

At this, he raises his head and presses his lips against mine. "I love you, Kendall."

The next thing I know, Lucas's body jerks against mine. "Shit, shit, shit."

I crack my eyes to find that it's at least mid-morning and Lucas is beside me freaking out, apparently, just waking up himself. He yanks the zipper down and I tumble out onto the frozen bed of the truck.

I yelp and try to crawl back into the warmth.

"I'm sorry baby. We've got to go. My parents are going to go fucking postal if the guys didn't cover for me," he says, jumping up to throw his underwear and pants on. It's a race to see who can dress the fastest and by the time that we jump in the truck we're both laughing so hard we're in tears.

He checks his phone. "Fuck. The guys have called eighteen times. If my parents don't kill me, they will for keeping you out like this."

I don't know why, but it makes me laugh again and Lucas smiles at me as he presses the call button. The sound of a ringing phone comes across the Bluetooth in the truck. Lucas pulls me to him. "No matter what the consequences, this was worth it."

"I couldn't agree more," I say and press my lips against his.

Mav's deep voice comes over the speakers, breaking us up, "What the fuck, dude? Please tell me Kendall is with you."

It is in no way funny, but I can't help the laugh that slips out of my lips at how much trouble we're in.

Chapter Twenty Three

Flowers

The week of Valentine's Day comes up fast on us and none of the guys have mentioned doing anything, which I must say is exciting. I've never been one for big, showy things, especially on that day. All it's good for is making lonely people feel even lonelier. Lucas better be glad Goose covered for him two weeks ago, or he'd be grounded and not doing anything anyways. Thinking back on that day puts a smile on my face.

First, because of that one stolen moment with Lucas. I never thought that I'd fall in love with anyone else after the accident. I was walking through life with blinders on, not truly living. It would sound insane if I said so out loud, but it seems as though all of my senses have awakened after being asleep for the past two years. Everything is more colorful, and even smells and sounds better.

Second, because of the shit-show that happened once we met up with the guys. Lucas and I talked about it on the ride back to my house that day, and decided it was best to tell them what had happened. Can't have a relationship like ours and not have honesty in every aspect.

Their reaction wasn't as bad as I was thinking it would be, which wasn't altogether a good thing. I honestly thought Mav was going to punch Lucas in the face for a minute, but he calmed down pretty quick. Goose wasn't pissed at all, said he was expecting it when they couldn't find us. Teagan was the one that worried me the most, because he was the quietest. Then he jumped in and said it's his turn next, and broke up the tension. We all laughed with him, but I'm not too sure that he was kidding.

"Your food say something funny?" Billy asks, sitting down across from me at the lunch table.

I shake my head. "Just thinking about something. I'm so fucking glad that it's Friday, though, for serious."

"Yeah, me, too," he says, before taking a bite of the burger on his plate. "I was thinking. You know tomorrow is Valentine's Day, right?"

Uh-oh. I know where this is headed, and it's not good. Billy is an okay guy, and is probably the only one in this school who isn't a giant douche, but I've got my hands full with the four that I have, not to mention the fact that I don't even see any other guys like that anymore. I try to play it off, "Yeah. I guess it is, huh."

Rhetorical question and he answers it anyways, "Yep, so I was thinking, why don't we go to the movies or something? It doesn't even have to be a real date if you don't want it to be."

"That would be fun," I say, trying to think of a way to let him down gently. "But, I can't. I've got stuff going on, and I'll be busy all day tomorrow." I'm just about to mention the fact that I have a boyfriend, or four, when the bell rings.

He shrugs. "That's fine. I'll pick you up tonight. See you at eight."

Then he walks away, leaving me with my jaw on the floor.

I search for him for the rest of the day, but he's nowhere to be found. It isn't until the final bell rings, and I'm headed out that I find him in the worst way possible.

The buses are getting ready to pull away as he jumps out in front of me with a dozen red roses in his hand. "Just thought I'd get an early start on tonight."

When I don't reach out to take them, he grabs my hand and I have a choice of grabbing them or letting them drop. I don't want to be rude, so my fingers close around the stems. Surprising me even further, he leans in and drops a kiss on my cheek as he says, "See you at eight."

I'm too shocked to say what I had planned to all day. Honestly, I can't do anything but watch him walk away once again, with my mouth open catching flies. It isn't until this moment that I realize that the buses have pulled away, and there stands Goose with his arms folded across his chest. Teagan is behind him, half in, half out of Goose's truck. Both of their faces war between hurt and pure rage.

Walking over to them, I want to hide the roses behind my back, but it's too late now. They've seen everything. I don't say anything as I walk beside Goose and toss the flowers in the bed of his truck and jump into the middle of the bench seat. The ride to my house is silent and tense as a motherfucker.

I think I hold my breath the entire way, and don't let it out until we're inside my house. That only lasts so long, though, as Mav is about ten minutes behind us.

He storms into the house with Lucas right behind him trying to talk some sense into him. I am slowly taking my time to put up the dishes from the drying rack just to busy my hands. Shit. There's going to be no easy way out of this. I feel his breath against my neck as his hands prop against the counter on either side of my hips, locking me in place.

"Who is he?" he asks in a voice that is barely containing the rage sitting under the surface.

Mav could have come at me in any other way than that one, and I wouldn't have gotten defensive. I can't explain it, but with those three words, I feel like he's accusing me of something that I didn't do.

So, naturally, it kick-starts my smartass mouth, "I'm afraid I don't know what you're talking about."

His nose makes a trail from my neck up to my ear as his tone turns darker. "Don't play with me, baby girl. Who was the guy who gave you the flowers and you let kiss you?"

I twist in his arms until we're face to face, and I snap, "I didn't let him do anything."

Mav crowds into my space, and out of the corner of my eye, I see Lucas and Teagan looming right over his shoulder, as Goose stands on the other side of the counter. All with their eyes on me, waiting for an answer same as Mav.

"I've told you before," he says, talking low, "I don't share well with others. The only reason this is working is because it's the four of us. I'm not doing this shit with anybody else."

This pisses me off more than anything else. "I might be trailer trash, but I'm not a fucking whore, Maverick."

"Don't talk about yourself like that," Goose says, speaking for the first time.

Without taking my eyes from Mav's, I reply defensively, "Well, that's what he's making me sound like."

At this, Teagan jumps in, "He's not meaning it that way. He's just asking the question that we're all wanting to know the answer to."

When I try to glance at him, Mav shifts his shoulder in my way. "Who is he, Kendall?"

I have no choice but to look him in the face as I answer, "It's just some guy at school. He sat down with me at lunch a couple months ago and started talking. We eat lunch together and that's it. Today, he brought out the bullshit about tomorrow being Valentine's Day, and asked me out. When I told him no, he said he'd pick me up tonight, and before I could say anything, he left. I tried finding him to tell him that it wasn't going to happen, but he disappeared, and I guess we've figured out where he went. Then, as I'm walking out to the parking lot, he ambushes me. Drops the flowers in my hand, kisses me on the cheek, and runs off with a promise to be here at eight."

Goose chuckles darkly under his breath, "He'll have a surprise waiting on him if he shows up here tonight."

"Now why couldn't you just say that?" Mav asks, still not moving.

I cross my arms against my chest. "Did you give me a chance to before you came in here with an attitude, acting like a crazy caveman? Me man. You woman. No share."

Catching sight of Teagan and Lucas over Mav's shoulder, I see them leaning on each other for support as they try to hold in their laughs.

Mav tries his damnedest, but eventually, a smile breaks free as the guys fail at holding theirs in. He pulls me to him and whispers in my ear, "I'm sorry. You just make me crazy sometimes."

I press my lips against his Adam's apple. "Just returning the favor I guess."

He chuckles, and I feel the sound all the way down to my toes.

"So, is this guy for real about showing up here today?" Goose asks.

I share a grim smile with him.

"Yeah, I think so."

"Guess he'll get a little more than what he bargained for then, huh?" Teagan asks as he fist bumps Goose.

Oh damn. This is going to be ugly.

We make a spaghetti dinner while we wait. Of course, that means Goose and I make dinner. The other three would burn boiling water. Well, maybe not Lucas. He's not that bad.

I mentally bite my nails waiting around for the clock to turn. I'm seriously kicking myself in the ass for not having his number so I could just tell him. Even though that might have made the situation worse earlier.

When lights cut across the front windows five minutes before eight, I jump up and beat the guys to the door. "Let me handle this. There's no reason for anyone to have to get arrested or go to the hospital tonight."

Goose and Teagan look disappointed, but nod almost at the same time. Then, surprising me, Lucas says, "He's got one chance to accept your answer. That's it."

I sigh and walk out onto the porch. The closer he is to his car, the better.

He's just walking around the front of an older-style Camaro as I walk down the steps, and the sight of it squeezes my chest like a vise. If things weren't already looking bad for him, that right there would have been the straw that broke the camel's back. I'd never ride in that car.

Billy smiles as he sees me. "Hey, Kendall." He moves in for a hug right before his eyes find the four looming shadows I'm sure are behind me on the porch, and pulls up to a stop.

"Hi, Billy. I'm sorry you went out of your way today, but I can't go out with you tonight, or any night actually," I tell him.

His face looks defeated for a second. "I didn't mean to come off so pushy earlier. I just didn't know how to get you to agree to a date with me."

I shake my head. "It's nothing you did. I'm in a relationship right now and I tried to tell you earlier, but you kept running off before I could. It would be best if you left now."

Stepping closer, he leans down so only I can hear it when he says, "If you feel threatened, I can help, you know."

The guys shift on the porch and one of them comes to stand behind me. Lucas's cologne hits my nose, and I have half a second to be thankful it isn't one of the others. That is until he opens his mouth, "Are you deaf? She said leave, dude."

His face turns into an ugly sneer, "Wow. Not straying too far from the trailer park with this one, are you?"

Confusion muddles my brain for a second before it clicks that he's talking about Lucas. He must have his sleeves pushed back so his tattoos are visible, and Billy assumed. "Are you fucking serious?" I demand, my temper going as red-hot at Mav's earlier.

"Look," he says, throwing up his hands in surrender and turning to walk away, "I didn't come here for any trouble. That's what I get for trying to be nice to the outcast, right? It's just amazing that you'd choose to stick with trash when you can have something better."

Lucas steps up against my back as I say, "Just get in your fucking piece-of-shit car and leave, Billy."

Then as if he just remembered something, Billy turns back around with a laugh, "Oh shit, that's what kind of car your other trailer trash boyfriends died in, wasn't it?"

Goose clears the side railing of the porch in one jump, and I get the pleasure of watching Billy's eyes go wide in fear. However, this isn't Goose's fight. Billy looks back at me, and I punch him harder than I've ever hit anyone in my life. One of my fingers pops, but I don't even feel the pain from it. His nose gushes blood, and all I can think is of hitting him again. Goose stops next to us, realizing that I've taken care of it. He's normally as sweet as Lucas, but the murderous look he's throwing Billy is scary, even to me.

"Goddamn it. You broke my fucking nose," Billy wheezes

out.

"You're fucking lucky that's all that's broken, asshole," Goose tells him.

He shakes his head and backs up toward his car without turning away. "This is so not worth the two hundred bucks."

My mouth drops open and there's no stopping Goose this time. He has him pinned against the side of his car before I can even move to stop him.

"What did you say?" he growls at him.

Billy looks pathetic with blood pouring down his chin and onto his shirt, as white as a ghost, facing Goose, "Derrik paid me months ago to woo, fuck, and leave her."

I catch Goose right before his fist connects with Billy's face, "Stop. Babe, please stop."

Billy's eyes widen. "I thought you were with the other one."

Neither of us bother to respond to him. I pull on the hand I have in mine until Goose lets him go completely.

I should have just let Goose punch him, because the next thing he says is, "Guess Derrik was right. You really will sleep with anybody."

Mav and Teagan, the two that I'm more afraid of getting in the middle of this, come down the steps at his words.

But I've had enough. I turn and knee Billy right in the balls. He drops like a stone. Goose gives him a full ten seconds before he lifts him up by the front of the shirt and hauls his ass around to the driver's side door. "Now get the fuck out of here."

"I'll have you guys locked up for this," he threatens, digging his keys out of his pocket.

Teagan laughs, "You can try, asshole. My dad is Steve Morgan. He'll bury your ass in paperwork for five years before I ever see the inside of a jail cell."

Apparently, the name rings a bell for Billy, because he jumps in the Camaro and spins out as he pulls away.

Lucas comes up on my right and grabs my hand. I let out a yelp and jerk my hand back.

"Did you hurt your hand, baby? Let me see," he says softly.

Goose looks over his shoulder. "If it's moving, then she just jammed it."

"Come inside," Lucas tells me, "let's take a look at it."

Passing by Mav and Teagan, the latter pulls me to him away from Lucas, "That was the hottest fucking thing I've ever seen in my life." He tucks his hands underneath my arms as he slams his mouth down on mine. Once he's had his fill, he picks me up and spins us in a circle.

"We need to get inside for real, though. Someone probably already called the cops," Lucas says as Teagan puts me down.

"Forget where you are, baby?" I ask him, using his pet name for me. "You're in the trailer park. They don't call the cops out here unless shit gets real bad."

Chapter Twenty Four

Words Of Wisdom

"Wakey, wakey," a girly voice says, shaking my ass above the covers.

I groan and roll myself up in the blanket, so not ready to be up yet. It feels like I just fell asleep. Peeling one of my eyes open, I find Ryleigh grinning at me. "Wake up sunshine."

"Oh my god, dude," I groan. "You sound just like your brother in the mornings."

She turns her nose up. "I don't know whether to take that as an insult or compliment, considering I know how much you looooove the sound of his voice."

Flipping my pillow on top of my head, I try to hide my pink cheeks. "What are you doing here anyways, and where's said brother?" The guys drew straws last night after the fiasco with Billy. Teagan won, but I passed out before anything could get interesting.

Shaking my bum again, she says, "I kicked said brother out a little while ago and told him to go do boy stuff. We're having a girls' day."

"Don't you and Eddie have plans today?" I ask, my voice still muffled with the pillow.

"Yeah, duh," she answers, "but not until tonight. I'm going to go get my hair and nails done. Plus, I need a new outfit. I haven't gone shopping without you, so my retail therapy has been at an all-time low this past month."

If I wasn't already feeling guilty about not calling her before, I am definitely feeling it now. I uncover my face and roll onto my back, so I can see her face, "I'm sorry I didn't call sooner, Ryleigh."

She smiles sadly at me, "No need for apologies. It's been a rough month or so. I'm just sorry that I couldn't be here for you when everything happened with your Gramps. If I had known, I wouldn't have given you a chance to not have me around. I would have been here."

Digging my way out of my blanket cave, I grab her hand, "Please don't. I know that you would have been here if you could. I should be the one apologizing. Everything happened so fast and yet so slow. If I'm honest about it, I don't really remember much over the past month. It's like living in a fishbowl. You know what's happening around you, but it's not happening to you, if that makes sense."

"Sounds kind of crazy," she says before a true smile lights her face. "But that's just one of the reasons why you're my bestie. Our crazies match each other." I laugh as she wiggles her eyebrows, "Besides, I know of two ways you can make it up to me."

"By getting my lazy ass out of bed and having a girls' day," I guess the first one.

Nodding she says, "And turning your fucking phone back on so someone can get in touch with you."

I laugh, and it makes her giggle. The thought hasn't even crossed my mind. I'm normally with one of the quad, except school, but they drop me off and pick me up. I haven't had the need for it, but I know that I need to. I tease her anyways, "You can always call me on the house phone. I never leave the house anymore."

"Yeah," she says sarcastically, "Unless you're off bumping uglies, or pretties I should say, with Lucas."

My gasp is loud, and it makes her giggle again, "They told

you about that?"

"Teagan did," she admits. "He needed someone who wasn't a dude to talk to about it. His words, not mine."

"What did he say?" I ask curiously.

A look of shock falls across her face, "You think that I'd betray my brother's trust like that, after he asked me not to say anything?" I must let my disappointment show, because she laughs again, "I'll tell you on the way if you'll get up and spend the day with me."

I was going to do that anyway, so this is just an added bonus, "Deal." Unwrapping myself, I make quick work of getting ready. Before we leave, though, I need to check the bank. There was money in there, but between bills for a month and me not having a job, it's dwindling down fast. I tried to find out who paid to have the lights turned back on, but the guys wouldn't tell me, even when I threatened maiming.

Sorting through the mess of crap on my dresser, I locate my phone and turn it on. Someone had it connected to the charger. That definitely wasn't me, unless it was one of those moments of non-clarity. When it finally fires up, I see that there's still service on it, which is weird because I thought that it ran out back in January. One of the guys has been paying it, had to be. Oh, they are in so much trouble. The phone beeps and chimes endlessly for at least a full three minutes before it quits.

"Jesus," I exclaim out loud.

Ryleigh is laid across my bed with her phone in her hand, "What is it?"

"There are three hundred and twenty-six fucking texts on here. And it says my voicemail is full," I marvel.

She lets out a small disbelieving snort, "That's what happens when you ignore people who care about you for over a month. I may or may not be half of all of that."

Her confession and the tone in which she says it have me laughing. Opening the bank app, I ignore the other stuff for now. It takes forever to pull up, but when it does, I almost sit on Ryleigh as I plop down on my bed to keep from hitting the floor.

"Hey!" she squeals trying to move out of my way.

I feel her look over my shoulder, "Don't mind me as I'm nosy for a second." Then she gasps as she sees what almost put my ass on the floor. "Is that for real?" she asks quietly.

"It has to be," I tell her when I can find my voice. "Gramps had a lawyer who handled all of his stuff before he passed. A will and a life insurance policy that I didn't even know that he had. He told me that the claim would be coming through within thirty days, but I never got the amount from him."

No wonder all of Gramps's checks were going to his policy. There's a quarter of a million dollars sitting in my bank account right now. The screen goes fuzzy as tears cloud my eyes. My heart wrenches hard, and the phone drops to the floor as I use my hand to cover it. Propping my elbows on my knees, my face falls into my hands as tears run into the carpet. Ryleigh's hand rubs smooth circles across my back as she lets me cry it out.

It's just so unbelievable. Not that he would do this, but that it was for so much. I could pay off all our debts on his and Nana's medical bills, go to college and still have some left over to have a decent start on a life away from the trailer park. Once the water works dry up, I apologize to Ryleigh again.

"There's nothing to be sorry for, Kendall," she reassures. "Some days are harder than others, right? Little shocks and surprises, good or bad, along the way don't help I'm sure. Want me to wait in the living room for a minute?"

This is the first time that we've seen each other in over a month, and the last thing I want is her to think that she's not important to me, but I need a second. There's a pressure in my chest that I can't seem to let go of. When I nod, she smiles and leaves me alone in the room.

Rescuing my phone from the floor, I find the number that I'm looking for and hit call.

Goose answers on the second ring, "Figures it would take Ryleigh to have you start using your phone again."

I want to laugh, but it comes out as a sob instead.

His voice drops the playful tone and goes serious instantly, "Are you okay, babe?" And when I don't answer, "Kendall?"

Mav's voice says something in the background. Should have known that they would be together. Another second has him on the line. "What's wrong, Kendall?"

"Nothing," I tell them, only half lying. Just hearing their voices has lifted off some of the weight off my chest.

"Try again," Mav coaxes in that deep voice of his.

I take a deep breath. "I just had a moment and I needed…" I trail off, not knowing if I should tell them just how deeply rooted my necessity of them actually is right now. Too late, though.

"Needed what, lovely?" T asks.

Smacking myself in the forehead, I answer honestly, "I just needed to hear your voices."

"There's nothing wrong with that, baby," Lucas pipes in.

"Need us to come over?" Goose asks.

My heart says so much yes, but they're out doing shit. Plus, it'll ruin a girls' day with Ryleigh that I owe her. "No, that's okay. I'm fine. Besides, Ryleigh would never let any of us live it down."

"Goddamn right she wouldn't," Teagan warns then adds, "but I'll face her wrath if you need us."

The laugh that he pulls out of me lifts the last little bit of weight and I can fully breathe again. I hear their laughter on the other end, even Mav's.

"I appreciate your willingness to sacrifice yourself, but I think I'll be okay," I smirk, and then making myself sound needy as fuck, I ask, "I'll see you guys later, right?"

"Of course, you will," Teagan says with a smile still in his voice. "We're just headed to go get…" There's some rustling around then he says, "Ow, shit. I mean, yes, you'll see us later."

Shaking my head, I roll my eyes at them as we say our goodbyes.

I stuff my phone and wallet in the inner pocket of my jacket as I walk out to find Ryleigh.

She's sitting on the couch laughing at her phone, and when she sees me watching her, she stands and says, "My brother is so stupid sometimes."

I don't comment, because there's something more on my mind. Waiting until we're in the Jeep and on our way, I ask, "So, what did Teagan say?"

She laughs like she's been waiting to see how long it would take me to ask, "Well, he told me pretty much everything. That you guys were all together, which any moron would be able to see that. But, he also said that you and Lucas had sex first the other day."

Looking out the window, I don't want to see the judgment there. I should have known better. She says, "Look, I think it's really cool that you guys are trying something out of the ordinary. I would never in a million years try it, because one is enough for me, thanks. I think you're exactly what they need, though. They'll never be happy being separated with four different women."

Her words leave a warm place in my chest, "Thanks. What did Teagan say about me and Lucas?"

Shrugging, she answers, "Not much, really. He said he was surprised that he wasn't really jealous. I think he wanted to be, but he wasn't. And, he said that Maverick told him that he wasn't pissed, either." Her face scrunches up like she's thinking of something unpleasant, "He said that it was quite the opposite, that it turned them on thinking about you and Lucas. And as much it makes me want to throw up in my mouth to think about my brother saying that, he asked if I thought that was a normal response."

"What did you tell him?" I question curiously.

She smiles over at me, "I told him that nothing about your relationship with the four of them is normal, so they're allowed to feel the way that they want to without thinking too hard on it."

God, I could kiss Ryleigh right now for her words of wisdom. I don't know how I got so lucky to have her in my life, but I know I'll never go a month without speaking to her again, "I missed you, Ry."

"Aww," she says, "I missed you, too."

We're gone for a little over five hours. She takes me with her to the salon and demands that I get a manicure and pedicure with her. After doing it, let's just say there will be more trips like that in my future. I watch her getting her hair styled and decide that maybe it's time for something new for me too, but not today. Then we eat lunch and shop for a new outfit for her, even though I'm beginning to think that the whole thing was for me as she throws yet another skirt at me.

Both of us leave with two new sets of clothes, and feeling like a million bucks from the salon. I hate being wasteful with the money in the bank, but I owe her several times over, and don't let her pay for anything.

As we pull back up to my house, I let out a huge yawn, and I think about going back to sleep. For some reason, today has completely worn me out.

"Uh-uh," Ryleigh says as she parks. "The guys would kill me if they came over to find you passed out."

"Why would they care if I'm asleep later?" I ask while watching her dig through a bag in the back.

She mumbles to herself and then says, "Ah-hah," as she finds what she was looking for. Handing me a slim silver can she says, "This is made with natural fruit juice and green tea. It's like a healthy energy drink."

I look from her to the can skeptically, but crack it open and take a swig anyways. It's not half as bad as it sounds.

The smile she shoots me is smug, "You'll thank me for that later."

Her attitude and playfulness remind me of Teagan, but not in a weird way. "I'm glad to have you back." I smile.

Returning it, she says, "Right back at you. Now get out of here and go get ready."

My face scrunches in confusion, "Ready for what?"

"Uh-uh," she says with a shake of her head, "I've managed to keep it a secret all day. Just trust me. Wear the second outfit."

I roll my eyes. Should have known that her and the guys were up to something. I take my time getting out all of my bags as a small act of rebellion, and she sighs dramatically in the front seat, "You'll have fun, I promise. Call me later…or on second thought. Maybe not." We both laugh as I shut the door and she pulls away.

Chapter Twenty Five

Beautiful Sweaty Messes

Juggling the bags and drink in my hands, I manage to get the front door open, only to be accosted with color everywhere. There are flowers on every inch of flat surface available. Bouquets of soft-pink roses, big, yellow sunflowers, deep-purple lilies, and tiny, white carnations cover the entire living room. It doesn't surprise me that the guys were in the house while I was gone. They all have their own key to get in, but the flowers are like a sucker punch to the gut. No one has ever gotten me flowers before, well, besides Billy, and I'm just going to go ahead and say that it doesn't count, considering.

I drop my bags at the door and walk to the counter where a note sits waiting. *Be ready to go by six.* That gives me about three hours to get ready and after this, I'm going to put as much effort as I can into looking nice for them. I'll have to trust Ryleigh since she seems to know where we're going.

After taking a long hot shower and shaving every inch of my body that needed it, I put my wet hair up in these old school rollers that I've had forever. Found them a long time ago at one of the thrift stores back when I used to dress up to go out. They're pretty cool. All I have to do is roll up my wet hair and then blow dry them. I used to put some hairspray kind of stuff on it before the rollers came out, but I haven't bought that stuff in a really long time. Let's just hope it'll hold up without it. I'll leave them in while I do my makeup and get dressed just in case.

Going as light as I can, I only put a little powder on my face and then do up my eyes with eyeliner and eyeshadow. Stepping back to look at my face, the black liner brings out the green in my hazel eyes, but something is still missing. Searching through my scantily-filled makeup bag, I find it. I dab some of the bright-red lipstick across my lips and blend it in with my finger. When I'm done, I nod at myself in the mirror. Fucking perfect.

I drag the bags from the shopping trip into my room. Once again trusting Ryleigh, I put on the outfit that she recommended, and when I look in the dresser mirror, it's hard to even recognize myself. I still haven't gained back all my weight, so I'm skinnier than what I normally am. The skirt is black with huge, red roses and their green leaves all over it. Sitting right above my belly button it leaves the bottom hem to stop mid-thigh. There's about a two-inch gap between that and my shirt, showing off a little skin between them. The shirt is what truly sold me on the outfit. There's a strip of black fabric that runs across my breasts. See through lace sleeves works from the bottom of my elbows up to an oval shaped neckline and covers that strip of fabric all the way down to the exposed skin. The back is definitely my favorite. It fastens like a bra at the bottom, leaving a big open hole exposing most of my back and tying at the top with lace strings that hang down to the skirt. Putting my feet into a pair of all black wedges and taking my hair out of the rollers, I stand for a good five minutes just staring at myself. Not to sound conceited, but I look good. Even I wouldn't guess that the person in front of me came from the trailer park.

All dressed up and nowhere to go, I sit on the couch and fidget with my phone as I admire all of the flowers. Just from knowing the guys as well as I do, I know who picked which flower. Lucas the pink roses. Teagan the sunflowers. Mav the purple lilies. Last but not least, Goose the white carnations. I'd bet my last dollar on that, which probably isn't such a good phrase to use anymore. I'm just thankful for all those days in the garden with Nana. At least now if the guys ask, I don't look like a complete idiot.

Lights flash across the front windows and my heart feels like it's going to beat out of my chest. All of us but Mav have been on some sort of date kind of thing before, and I'm not sure what to expect. The rap on my door makes my heart skip a beat, which is weird because they never knock. As soon as the thought fires in my head, the door opens and Teagan walks in.

Holy fucking sexiness. His hair is pulled up into a messy man bun thing on the top of his head, and the smile he throws me would melt ice. There's a blue, open, long-sleeve flannel shirt covering his t-shirt and the tight blue jeans hug his legs just to show off all the muscle there. His smile turns dark as he takes me in from head to toe. When I make a move towards him, he holds up a hand and in a husky voice says, "Wait right there. They need to see this as I did."

Less than two seconds later Goose comes in complaining, "Dude, you could have at least waited until the car was in p…" He trails off as he catches sight of me standing across from them. Damn it, Goose looks just as good as Teagan in his own way. His black dress shirt is buttoned all the way up except the last few, and his sleeves are rolled up, like always, displaying his massive forearms. Just as T, his light blue jeans look like they were tailored to fit him. He opens his mouth to say something, but closes it just as fast.

Lucas, who was right on Goose's heels, grins at me as he says, "You look down-right fucking sexy, baby." He's the first one to come over and wrap me up in both his arms and his scent. As always, he's in his jeans and leather jacket. A look that has become one of my favorites. He should patent that shit.

When he lets go, my eyes lock on Mav's face as he does a

head to toe inspection of my body. My cheeks turn pink as his eyes linger on the open space on my stomach. His eyes meet mine, and I see the fire there that he's trying so hard to hide. He arches an eyebrow as he shoots me a wicked half smile. That's all the invitation that I need. I move to stand in front of him, and he keeps that same look on his face, almost daring me to make the first move. Teagan and Goose are standing close enough for me to see them watching us out of the corner of my eye. Dressed just like Goose, his dark button up has every one done up to his neck, and paired with a lighter pair of jeans.

His hands twitch like he wants to reach out for me, but he puts them in the pockets of his jeans instead. Challenging me to make the first move, his head tilts back to look down to me with that sexy fucking eyebrow still arched. The wedges have given me some extra height. Wrapping my arms around him, I'm able to go up on my tiptoes to kiss him right underneath the chin. It dips, and his lips find mine as his arms go around me. The naked skin of my back meets his fingertips and then his palms as his kiss deepens.

It's a good minute before we pull away from each other, the fire still burning in his eyes. A laugh slips from my lips as he goes to smooth his black hair that I messed up just now without even realizing I was doing it. Letting go, I take the one step to Goose and throw my arms around his neck. He pulls me into a big bear hug, lifting me off my feet, as he whispers in my ear, "You look beautiful."

I grin like an idiot and give him a quick kiss. Almost as soon as my feet touch the floor, T has my hand and spins me to him. Surprising me, he dips me back and kisses my chin as a laugh falls from my lips. Always expect the unexpected with him. After he pulls me back up and kisses me thoroughly, I thank them all for the flowers.

T circles his arms around me from behind as Lucas says, "We weren't sure what your favorite was, so you got four different kinds."

"Which one is your favorite?" T asks in my ear.

I throw him a look over my shoulder. "I don't choose favorites."

The four of them laugh and Goose says, "Even in flowers?"

"I don't really know if I had a favorite flower before today, but I now have four," I confess to them.

They laugh again, and I take a second to consider what a lucky girl I am to have them. "So, where are we going tonight?"

"How do you feel about going to a concert?" Mav asks.

I shrug. "Never been, so I can't say."

Goose tips his head back and shakes it at the ceiling before looking back to me, "You have no idea what you're missing."

"That means we get to pop your concert cherry," T says, still behind me.

I roll my eyes and slap his arm playfully. "Who are we going to see?"

Lucas, practically vibrating with excitement, says, "Beauty in Lies."

"Their shows are always sold out," Goose adds. "It took Mav pulling some strings to get us tickets."

That's interesting. I wonder who he knows in the business that allows for those kinds of strings, maybe I could get him to tell me someday.

Mav interrupts my inner thoughts, "Speaking of which, we need to get going or we're going to be late."

I throw on my jacket and check to make sure I have all of my stuff in my pockets before we lock up. Teagan makes a sound and I turn to find him looking angrily toward the, apparently, offensive jacket, and it makes me laugh.

"Why are we not taking the Rover tonight?" I ask as I see

Lucas's truck in the driveway. I've gotten so used to taking it when all of us are together, that it's weird not seeing it here.

Lucas throws his arm around my shoulders as we walk. "We've got to head into the city, and Mav tends to get road rage there." Said subject throws Lucas a 'fuck you' look and Lucas laughs as he adds, "Besides, I'm more partial to my truck now. What about you?"

My face goes red all the way to my ears as Teagan groans, "Seriously, dude? Rub it in, why don't you?"

Lucas laughs and kisses me on the cheek before walking around to the driver's side. Teagan reaches out for my hand to help me into the back where Mav is already waiting. It's been so long since I've been in a skirt that I don't think about it raising up in the back as I lean over to get in.

I yelp in surprise as teeth catch me right under my right ass cheek.

"Sorry, not sorry," T says, jumping in behind me. "You can't put that right in my face without repercussions."

Lucas laughs in the front seat as Goose shakes his head with a smile. Mav looks jealous as fuck, but not at Teagan. I'd wager to say that I'll be getting in on his side next time.

"Here, let me help you out of this," T says, working my jacket off my shoulders. "If you get cold, you've got us to warm you up."

I have a feeling tonight is going to be filled with those sexual innuendos, and it's just getting started.

It takes us about an hour and a half to drive into the city. Goose turns on the band that we're going to see, and plays their music the whole way. I must say that I'm in fucking love with their sound. When we pull up outside of the venue, I'm bouncing off my seat excited.

Lines to get in that wrap around the venue can't even put a

damper on my mood. Luckily for us, Mav knows his people. He got us VIP passes that let us just walk right in. There's some kind of meet and greet thing after, but all I'm worried about right now is seeing if they sound as good on stage as they did in the truck.

We find our spots close to the side of the stage just in time to see the opening act take their places. The open space around us disappears quickly as more people flood into the arena. Thankfully, I have my own personal bodyguards who make four separate walls around me. Mav stands behind me with his hands on my hips, T to my left, Goose on my right and Lucas takes point in front of me. They aren't going to let me get lost in the crowd, which I couldn't be any more grateful for.

The band on stage kills it, but waiting on the sound that I heard in the truck makes me feel like all of the molecules in my body are bouncing around trying to escape.

As they finish, and the lights go dark, Goose leans down to my ear and asks, "Having fun?"

It's still so loud from all of the people that I don't bother trying to answer. I just nod, and he grins at me. The announcement for the main band is made, and I go up on my tiptoes to throw my arms around Lucas's neck. He leans back so I can reach his ear, "Here they come."

Turning his face, he captures my lips for a quick kiss just as the first notes pour from the stage. I can honestly say that the only thing more beautiful than the sound that hits my ears in that moment would be my guys' voices. They must be attractive, too, considering the squealing of the girls around us. It makes them sound like a bunch of groupies. Me, however, I only have eyes for my sexy quad.

Always the first one to start dancing, Teagan sways us in time with the beat, and before I know it, I find myself dancing with Mav as the other three provide a buffer against the crowd. Hands slip under my skirt and palm my ass as we grind against each other. His lips find my neck as my fingers weave into that perfectly-styled hair. I love being the one who gives it that 'fresh rolled out of bed' look. One of the guys on stage has a voice that reminds me of Mav, and the sound has me wishing that he'd sing to me. Or better yet, take advantage of the human walls around us and fuck me where we stand.

In what feels like no time at all, they play their final song and I'm left wanting more of both them and of Mav.

It's all I can do to follow the guys as we flow with the crowd out into the hallways. All I want to do is pull Mav into a dark corner somewhere to release all the tension inside my body right now.

"Are we battling our way to the meet and greet?" Lucas asks above the noise.

The guys shrug like they don't care one way or another, so I guess I'm left with the decision. As much as I'd love to meet them, I honestly just can't get my brain off Mav and the way he felt against me, so I shake my head, "Maybe next time."

I figured Lucas would be disappointed, but he actually looks relieved. It seems he isn't much of a fan of the hordes of people. Mav and Goose grab my hands and don't let go as we weave through the masses toward the truck. My suspicions were correct as Mav tows me to his side and helps me in when we get there. The slip up with T earlier was truly an accident, but this time, I purposely move slowly getting in, while giving Maverick a full show. The adrenaline from the show and sexual tension between us has left me feeling wanton. Sweet baby Jesus, please let one of them stay with me tonight. I secretly hope it's Mav, but I'm not getting my hopes up. He's only stayed two nights and that was when all of them were there with me.

The ride back home is quiet, even with the music of the band still playing through the speakers. I think the other three can feel the tension coming from Mav and me. His hand sits high on the inside of my thigh, almost in a dominant, claiming kind of way, every second that we are in the truck.

When we make it to my house, Mav hops down to let me out. I'm not sure what the plan is tonight or who, if anyone is staying, but I ask him anyways, "Stay?"

His eyebrow goes up in question as that fire comes back into his eyes and he nods. My insides feel like there are a million butterflies flittering around at that one small movement. I make my rounds giving the other three kisses, and telling them thank you for an awesome night. Lucas backs up and waits until the door is open before pulling away.

We've no sooner made it in the door before I practically jump Mav. At first, he stands as still as a statue, as if I took him by surprise, but that only lasts for a second as he literally growls into my mouth. The sound does something to my brain, because my muscles turn to Jell-O in his arms. Doesn't matter, he's ready to catch me as if he expected it.

Lifting me underneath the back of my thighs, I wrap my legs around his waist as he stalks his way to my bedroom. I wait for the drop to the bed, but it never comes. Instead, the cold dresser meets my almost bare ass and thighs. Mav grabs the back of my head and dominates my mouth until there's no fully functioning thought running through my brain except the need to have him naked.

The button on the top of his shirt is the only one that survives as I undo it and rip it open the rest of the way, only to be met with another obstacle of an undershirt. He stops long enough to yank them both off his body and toss them in the corner somewhere. My lips find his now naked chest and the sound that falls from his lips makes me want to kiss every inch of his body just to see if he'll keep making it.

When he kisses me again, his hands go to undo my shirt. I feel him getting frustrated and ready to tear it to shreds in impatience.

"Wait a second," I tell him.

He does that growling thing again, "No."

Some of the material groans in protest and I shove at his chest. I'm so hot for him that I can barely fucking breath, but I don't want him ruining a brand-new shirt.

"I'll buy you five more just like it," he says, reaching for it again.

I push his chest. "I don't want five more like it. I want this one, just wait."

Seemingly out of patience, he pulls me off the dresser and as soon as my feet hit the floor, he spins me around. Now, I get to watch his face as he works the back of it free and it falls away somewhere. His hands find my breasts as he grinds against me.

I lean back and close my eyes as different sensations assault me.

"Open your eyes and watch, baby girl," that deep voice says in my ear.

No one would argue with that voice and I'm no exception. Being able to see where his face and hands go gives me a thrill that I never knew existed.

He finds the zipper on my skirt, and meets my eyes as he makes slow work of sliding it from my hips. Standing in nothing but a pair of black, almost see through, panties and my shoes, my heart stops and starts again as I watch his face take in what's standing in front of him. I'm for sure thanking Ryleigh later for making me buy new bras and panties.

Mav's jeans rub against the back of my legs as he brings himself against me again. His hands travel up my back and then down my arms before closing around my wrists. Placing my palms flat on top of the dresser he warns, "Keep them here. No matter what. If you move them then I'll have to punish you."

My knees go weak at his words as my heart races. I never thought the dominant thing would turn me on as much as it is right now. I follow his instructions as he kisses his way down my back. When he gets to my ass, I feel the sting of his teeth through my panties on each cheek before the soft kiss after. At the angle of my mirror, I can see the top of Mav's head and shoulders as he drops to his knees. Standing in front of him like this, unable to move at his demand, as I bring such a powerful creature to his knees makes me feel stronger than I ever have.

His warm fingers make a trail from my ankles up to my hips underneath the panties right before he painstakingly and slowly pulls them down my legs. He taps the inside of my ankles letting me know he wants me to open my legs for him. I want to defy him just to see what would happen, but I open them anyway.

Once I do, it doesn't take long for his mouth to find the sweet spot between them. Losing concentration, I grab a fistful of his hair and he immediately pulls away.

"What did I tell you?" he scolds, standing up behind me. The sting on my right ass cheek from his slap puts heat in more than that one spot. I rub against him like a cat without moving my hands.

I hear his muttered, "Fuck," before he pulls me away from the dresser and lays me on the bed. Without removing the rest of his clothes or my shoes, he's inside of me without any kind of warning.

Maverick fucks me until I'm not sure where I start, and he ends. By the time that he's done, we're nothing more than beautiful sweaty messes.

He takes his time cleaning us up and getting the rest of our clothing off as he kisses everywhere his fingers touch. When he finally pulls my back to his chest and covers our naked bodies with my blanket, I'm exhausted.

"Hey, Mav?" I ask in the quiet of the room.

The sound of his, "Hmm," vibrates through his chest into my back.

"Why have you not stayed before now?" I ask him.

His breath is hot in my ear, sending chills down my skin, "Because you haven't asked, baby girl."

Chapter Twenty-Six

Poking The Bear

"Stop fidgeting, baby. You look perfect," Lucas tells me.

Sitting by him in the front of the truck with the other guys in the back, I can't help but to be nervous. It's well into March now and all four of them just found out that they are getting picked up for their choice of school to play football, so Lucas's family is throwing a small get together to celebrate. According to him, no one knows that I'm coming. So, not only am I unexpected, but I'm worried that I'm going to slip up with the guys and make everyone uncomfortable.

"Are you sure you want me to be here today?" I ask for the millionth time.

He grabs my hand and kisses the back of it. "Yes. It won't be much of a celebration without all of the people we love around us."

Which brings me to the other reason why I'd rather not be here, thinking about them leaving me hurts. The school that they're going off to is a good six hours away and it makes my heart hurt to think about them being so far.

I feel a tap on my shoulder by the window, when I raise my eyes I find Teagan watching me in the side mirror of the truck, "What cha thinkin about?"

"Nothing," I lie.

"Then why do you look like you're about to cry?" he asks. "You don't have to go if you really don't want to."

I shake my head, "It's not that. I just had this flash forward to

August when you guys are going to be six hours away."

Lucas squeezes the hand that he's still holding as Mav asks, "Have you applied to go anywhere for college yet?"

Throwing him a disbelieving look over my shoulder I say, "Why would I? Up until last month I didn't think that I would have the money to go anywhere."

His eyebrow quirks up, "And what have you been doing with your time since then?"

I look at him with a 'duh' look on my face. *You.* Goose gets it by my facial expression without me having to say it and cracks up beside him. It takes the others a few seconds to catch up, but they're laughing, too, by the time that we pull into Lucas's driveway.

Out of all their houses, I have to say that this one is my favorite. It's two stories, and has the triangle shape on the second floor on all four sides. The massive front porch runs from one side of the house to the other. There's a swing attached to the ceiling of the porch with a few pillows on the seat. It looks comfy and homey, just how my dream house would.

"Look," Lucas says as we walk up the stairs, "I'm going to go ahead and apologize for anything that you're about to be subjected to. My brothers have no filters or boundaries."

"Yeah, they'll be keeping their hands to themselves today," Teagan warns.

Lucas huffs under his breath as if saying 'yeah right.' Oh jeez, just like the white trash to start a fight at the barbeque. When he opens the door, the inside isn't what gets my attention first. It's the smell. Even without the scent of food coming from the kitchen, it has that homey smell to it.

"Dude, it's about fucking time that you got here," a male voice booms from the living room on the right.

Glancing in there, I see the backs of two heads sitting in front of a TV playing some shooting game. There's a bigger guy sitting in a chair off to the side watching them, and another smaller guy sitting across from him with a book in his lap.

He looks up and catches my eye, "Umm, Leo, you're going to have to watch your language today."

"What the fuck are you talking about now, Lincoln?" he asks looking over to him.

Lincoln motions towards the door where we're still standing, and all three of the other heads turn our way.

The game gets forgotten as Leo jumps over the back of the couch and the brother who was sitting beside him says, "Dude, mom will have your ass for doing that."

Leo ignores him as he puffs out his chest and walks to us, "I didn't know you were bringing company, little brother."

"Hey," Teagan complains, "What are we? Chopped liver?"

"You're over here enough to be family," one of Lucas's brothers tells him as he offers me a hand, "Lathan. And you are, pretty lady?"

I shake his hand with more confidence than I feel. "Kendall."

He smiles at me, and it's so much like Lucas's, that I feel my nerves loosen up a little. Both he and Leo have buzzed hair on the sides with a little left on top. Pointing to the other brothers he says, "Logan, Lincoln, and Leo."

Bloody hell. What are these boys drinking on the farm out here? Leo, Logan, and Lathan are all just as big as Lucas and my guys. Lincoln is the only one that is smaller than the rest, with almost feminine attributes. His curly, dark hair is pushed back away from his face, completely opposite Logan, who has shaggy hair falling everywhere.

I take turns shaking all of their hands.

Leo is last, and he kisses the back of my hand as he watches Lucas. He must assume that I'm with him, and is just trying to get a rise out of him. I pull my hand back as soon as it's polite to. No reason to start war just yet, because he doesn't realize that he's not just poking a bear, he's waking a whole goddamn den of them.

"Are you thirsty or hungry? The food is still cooking, but we can scrounge something up. Come on," Logan says, putting my hand in the crook of his elbow and leading us to the kitchen.

I hear Lathan tell Lucas behind me, "So rude, dude." And I have to bite my tongue to keep from laughing.

We walk into the kitchen and I fall in love with the house all over again. Everything looks like it just stepped out of one of those country life magazines, from the light brown cabinets to the frosted looking counter tops. There's a bar in the middle of the room with at least eight chairs around three sides of it. As Logan pulls me to the fridge, the rest of the guys take a seat around the bar. I grab a bottle of water before he tows me back to the counter.

Once we're there, he won't let me pull my hand free. "So, tell me, Kendall, how is it that you came to know these four troublemakers?"

With all eyes on me, the nerves come back, and my hands get all clammy. "We met at a restaurant I used to work at a couple months ago."

"What?!" Leo exclaims in fake surprise at Lucas, "You've known her for this long and are just now sharing?"

The others laugh, all except Mav. He can't seem to pry his eyes away from my hand on Logan's arm. When I try to pull away again, he just tightens his hold.

Lincoln sits on the counter off to the side of the bar and

observes everything that's going on. If I didn't know any better, I'd say that he has already discovered the dynamics of what we are. Definitely the smarter one out of Lucas's older brothers, or at least the more cautious one.

I try to answer as many of their questions as I can as they fire them at me. Even Lucas is no help when he tries to tell them to shove off. That only makes it worse.

"Ok, I've heard all I need to hear," Leo says, standing up on my other side. "You have to ditch whichever one of these bozos you're with and choose me instead."

He throws his arm around my shoulder and presses a kiss to my temple.

"Stop fucking touching her," Mav growls, apparently, at his breaking point.

There's a good fifteen seconds where no one in the room says anything, and a pin could be heard dropping.

Logan breaks the silence as he finally lets go of my arm. "Well, well, well, the good ole Mav. Didn't know you'd be the first one to land a girl like this. Being all mean and shit all the time."

My eyes go wide, but it must be a standing joke around here, because Mav just shrugs. I don't know if I should correct them, so my eyes find Lucas's and he winks at me. Ohhhh shit.

"Yeah, about that," Lucas says as all eyes turn to him, "She's my girlfriend, too."

This silence is even better than the last, because it leaves three of the brothers looking at Lucas like they don't know whether to congratulate him or beat his ass for lying to them.

"And mine," Goose chimes in.

Teagan simply raises his hand, laying claim to me with nothing more than a look.

Lathan bursts out laughing, “Come on, man. Why do you guys always fuck with us like that? Haven’t we always been nice to you?”

“I hope that’s a rhetorical question,” Teagan teases.

Leo and Lathan laugh, but I feel Logan and Lincoln staring at me.

“What’s the truth, pretty lady?” Logan asks, turning all the attention back on us. “Are you with any of them?”

If the guys aren’t ashamed to tell them about us, then I’m damn sure not going to be, no matter how it makes us look. I meet his eyes as I confess, “They weren’t lying. I’m theirs.”

My guys are smiling at me, especially Lucas. Telling them the truth, I’m waiting on the other shoe to drop, and people to start throwing accusations around. What I get is not what I expect.

“Mom!” Leo yells, “Lucas has a girlfriend!”

I see Lincoln, out of the corner of my eye, smile and shake his head as all of the brothers crack up, Lucas included.

“You don’t have to yell, Leonard,” a female voice says, walking around the corner. “I’m right here, and well aware that your brother has a girlfriend, even though I fail to see how that’s any of your business.”

“Buurrrn,” Logan says, slapping him on the arm while the others crack up again.

She walks over and pulls me into an unexpected hug. “Sorry if my boys are pestering you. They seem to lose their manners around pretty girls. I’m Elaine. You can call me Lane or just Mom like the rest of the crew here.”

I smile at her as I say, “Kendall. Nice to meet you.”

Walking around the kitchen and pulling things out of a couple of the cabinets, she says, “Nice to finally meet you, too, honey. Lucas talks about you non-stop. It's nice to be able to put a face with his Kendall."

Her words make me smile, and I realize I must look like a fool standing in the middle of the kitchen grinning like the Cheshire cat. I can't stop my face from going pink as I see all of the guys' attention on us. Trying to distract myself as well as not to be rude, I ask if there's anything I can do to help. She just turns me down, and says company doesn't cook or clean, then smacks Leo and Lathan on the back of the head for being rude and not offering me one of their chairs.

Oh, I love this woman as much as I love her house and almost as much as I love her son.

Chapter Twenty-Seven

Grant

To say that I'm shocked that none of the other families show up besides Ryleigh and Cynthia is an understatement. They don't even stay that long. Cynthia gives some excuse about having some company thing for Teagan's dad, but I honestly just think that the country life makes her uncomfortable. Ryleigh leaves with her. I doubt her reasons are the same, though. Especially if the look that she throws Logan is any indication. Oh, I'm definitely getting the inside scoop on that one later.

Now with seven of the guys out in the yard playing some weird version of football, and Lane in the kitchen cleaning up with Lucas's dad, I sit on the porch swing and laugh at the antics going on in the yard in front of me. I offered my services in the kitchen, but neither of them would hear of it.

Lincoln walks out the screen door and makes his way over to me. I motion for him to take the seat next to me, and we swing in silence for a few minutes just watching the guys.

"It's true isn't it?" he asks.

"What?" I reply.

His head tilts toward the yard where Mav and Lucas have teamed up on Lathan, trying to take him down, "That you're all together."

I nod even though he's not looking at me, "Very much so."

He turns to me and those eyes that are the same shade as

Lucas's focus on mine, "How do you do it? Not sex or anything, just balance them all."

If it was one of the others asking, I'd question their motives for wanting to know, but there's something about Lincoln. Some sadness that he tries to hide from the world. I guess it takes one lonely soul to recognize another.

"It's not so much balance," I tell him honestly. "We're all together almost every day anyways."

Looking at me like he's trying to figure out how to say something, he finally points at his chest as he says, "But do you have enough here for them? Can you honestly say that you love them all the same?"

Without a second thought, I say, "Yes, I can. They're all different in their own way, which makes it easier. But there's no rule saying that your heart is only big enough to fit one person." It takes me a few minutes into the conversation, but I eventually get a feeling that Lincoln is asking for more personal reasons. "You shouldn't give a shit what society thinks," I say, slipping up and letting my sailor mouth come out. He doesn't seem to get offended, though, as he just smiles at me and I continue, "You can't help who you love. If it's there, then it's there, and if people can't deal, then you don't need those people in your life."

He nods and looks to the floor, "I came out to everyone when I was fifteen. My parents, and even my brothers, have been nothing but supportive. They don't treat me any different, which takes a ton of pressure off."

"I bet," I agree softly. "You've got an amazing family."

The smile he shoots me lights up his face, "Yeah, I got really lucky in that department."

When it falls, he looks out to the yard again, "I fell in love with this guy a year or so ago. We dated for about four months before he told me that he was bi and has a girlfriend."

"People suck, Lincoln," I tell him.

He lets out a sad laugh, "That they do."

"And you still love him?" I ask curiously.

"Yeah," he answers, "how pathetic is that?"

I think on it for a second before I say anything, "It's not pathetic at all. He should have been honest with you. If anyone is pathetic, it's him for stringing you along like he did, and then just dropping you."

"That's the kicker," he says getting angry, "he didn't drop me. I left him because he asked me to be with them both. His girlfriend knew the whole time, and he told me that she was half in love with me already from just what he told her."

"And you're not attracted to girls," I state.

He shakes his head, "No, I am. I'm bi. Take you for example, I think you're insanely gorgeous and I probably would be acting just as bad as the others did earlier if I wasn't already taken. I'm just so confused. I love him more than anything, and I tried a few times to get to know her. I'm sure I could love her, too. It's just the thought of loving two people at once, and everything that comes with that, scares the shit out of me. Excuse my language."

His words are flattering, and the last bit makes me smile, considering I used the same words just minutes ago, "The best advice I can give you is you'll never know if you don't try. Even if you lose him, you won't have to go through life wondering what could have happened."

"Yeah," he says, "After seeing you guys today, it gives me a little hope that maybe it's possible, so thank you. Both for that, and your advice, and for loving Lucas. He's always been the nicer one of us, and he deserves someone like you."

"Thanks." I smile.

"Don't tell me I've got even more competition for your heart, Kendall," Leo says, coming up the stairs. "This is just getting ridiculous."

Lincoln and I look at each other and laugh until we're crying.

Later, as we're driving to Teagan's house to pick up Goose's truck, Lucas takes my hand in his and kisses the back like he did earlier, "I don't know what you said to Lincoln today, but thank you. I haven't seen him smile like that in a long time."

"It wasn't me," I tell him honestly, "I think that he just needed to get some stuff off of his chest."

"Well, whatever you guys talked about helped, so thank you," he says.

I nod and get lost in the conversation from earlier. I truly hope it turns out okay for him. I'd never say this aloud but he's probably my favorite of the brothers, besides Lucas, of course.

When we make it to Teagan's, I hop over to Goose's truck, so he can run me home while the other three head over to Mav's. He was supposed to go, too, but decided to stay with me instead.

Just as we pull into Sleepy Pines, Lucas calls to tell me that I left my jacket in the truck and that he'd bring it to me in the morning. I'm about to tell him thanks as Goose opens the door to the trailer and gets smashed in the side of the head with something.

He falls to the floor, and I scream.

Lucas is yelling into the phone, but it gets lost as a thick hand grabs me by the neck and slams me back against the trailer wall hard enough to make the glass in the windows rattle.

The repulsive smell of cigarettes and stale beer hit my nose as a raspy voice says, "Your mom and dad send their best, little girl."

My feet are at least six inches off the floor, and I'm starting to see spots dancing around the edges of my vision. Just as I feel that tunnel narrowing in warning from lack of oxygen, Goose comes out of nowhere and tackles the guy to the floor. They roll around a few times and a gun clangs against the linoleum as Goose knocks it out of his hand. I didn't even see that he had one. I'm useless on my knees by the door, still trying to catch my breath. It's almost like I can't get enough air.

By the time that I finally get the rhythm down again, Goose is straddling the guy's body as he pounds on his face. I go in search of my phone to call 911. No sooner than my hand closes around it, the front door flies open again, and I scramble backwards away from it.

Teagan and Lucas kneel next to me, asking me if I'm okay while Mav is trying to pull Goose off the now unconscious stranger. I ignore the two in front of me and crawl over to him as he falls back on his ass against the wall. There's blood running down his temple, and his right hand looks worse for wear.

"Are you okay?" I ask, my voice coming out with a strange rasp to it.

He nods, and I take off my flannel to put pressure against the blood still pouring down his face.

Hugging me to him, he asks, "What about you? I think I may have blacked out for a few minutes. I'm so sorry, babe."

I try to reassure him that he did fucking awesome as I hear the guys talking at the door. Blue lights flash around the living room and highlight the mess that was made during the fight. One of the officers steps in and flips the light switch. Yeah, it's trashed.

"What happened here?" he asks, looking from us to the guy on the floor and the gun now sitting in the corner of the kitchen. "I'm going to need you to get up and come with us, son," he says to Goose.

"What?" I demand, and point to the unconscious man on the floor. "That asshole is the one that broke into the house."

"Do you live here, ma'am?" he asks.

"Yessir," I answer.

He flips out his notebook. "Who lives here with you?"

A pang shoots through my heart. "It's just me now. My grandpa passed away in January."

Looking from me and Goose to the others standing off to the side, his face turns stern, but he doesn't say anything. "Can you tell me what happened here tonight?"

I recall everything that happened, and at the very last of it, the stranger on the floor starts groaning and moving around. He looks like a biker, but like a biker who just got off a two-week binge of meth. His jeans and shirt are dirty, and his facial hair looks like a dog with mange. The officers move in and have him in handcuffs before he's fully awake. When they lift him and walk by us, he snarls down at me through a bloody face, "I'll be seeing you, girl. They know you got money from the old man dying. That's your mama's money, girl, so you better be prepared to hand it over."

"Let's go," the second officer tells him as he shoves him out the door.

Letting out a sigh of relief, I listen to the officer explain that they'll be leaving an empty patrol car out front just in case, but he wouldn't recommend I stay here tonight because of the broken window the guy used to get in.

"She won't be here tonight," Goose tells him with his eyes trying to focus. "We have a spare room and my parents said it's okay if she crashes at my house for now."

At the word 'parents,' the cop nods and some of the sternness drops from his face, "Good, good. I still want the both of you checked out by the EMT outside, and I'll need you to come in tomorrow to sign a statement if you're wanting to press charges."

We follow him out to the waiting ambulance, where they tell us that Goose has a mild concussion and shouldn't be allowed to sleep for the next few hours. The good news is that his hand is only banged up. There's nothing broken, which is surprising with how hard he was beating that guy into the floor. My throat is severely bruised, but they said I should be back to normal in about a week or so.

After all of the people leave, Lucas is the first to pull me away from Goose. "Goddamn it, baby. You scared the shit out of me. I don't want to ever let you out of my sight again."

Teagan hugs me from behind. "What he just said."

"You guys do realize that Goose took the worst of it right?" I ask them.

"Goose can handle his own," Mav says, stepping closer and bending down to examine the marks on my neck in the little bit of light spilling out the front door. A look of pure fury crosses his face before he masks it.

"I'm sorry, man," Goose apologizes as he catches the same thing I saw. "I fucking tried. It was pitch black and he hit me before I even saw him."

"There's nothing to be sorry for," I assure him, staring pointedly at Mav, who finally takes the hint and agrees with me.

"Come on. Let's find something to put across the window," Mav says. "Pack yourself a couple of days' worth of clothes, Kendall."

I want to argue and say I'll be fine, but tonight scared me shitless. Thinking about if it had been just me and Gramps, makes me sick to my stomach. So, without saying anything, I pack my bag as the three of them move some shit in front of the gaping hole.

"It'll have to do for now," Lucas tells me as we lock up.

"We'll get it fixed first thing tomorrow."

Mav drives me and Goose to his house as Lucas and T follow behind us. Once we get there, I promise to take care of Goose, and to call if we need them, so that they can go do what they needed to at Mav's across the street.

Helping Goose down the stairs, I make him sit in one of the chairs. "What happened to your ice pack?"

He shrugs, "Must have left it in the back of the ambulance. I'm okay. I don't need one."

I run my fingers across his jawline to underneath his chin until he looks up to me, "You're always trying to take care of and protect everyone else. Let me do it for you this time. I'm going to go get you some ice from the kitchen. Don't move."

Turning his head to the side, he kisses the inside of my palm before closing his eyes and relaxing in the chair.

Finding some Ziploc bags in one of the cabinets, I fill it with ice, and find a dish towel to wrap around it, the whole while kicking myself. This is all my fucking fault. If he wasn't with me, he wouldn't have gotten hurt. A cold chill racks my body thinking about how it would have ended if he hadn't been there.

When I make it back downstairs, it sounds like he's snoring. I shake his shoulder softly, "Babe, you can't go to sleep for a little while. Doctor's orders. Remember?"

He makes a 'mmm' sound and wraps his arm around my waist, pulling me down to straddle his lap, "That's better. I definitely won't be going to sleep now."

I shake my head with a smile, even though he can't see it with his eyes still closed. Putting the ice against the side of his head gently, I tell him, "I put some ice in a baggie, and I can keep refilling it if it melts."

"You know there's an icepack in the freezer just for this reason, right?" he teases, cracking an eye open with a smile.

"And you're just now telling me?" I accuse.

He grins at me. "You told me to let you take care of me, so I'm just doing what I was told."

"Ok, smartass," I smile.

"Better than being a dumbass, right?" he retorts. A full laugh falls from my mouth, and he hums in approval underneath me, "That's my favorite sound in the world."

"Well, you just so happen to be my favorite person in the world right now," I admit softly.

His cheeks pull up in a tired smile,."I thought you didn't pick favorites."

"I don't," I say, running my fingers across the short hairs on his jawline that he has still yet to shave, "But I have moments."

He closes his eyes again, "Do you love me, Kendall?"

A sliver of hurt goes through my chest that he would even have to ask. That means that I'm not holding up my side of this relationship with the four of them like I'm supposed to do.

"Do you really not know the answer to that question?" I ask him.

"Sometimes, I just need to hear it," he says sadly with a shrug.

I press the front of my body against him until we're almost laid back in the chair, "I love you, Grant Michaels. I'll tell you every day until I take my last breath if that's what it takes for you to accept it."

"Say it again," he whispers.

"I love you," I say.

He shakes his head, "No, the part where you said my name."

I laugh as I recognize the line from the Cinderella movie we just watched the other day. Only he would be quoting movies at a moment like this.

Staring him straight in the eyes, I say, "I love you, Grant."

My lips find those hairs lining his jaw. It feels just as good as it does against my fingers, "I love you." With my nose skimming his skin, I move down the side of his neck and press my lips there, "I love you." Back up to the corner of his mouth, "I love you." Other side of his jaw, "I love you." When I make it up to his ear, I whisper, "I love you," and nip at his ear.

The sound that he makes in return could rival Mav any day of the week. His hands jerk my hips against him as I smash my lips against his. No one who looks at him would ever think that he'd be the type to let me take control the way that he is right now. I take my time exploring and devouring every inch of his mouth that I can. His hands find the bottom hem of my shirt and he hesitates like he's asking for permission. He'll never need that from me.

Taking his hands in mine, I help him lift it over my head. Without giving him the chance to question it, I unsnap my bra and drop it to the floor, too. His eyes fill with so much emotion as he watches me, that all I want to do is erase any doubt that he's ever had about us.

I pull his hands to my breasts and my head falls back as I help him knead them.

He has me looking back at him as he says, "You're so beautiful."

No, what's beautiful is the way that his large hands cover every inch of my breasts, leaving none to spill over. Yet, they're still so gentle. "You make me feel that way," I insist.

"Then I must be doing something right," he says, pulling my face back to his.

I pull away to stand in front of him. Taking my time, I watch his eyes mark my body as I slowly take off the rest of my clothes. When I reach out a hand to him, he doesn't hesitate to take it. Carefully, I pull him to his feet, "We probably shouldn't be doing this. You do have a concussion, and all."

"I could be bleeding out right here in the middle of the floor and wouldn't change a damn thing that's happening. I'd die a happy man," he brags.

Shaking my head, I grin like a fool. I'm such a sucker for his words, even when they're nothing more than movie quotes or poems that he's memorized.

Taking his hand, I walk us over to the bed against the side wall. Stark naked, I climb up to stand on the edge, so I can lift his shirt off without him trying to bend down.

"I can do that, you know?" he teases.

"You could," I tell him, stepping down, "but it wouldn't be as much fun as this." And I press my lips against the middle of his chest and work my way down the line that runs straight through his six-pack abs. I've never been one to be heavily attracted to hardcore muscles, but it looks so fucking sexy on my guys. When I make it to the top of his pants, his hand finds the back of my head and weaves into my hair. With his pants riding lower, that sexy man v is on display, and I can't help but to flick my tongue out to taste it.

His hips buck a little toward me, almost as if it's uncontrollable. I feel a small tug on my hair as if he's trying to get me to stop. Not happening. Sitting on the bed, I pull him by a belt loop to stand in front of me. A quick glance up shows his eyes trained on my every move, so I watch his face as I unbuckle and unzip his jeans. His eyes close and his head falls back as I hook my fingers in the waistband of his boxer briefs, and pull them down with his jeans.

It's probably a good thing that he's not watching, because I can feel my face flush with heat as he's fully freed from restraints. He's bigger than Lucas or Mav, which isn't surprising, because he is big body wise. When my fingers slide down the length of him, he looks like he's going to fall over.

Yeah, worst girlfriend of the year award right here. Give him another concussion while giving him a blowjob. Perfect.

I decide to trade our positions instead. Making him lay face-up on the bed, I'm able to strip him down the rest of the way and holy fucking hell. It's like I told Lincoln, each guy is different in their own way and physique is no different. There's just something about their bodies, no matter how different they are, that makes me feel like I'm going to spontaneously combust just looking at them.

With one leg hooked off the bed and the other knee bent, he lays with his arms above his head and it flexes the muscles in his arms. Skimming my fingertips up his thighs, I make my way back up to face level with where I was before. A groan slips from his lips as I wrap my hand around the base and take him into my mouth. His hand finds my hair again, but he doesn't try to control. No, he lets me take my time exploring and figuring out what he likes. When I feel like neither of us can take anymore, I straddle him and guide him into me with a few rocks of my hips.

"Grant," I whisper.

He moans underneath me at the sound of his name and his hands come back up to find my breasts again. The bruising across his knuckles sends a jolt down my spine. It was sexy as fuck not only having him defend me the way that he did, but to watch him take out a full-grown man just as big as he is. I kiss the swollen discolored spots before he grabs me at the hips and takes control of the pace. When we go over, it's together.

I feel like a jellyfish just lying on top of him, but I don't want to move, and he doesn't seem to mind. His hands skim over every inch of skin that he can find, and it sends chill bumps following after. Following the EMTs orders, I keep him awake for the next couple of hours, just talking about anything and everything. Never once does he ask me to move. The only complaint he has is after I do allow him to fall asleep, I have to wake him up again, so we can lay the right way on the bed.

It's a few hours more before I wake straight up out of a deep sleep. Goose's soft snores behind me never miss a beat as I look around the room. I don't know what woke me up, but I feel like someone is watching us. A figure steps from the shadows of the stairs and I almost scream like a little girl before I catch sight of a familiar leather jacket. Lucas.

"You scared the shit out of me," I whisper.

His quiet laugh echoes around the room before he whispers back, "I'm sorry, baby. I just wanted to check on you guys before I left. Feeling okay?"

I nod and reach for him. When he sits down on the side of the bed, I raise up to give him a quick kiss, not caring that the blanket falls away to bare my breasts to him, not like he hasn't seen them before anyway.

"You don't have to go," I tell him. The bed is plenty big enough and I know that Goose won't mind.

He thinks on it for a good thirty seconds, before he stands up to strip down to his boxer briefs. As he climbs into bed with us, it wedges me closer to Goose who tightens his arm around me. He accidentally rubs against Lucas's stomach and jerks up next to me.

It takes him a second glance to recognize who's lying in front of us, but once he does he just says, "What's up, dude?" and lays back down to snuggle against my back.

Lucas kisses me lightly on the lips, “Good night, baby.”

Chapter Twenty Eight

Hot Poker To The Heart

The guys have been coming up MIA for short periods of time for the past few weeks. I've been doing better about not needing them around so much, but it doesn't make me miss them any less. On days like today, when I get a little lonely, I'll be with Ryleigh or at Lucas's house with Lincoln.

Lincoln is almost always home. I learned during the first visit that he got so depressed that he dropped out of college his sophomore year, and has practically become a hermit. Lucas says that he's been going out more since I started coming around, and even said something about trying to get back into classes in the fall, so that, in itself, makes the trip over worthwhile.

Today, we're laid out on a quilt in the backyard. With our heads next to each other and feet opposite, it makes it easier to hear lying on our backs.

"Did I tell you that I'm going to try to get my shit together to get into classes in the fall?" he asks.

"Lucas did," I admit.

He lets out a small laugh, "It was more than just Dallas, you know? Yeah, I love him and everything that happened didn't help, but I was so stressed out from classes and everything else that I felt like I was having a nervous breakdown. Figured I could take a year off. It'll still be there for when I'm ready to go back."

I tilt my head to the side to look at him. "You know that I

don't judge you anyways, but I'm glad that you feel ready enough to get back to it."

Nodding he adds, "I talked to Dallas the other day, too."

Now this does come as a surprise. "What happened?"

He shrugs. "We just asked how the other was doing. Polite chit chat and whatnot."

"Have you decided to give it a shot?" I ask gently as I roll on my side and prop up on my elbow to look down to him.

"I don't know," he answers honestly. "You've given me hope that it could work. I'm just not sure that I want to let her in. I don't know. I'm just a confused mess, and I want to get myself straight before trying anything."

"You speak such wisdom for such a mighty youth, young grasshopper," I kid.

My words work in turning his frown into a smile, "I think Goose is rubbing off on you. Is that a movie quote?"

I grin. "I don't know, but it should be."

"Ohhhh, Kendaaallll," Goose calls, sticking his head off the back porch.

"Speak of the devil," Lincoln says with a wink.

Goose and Teagan walk out to where we are laying in the yard, and T says, "Yeah and the devil's going to come calling if you're out here trying to steal Kendall's heart."

He laughs and jumps up to pull me to my feet, "Don't tempt me. I'm no stranger to dancing with the devil, but I think little K has enough testosterone in her life right now."

Wrapping me up in his arms, Goose pulls me to his lap as he sits down. "We're not going anywhere just yet."

"I thought we were going back to your house for movie night?" I ask.

"We are," Teagan answers for him as he sits down and then looks to Lincoln, "You're more than welcome to stay out here with us."

Lincoln shakes his head. "I'm good. I've got some stuff to take care of inside anyways. See you later, little K."

"Bye," I tell him.

Passing Mav and Lucas coming down the stairs, they nod to each other. What are they up to?

The pair walk down to the blanket and sit across from the three of us. It's a good thirty seconds of no one saying anything and it's driving me crazy. "Ok, what's the deal?" I ask.

The words out of Maverick's mouth sends my heart into my ass, "There's two things on the table that we need to discuss. First up, we need to talk about us leaving in the fall."

"Ok," I manage to squeeze out through the lump in my throat.

"Well," he starts, "I think it's a safe bet to say that a long-distance relationship is never going to work, especially since there's four of us and not just one."

Tears fill my eyes, but I try to swallow the sick feeling in my chest as I look toward the ground. I knew it was coming and I knew that it would hurt, but this feels like taking a hot poker to the heart. They, apparently, didn't want to be burdened with me through their last high-school summer. That's understandable. I feel the warm tears as they start their trek down my face and I don't want them to pity me. The last thing I want is for them to feel bad and try to stick around when they see me cry. I'm not that girl.

Pushing Goose's arms away from me, I stand up in one quick motion. Maverick tries to grab my hand, but a quick side-step maneuver puts me out of reach. Teagan is smarter. He hits his feet when I do and captures me around the waist.

He twists me to face him. "Kendall, what's wrong?"

Really? That stings some, like I'm not supposed to give a shit that they are dropping me and moving on. I find a spot in the trees to stare at to his right and don't answer.

Mav steps into my line of sight and I have no choice but to look up to his face. "Where are you going? You didn't even let me finish what I was saying, and why the hell are you crying?"

"I'm confused," I choke out, "You're breaking up with me, right? That's what this distance speech was for. It's okay, you know. There's going to be plenty of girls where you're going and with you being hot football stars, you'll have your pick, I'm sure. You deserve a chance to live a little, so I understand."

Mav's and T's facial expressions are almost identical as they go from confused to pissed to comprehension by the end of my words.

Maverick steps up like he's going to take me from Teagan, but the latter tightens his arms around me and smooshes my face against his chest. "Oh, sweet K. We aren't leaving you, lovely. Quite the contrary, actually."

"I don't understand," I say, my voice muffled by his shirt.

"If you would have stopped long enough to let me finish, this wouldn't even be an issue right now," Mav tells me as he reaches around T and lifts my chin.

"Will you come sit back down and let us explain?" he asks in a very unlike-Mav manner.

When I nod, I'm pulled back to the quilt on the ground. I didn't realize Lucas and Goose both stood and were right behind Mav the whole time. We do a little rearranging and I end up sitting in between Teagan's legs with Lucas on my right, and Goose's head in my lap. Using the hand that Lucas doesn't have hostage, I run it through what little hair Goose has on top. There's a lapse in conversation for a few, and I feel completely immature for my reaction.

Goose makes a humming sound of approval before he says, "I can't believe you thought that we would drop you just like that."

Even though he can't see me, I shrug anyway "Mav didn't start that conversation out too well."

"Yeah, dude," T says from behind me, "I think you should have thought that through a little better."

Mav just rolls his eyes. "That may be so, but my bigger concern is the fact that she has no faith in us. Looks like we need to rectify that situation, but first, we need to get back to the other things."

I know they said they weren't ditching me, but my heart thumps harder in my chest anyways.

Lucas pulls a packet of papers from inside his jacket and hands them to me. There's a stamp of a college I've never heard of on the front, "What's this?"

After a minute or so, Mav drops the bomb, "It's an acceptance letter to a smaller sister college to ours."

I shake my head. "Then they sent it to the wrong person. I still haven't applied anywhere."

Goose points to the small print on the front of the envelope. "You're Kendall Davis, right?"

"Yeah," I answer looking closer, "but that's not my address, so they've got the wrong one."

When I try to hand it back to Lucas, he laughs, "That's my address."

"I sent over all of your credentials and application," Mav informs me, looking not the least bit sheepish. "And you won't have to worry about tuition for the first two years, either," he adds.

Applying to college for me is one thing. I will not allow them to pay my tuition, too. Just as I open my mouth to say so, he cuts me off, "Don't even start. We didn't pay for it."

"Dad has been looking for some PR for the firm, so I suggested a scholarship," Teagan tells me in my ear. Between the feel of his breath and Goose lying in my lap, it sends chills down my arms.

"They didn't even tell you the best part yet," Goose says, looking upside down at me. "This one is only thirty minutes away from ours."

"And," Lucas cuts in, "We've already found a house to rent. It's paid out for the next two years, so we don't risk losing it."

"Also," Mav says, "I didn't put you in for a major. You can do that when we get there in July. We can go online, so you can see all the programs that they offer. There's even a photography major, if that's what you're feeling so inclined to do."

Dropping the papers between Lucas and I, the heels of my hands dig into my eyes and they flood with tears again. Only it's a different kind this time.

"Don't cry again, baby," Lucas says, sounding close. "Are you not happy?"

I nod around my hands, "So much that you guys made me cry again."

They laugh, and it isn't long before I'm joining them. When I feel like I can breathe again, I tell them, "Thank you so much for this. It means the world to me."

Lucas winks as Goose and T reply. Once they're done, Mav throws me an arched brow and half smirk, "We did it for purely selfish reasons."

He can say that a million times and I'll still never believe him. Some of the motivations may have been, but they really are just that kind of heart. Making Goose raise up, I knee-walk around the four of them handing out hugs and a kiss to the cheek.

Lucas is last, and he lies back until I'm draped across his

chest, "You may want to hold up on celebrating just yet. We still have number two. You may hate us after this one."

In all of the excitement, I totally forgot that there was a number two. Propping up on my elbow so I can see all of their faces, I ask, "What is it?"

Mav looks to the same tree that I used before as Teagan laughs and thumb points to him, "Well, someone had to go and get himself nominated for Prom King and we're being jerks and making him go."

I smile. "Why would you not want to go, Mav?"

He rolls his eyes again. "Just didn't want to, but I guess we are."

"We? As in 'I get to go, too?'" I ask excitedly as I sit up.

"Woah," Goose says, "You sound happy about this."

I grin at him, "I am actually. I've never been to prom. Plus, we get to torture Mav for the night."

Mav's eyebrow shoots up as he gives me one of those looks that turns my insides to mush and puts a blush on my cheeks. I'm the first one to break eye contact, as I resort to playing with a string on Lucas's pants. I see the other three watching us, but no one says anything.

Goose breaks the silence, "We still on for movie night or are we going out to celebrate Kendall's acceptance?"

Lucas looks at me, "Up to you, baby."

A night with nothing but my boys is exactly what I need, and I tell them so. With it decided, Lucas and Teagan fold up the blanket to take back inside after shaking it out.

As Goose turns toward the house, I say, "Catch," and jump on his back.

Never missing a beat, his arms wrap around my legs to hold

me in place. I kiss his neck right under his ear, “I don’t think I’ve told you today, Grant Michaels. I love you.

Chapter Twenty Nine

A Good Dose of Payback

The black dress I'm wearing is one of those lace over-dress kind of things. Thin spaghetti straps cover my shoulders and lead down into a u-shaped neckline. Its soft material goes all the way down to almost mid-thigh. A piece of lace is layered over each strap and goes down to almost my knees in the front and mid-calf in the back. Pulling my long hair up into a clip behind my head, I put on a little makeup. The only color on my entire body is a pair of bright-red wedges. They called my name when Ryleigh and I went dress shopping. With a peep-toe front and three sandal straps across the front, they zip up the back and I fell in love instantly. I give myself a once over in her stand-up mirror before stepping out of the closet.

She's standing in front of a vanity mirror doing a quick touch up on her makeup. When she catches sight of me in the mirror she lets out a catcall whistle. She turns, and I do a quick pirouette to show her the back, too.

Grinning ear to ear she says, "Oh my god. You look amazing and sexy as hell. I wish I could pull something like that off."

"Oh, whatever. You totally could, and you know it," I say and motion for her to spin.

Her dress looks like something out of a fairy tale. Straight Cinderella. It's pale peach and hangs to the floor with cream-colored tulle material underneath.

"Wow," I say, literally stunned. "You look like a fucking

princess."

She laughs, "Good that's what I was going for."

I laugh with her right before my phone rings on the bed. Not even bothering to look to see which one of the guys it is, I answer, "Hello."

"Ready to go, gorgeous?" Mav asks, that deep voice giving me tingles.

"I think so," I say honestly as I watch Ryleigh playing with a shawl.

I let out a girly giggle at her struggles, making Mav laugh on the other end. "Well, we're down here when you ladies are ready."

"We'll be down in just a sec," I promise.

Stuffing the phone in my little change purse thing, I rush Ryleigh, "Come on, they're waiting on us."

She winks. "Patience is a virtue."

"Not right now it isn't," I tell her.

When she cocks her head at me, I laugh again, "Sorry. Movie quote."

She rolls her eyes, "Fine, fine. Let's go."

I follow her down the stairs, so she's the first one to see the guys. "You've ruined my best friend, Goose," she tells them.

He comes into my sight just as her words sink in and the confusion shows on his face.

"She talks in movie quotes now," she tells him as she walks over to a waiting Eddie.

The pride on his face could only be bested by the look that crosses when he sees me. It's hard to watch all of them at the same time, but I can tell that each of them do their own version of a once over starting with the bright-red nail polish on the ends of my toes. In those few moments, they make me feel sexier than I ever have in my life.

Lucas is the first to move, coming to stand in front of me. What little shag there is to his brown hair is tamed into a style against his head. He gives me a soft kiss on the lips before slipping a tiny corsage around my wrist with a red rose on it. "You look absolutely stunning."

"Thank you, baby," I tell him as I pretend to straighten the red vest underneath his jacket. "You look pretty amazing yourself."

He smiles down at me and gives me another quick kiss before stepping to the side.

Teagan steps up next. The only color on his tux being the red cummerbund thing and the tiny, red daisy that looks similar to a sunflower in his hand. He slips it on my wrist before picking me up to spin me around in a circle and place a kiss against my lips. "Breathtaking as always." His long locks hang down around his face and I love the way that they feather across my skin when he gets close.

"Yes, you are," I reply, making his smile pull into a thousand-watt grin.

T stands off to the other side of Lucas to make way for Goose, who puts a small, red carnation on my wrist. He buries his face into the side of my neck as he lifts me a little off the ground. "You're beautiful, babe."

I wait until he puts me down and pulls away before I say, "I love you, Grant." The red handkerchief in his front pocket is crooked, so I fix it before he moves next to Teagan.

Finally, Maverick. There aren't many guys who could pull off a red bowtie, but he does, and makes that shit look good. His hair is laid back against his head and I find myself wanting to mess it up just to see if he'll let me. Before I can, he pushes a red lily down my wrist to sit against the other flowers already there. Lined up together, they make the cutest fucking corsage I've ever seen. Might not be saying much considering I've never had one before, but it means more than words to me.

Mav grabs the sides of my face and pulls my lips to his before saying, "I had it right the first time. Fucking gorgeous."

All I can do is smile at him like a fool. They've made me feel more special in the past almost eight months than I ever have in my life.

Ryleigh, of course, kills the moment, "This is so exciting. It's like a real-life version of The Bachelorette, only you don't have to choose at the end."

All of us, including Eddie, laugh with her. She makes us all do pictures in front of the house, several group pictures and then one with each of my guys. Then I do the ones of her and Eddie. It's at least a half hour before we're on the road.

They rented one of those stretch Hummers, and I must say, it's pretty awesome to even look at. I wonder if there's going to be enough room on the inside for all of us, even being as big as it is. No need to worry though, we all fit without a hitch. Ryleigh and Eddie sit directly behind the driver which is straight across from me, Mav, and Lucas. Teagan and Goose have their own seat to the left.

It only takes us thirty minutes or so to get to the hotel where their prom is being held. All heads turn to us as we step out. It's like being a celebrity or something, and I must say, I'm not a fan of the feeling.

Ryleigh and Eddie make their way up the little staircase and I go to follow. Mav's arm wraps around my waist and pulls me to him. Putting my arm in the crook of his elbow he says, "You're walking in with me. A good dose of payback."

I laugh quietly so as not to bring more attention to us, "You call being escorted by one of the four sexiest guys at this shindig, payback? I'd love to see what you'd have in mind for my reward."

He pulls us to a stop right in the middle of the hallway so fast that I feel one of the guys brush against my back. Then not caring that he's holding up the flow of people or that everyone around us is staring, he slams his mouth down across mine and conquers me until there's some throat clearing and a whistle or two.

My brain is a mushy mess, and it takes me a minute to put words together as we walk the rest of the way to the room, "So, we're a couple tonight?"

He lifts an eyebrow and looks down to me, "You don't want anyone to know that you're with me, baby girl?"

I would laugh, but he's completely serious and it breaks my heart a little. "I didn't mean it like that," I say low enough that the people around us can't hear. "I just wasn't sure if you guys wanted our business out there for your friends to see."

"Does it make you uncomfortable?" he asks.

Shaking my head, I don't even need the time to think on it.

One side of his mouth tilts up. "Us, either. We love you, Kendall Davis, and if we're going to do this then we have to start somewhere, right?"

This is the first time that Mav has said he loves me and it makes my stomach do a funny flip. Yeah, it's in plural form, but it's still something coming from him.

Letting go of his elbow, I squeeze him around the waist in a hug. He pulls me tighter as we make our way to one of the only empty tables.

Just as I go to sit down, Teagan grabs my empty hand. "Oh no way, ma'am. You're coming to dance with me."

Maverick gives me a quick kiss on the lips before T pulls me away to one of the many dances that happen over the next few hours. I make sure to give all of them equal time, even if T watches like a hawk for his next turn. It makes me laugh, because he's so hyped up. There's no doubt that he loves to dance, and even tries to steal a turn from Lucas. Which, of course, he doesn't give up, so I end up dancing with them both.

People give us funny looks, but I have a feeling that it's going to be a normal thing. At least the guys don't seem to notice.

Another hour and Maverick is crowned prom king. My first real bout of jealousy hits when he dances with the queen, but Goose never lets go of my hand, almost like he already knows what I'm feeling. In less than three minutes, the song is over and she's back with her date as he walks to me. Turning crazy cavewoman, I use his jacket to jerk him towards me so I can reach up on my toes to claim his mouth. His hum of approval lights a fire under my skin.

A voice clears behind me and he pulls away, "Break it up, Casanova."

"We need you over here for a picture, Maverick," a small, mousy girl says, coming up to us. He glares at her, which makes me feel kind of bad. Just by looking at her, anyone could see that she's the shy type, and Mav is intimidating, anyways.

"Stop it," I chastise as I push him toward her.

Once he's over at the photographer's backdrop, Goose drops a kiss on my cheek before he and Lucas go to get us something to drink. I actually manage to get T to sit down for a minute while they're gone.

We haven't even had a chance to say a word to each other, before a rando dude walks up and starts trying to talk to us. I don't know who he is, but T obviously does, and the disdain is written clearly on his face. The guy looks like a decent person, and not that unattractive, one of those pretty prep boys who styles his hair with way too much gel, standing there in his tux.

When Teagan doesn't answer him, the guy turns to me, "I

don't believe we've met before."

I reach out to shake his hand when he offers as he tells me his name is Richard.

"You're not from around here, huh?" he asks. "There were a couple people talking about it earlier." He slaps T on the back. "We knew the girls around here weren't good enough for the kings of school, but there must be something to this slumming thing."

The words have barely left his mouth when Teagan pulls his arm back and elbows Richard right in the crotch. He's not paying attention, and it takes him by surprise. Doubling over, he smacks his forehead on the table and falls to the floor groaning. The people around us are either whispering or laughing.

"What do you think you're doing, Mr. Morgan?" that same teacher who called Mav Casanova asks, stalking over to our table.

Teagan grabs my hand before he pulls us both to our feet and takes off at a dead sprint away from her. He makes a weird circle motion above his head right before we're out the door. We make it halfway to the main door before I pull him to a stop.

"Wait a minute," I say, trying to catch my breath between the running and laughing. "I can't run anymore in these shoes."

He grins down at me, "You have less than thirty seconds to take them off or I'll throw you over my shoulder and carry you."

I get them off in less than ten, but it's given the others time to catch up with us.

"What's going on?" Goose asks.

"T just cock-punched some dude named Richard," I laugh.

"Technically, it was an elbow, and he's a dick anyway," he says defensively.

The guys laugh right before that teacher rounds the corner and shouts for Teagan.

Off we go again, like a horde of zombies is on our ass. It's one of the weirdest times to notice, but I can't help but to stare at them as they run. I don't know why, but there's something about it that is sexy as fuck. I would love to be a fly on the wall wherever they work out at.

Distracted the whole way, I don't realize that we're at the Rover until we're right in front of it. Teagan picks me up and throws me into the back between him and Lucas.

"When did this get here?" I ask them.

"We dropped it off earlier," Goose answers as Mav gets us on the road.

Teagan is brooding as he stares out the window. I feel like the whole thing is my fault. He only got pissed on my behalf.

I try to make amends, "Hey, T, I'm really sorry that I ruined the night. You really didn't have to hit him for saying—"

Before I can finish, Teagan unsnaps my seat belt and pulls me to a straddling position on his lap. Between his lips capturing mine and the adrenaline left over, my body is demanding attention. His hands go to the outside of my thighs and push my dress all the way up almost to my hips. He never breaks the kiss, but groans into my mouth as they find the outline of my panties. My hands weave into the back of his long hair and I pull his head back for a better angle.

On the side, I register that Lucas is shifting, but it's not until his leg brushes against mine that it really hits me. Breaking away from Teagan, I find Lucas watching us with a dark look on his face. Coming up fully on my knees, I lean over to steal a kiss from him.

There's no explaining the feeling that rushes through my body at the feel of Teagan's hands still caressing my hips as Lucas's lips are on mine. The only thing that could pull me away is a soft tug on the back of my hair. Someone has taken the clip out and I feel my hair fall down to my back. Casting a quick look over my shoulder, I catch the eyes of Mav in the mirror watching us, but it's Goose that holds my clip in his hand. He's turned all the way around in his seat, almost like he's waiting for me.

Taking a good hold of Lucas's arm, I lean backwards until my lips are close enough to Goose for him to dip and press his lips against mine. Between the three of them and knowing that Mav is watching, my heart practically beats out of my chest thinking about what could happen. And I will say that upside down kissing has now been added to one of my favorite things list. I love the way that our tongues feel against each other from this angle. My free hand wraps around the back of his head, with my fingers playing with what little hair he has there.

All too soon, the car comes to a stop. Mav hops out as he mumbles something about making someone wreck. I beat Teagan to the door handle and hop down.

He's already walking toward the house, but turns when I call out, "Hey, Mav!"

I rush the couple of steps between us and when I jump, he's ready to catch me. Wasting no time at all, I cover his mouth with mine. Just knowing how dominant his personality is makes the fact that he's letting me take control this one time all the more exciting.

Chapter Thirty

Content As A Kitten

The guys build a fire in the pit behind Teagan's house and when it starts to get a little chilly out, Goose's jacket goes around my shoulders. I fret about him being cold, but he waves it off. It swallows me whole, but I love it, only to be rivaled by his masculine scent coming off of it. I don't think I'll ever get tired of that smell.

We sit around the fire long after midnight, just talking and laughing. It isn't until I start nodding off that Teagan pulls me to my feet, "Come on, lovely."

"Where are we going?" I ask with a yawn.

"Dad and Cynth are gone for the weekend, so you're staying with me tonight." He smiles towing me toward the house.

"Ugh," I groan. "I'll never get sleep then."

I hear a couple snickers behind us, but T is unmoved by them, "That was the plan."

His words take a minute to sink into my head, but when it does, I'm instantly awake.

Just as we step into the house, I pull my hand loose and take off running toward the stairs. I hear his chuckle before he starts after me. Making it halfway up, he finally catches up with me. No surprise, since I see him out of the corner of my eye taking the stairs two at a time. Curse those long, sexy legs of his.

It's not until I'm at the very top that I realize I have a problem. I don't remember which room is his. Ryleigh pointed it out one day a long time ago, and I can't recall which one it is. Doesn't matter, in one quick movement he's got me flipped over his shoulder in a fireman's hold.

His hand caresses the back of my thigh and I have to stop the sound that tries to escape my mouth. When we make it to his room at the end of the hall, he dumps me on the bed. I want to take a moment to look around at his personal space, especially considering I've only seen his and Goose's, but there couldn't possibly be anything better in here than what's standing in front of me. He reaches over to the little night stand beside the bed and uses a remote to turn on music from somewhere. I recognize the song as one from the show we went to back in February.

The bed sits way high off the floor, so much that I'd have to jump to get up here. It puts us at the perfect height when he leans back up. Untucking both shirts from his pants, I lift them over his head without unbuttoning the top one. I toss them to the floor. The mere sight of him makes my heart skip a beat.

His tattoos stand out against his skin. There's a dragon wrapped around his right bicep with a Japanese cherry blossom tree in the background. A Koi fish swims playfully up the left side of his torso. That one is more surprising than the dragon and even the one peeking out under the top of his pants. It's got crazy insane detail and coloring and must have hurt like a bitch. Pushing his pants down a little on his hips, I'm able to fully read the other one. It's written in some calligraphy script and matches the words perfectly, 'Never Back Down.'

When I glance up to meet his eyes, he grins down at me before pushing Goose's jacket off my shoulders. I don't give him a chance with the dress. Taking the bottom hem, I watch his face as I slowly inch it off my body. Pausing for only a second longer once I get to the bottom of my breasts, I let him get a good look in before pulling it off over my head. It has a built-in bra type thing, so I didn't bother wearing one.

"Holy shit, Kendall," he murmurs. "You are the sexiest thing I've ever seen."

Even though it's not funny, I laugh. Teagan is hardly ever serious, and just being around him makes you want to smile.

I reach out for his belt, but his hands stop me, "Oh no. You made me wait til last, so I get to have a little fun first."

"It's not like that was planned or anything. It just happened," I argue.

He shakes his head, "Doesn't matter. Done now, so you have to face the consequences."

Climbing up to the bed with me, he stalks me until I'm flat on my back. That long, blond hair tickles my skin as it trails after him while he tortures me with kisses on every inch of my naked body. As he makes his way to the lace panties still covering me, I feel his teeth graze my hip. Who would have ever thought that one little spot could literally make my toes curl? Little by little, he eases the material down my legs. By the time that they're off, my entire body feels like it's on fire.

I reach for him, but he grabs my wrists and puts them above my head as he comes chest to chest with me. Arching my back up, I rub against him and he lets out a low sound in my ear, which does nothing but make me want to do it again.

"I wanted to have some fun first, but I don't think I'll be able to," he says in my ear before he nips it. "We may need to invest in a pair of handcuffs. I have a few ties. Those might work."

I've never considered being restrained before and I'd be lying if I said that the thought of being at the mercy of Teagan doesn't turn me on. "Please," I beg. At this point, I don't care what he does as long as he puts out the fire.

His lips smash against mine and he devours me as if he'll never get the chance to again. With my arms still trapped above us, I wrap my legs around his waist and rub against him again.

"Fuck," he mutters jumping up off the bed. I rise up on my elbows to watch him take his pants off and reach for the nightstand again. As he rolls a condom on, I realize that neither Mav or Goose used one. That was so stupid of us, but thank fuck for birth control.

I'm not left to dwell on it for too long, because Teagan hops back up to the bed. Expecting him to come back to where he was, I lie back. He shocks me by grabbing my hips and flipping me over to my hands and knees. Stealing all of the thoughts rolling through my head, he's inside of me in one swift stroke. All playfulness is gone, and that's made pointedly clear in how rough he is, which is another nice surprise from him. Fisting the blanket covering his bed, I hang on as the sound of flesh meeting flesh fills the room. Taking a quick glance over my shoulder is my undoing. Teagan is fucking glorious and I'm pretty sure I moan his name right before he jerks against me and we crash to the bed together.

His lips trail down my back and up again before finding my ear. "Kendall?"

"Hmm?" I hum into the mattress. I'm as content as a kitten and don't want to move.

The warmth of his hands heats my skin as he makes paths all over it as if he's trying to memorize it. "I just wanted to say thank you."

I turn my head so that I'm looking at him. "Why?"

He lets out a short laugh, "For giving us a chance. For giving me a chance. I was worried that when we got to college, we'd all end up going our own ways. You're our glue now, and I don't think I could see life without you. It's going to sound really fucking cheesy to say this right after, but I do love you."

Smiling, I put a kiss on his lips, "I'll always be grateful for you guys not only finding me, but reviving me. Twice. I'm not going anywhere until you guys decide you don't want me anymore."

"Never going to happen," he says, wrapping his arms around me and tucking me into his chest.

Lifting my face, I kiss the bottom of his chin, "I love you, T."

Epilogue

Since it wasn't going to be put to use, I sold the trailer and the lot for cheap to a family who looked like they needed it more than I did a few weeks ago. When it came time to pack up Gramps's room, I wondered if I made the right decision. Crying non-stop, there's no way that I would have gotten through that task alone. If it hadn't been for my guys, I would have backed out on selling the place and just stayed here forever. Just the smell and thought of Gramps weighed heavily on my shoulders. We moved what little stuff that he and I had into a tiny storage place and paid it out for the year.

I stand now in the empty trailer looking around at where all of our things used to be. There have been so many memories here, good and bad. My throat swells up at my attempt to not cry. We're leaving today and now that the time has come for us to go, it makes my heart hurt. I know Gramps would want everything to have happened the way that they did, and that is the only thought that allows me to put one foot in front of the other out the door.

Once outside, I close my eyes and take a deep breath of summer air. When I open them, I see the guys sitting in a packed down Rover waiting on me. It brings a smile to my face, and lifts some of that weight. Every step I take toward them lifts a little more.

As one book closes, another one opens, and I for one cannot wait for this chapter.

From the Author

Thank you for taking the time to read the story of Kendall Davis. I hope you've enjoyed it as much as I've loved writing and sharing it with you! Pick up your copies of the next two books in the series, Refusing Kendall and Reclaiming Kendall on Amazon today!

Did You Know?

Did you know that Beauty in Lies mentioned in Reviving Kendall have their own reverse harem story?

About the Author

Brandy Slaven lives in Tennessee with her husband and two wild children. If you can't find her creating worlds with her words, you will find her with her nose in a book at the beach or hiking at a state park.

Find her anywhere online!

www.authorbrandyslaven.com

Made in United States
Troutdale, OR
03/26/2024